**Wait
for Me**

Wait
for Me

Selected Poems of
Konstantin Simonov

Translated by
Mike Munford

SMOKE

**STACK
BOOKS**

Smokestack Books
1 Lake Terrace, Grewelthorpe, Ripon HG4 3BU
e-mail: info@smokestack-books.co.uk
www.smokestack-books.co.uk

ISBN 9781916139237

Smokestack Books
is represented
by Inpress Ltd

Содержание

Contents

Preface

The translations in this book started life on a website, www.simonov.co.uk, in 2003. The site has always attracted quite a lot of traffic, much of it from Russia. My original translation of the poem 'Wait for Me' is even sometimes used in the English lesson in Russian schools!

The translations on the site are almost all included in this book, with some improvements of wording. In addition, a number of quite new translations appear here, notably those of the important longer poems 'An Open Letter' and 'The Colonel's Son'. I have also included one or two poems published by Simonov during the War, but not to be found in modern editions of Simonov in Russian – particularly 'Blindness', which I think is one of his best poems to Valentina.

Most of Simonov's short poems have no titles and in Russian, are identified by their first lines. But translations vary; so where Simonov has not given a poem a title, the translation has been given a short title related to content. These are not meant to be definitive; they are just there for identification.

The poems appear in the probable order in which they were written, except that 'Wait for Me' is given pride of place, before 'I love you!' which was probably written earlier. And at the end, I have appended 'The Old Lieutenant', the best of Simonov's early poems, written in 1939.

Mike Munford

Introduction

Kirill (later called Konstantin) Simonov was born in Petrograd (St Petersburg) in 1914. His mother had been born Princess Obolenskaya, in one of the oldest noble families of Russia. His father was a senior army officer: he went missing in the First World War and Kirill never knew him. The War led to the chaos of revolution and civil conflict; Simonova and her little son found themselves in the provincial town of Ryazan, where she met and married another ex-Tsarist officer – Colonel Alexander Ivanischev. He brought up Kirill as his own son and no other children were born.

Kirill's stepfather was now an instructor in a Red Army military college. Kirill's earliest memories were of barracks life – the parade ground was outside the window of their flat. He was close to his stepfather; Ivanischev was a strict disciplinarian for whom everything had its time and place, but he was also very fond of his stepson: When the older man was preparing lessons in strategy and tactics, he sometimes let Kirill help him; military matters became familiar to the future war poet very young.

At the same time, the softer Obolensky influence pulled him another way. His mother wrote verse; and in the Leningrad home of his librarian aunt Sofia Obolenskaya he wrote his first poem. These two influences – the military traditions of the old Russian army and the cultural legacy of the Russian aristocracy – contributed to the man he became.

Kirill was a sensitive, lonely boy, conscious of belonging to a barely tolerated pre-revolutionary minority and suffering from the embarrassing disadvantage of not being able to pronounce his own first name properly. (His later recordings suggest that that he always had difficulty in pronouncing the Russian 'r' and hard 'l' sounds). But he was ambitious; and he knew how to achieve success in the new Russia in which he found himself. Against the opposition of his stepfather, he left school early and become an engineering apprentice. In the new Communist Russia, this proletarian background would be an advantage rather than the reverse.

Not long after he left school, his stepfather was arrested and Kirill and his mother were thrown out of their home. Six months later, Ivanishchev was released and rehabilitated – there had been a 'mistake'. But as a result of this experience, the family moved to Moscow. Kirill found engineering work in a film studio and managed to publish a few poems. Encouraged by the publisher, he started a course at the Gorky Literary Institute.

The Gorky Institute was a forcing ground for the new generation of Russian writers who were to help build socialism in Russia. It offered encouraging opportunities to publish and be performed and it attracted some talented students. In this exciting new environment, Simonov found his feet for the first time. He changed his name to Konstantin and left the embarrassment of Kirill behind him. He had poems published; he married and his first child was born. Then he had a play accepted for performance and found himself in the intoxicating but dangerous world of the Russian theatre. He fell passionately in love with the actress Valentina Serova.

Valentina was a rising star of stage and screen. Two years before, she had married Anatoly Serov, a fighter ace hero of the Spanish Civil War. But after only one year of marriage, he was killed in a flying accident. Soon afterwards, she gave birth to their child.

Valentina had many lovers, but she judged every other man by the standard of Serov. The contrast between the very mature and masculine Serov and the brilliant student Simonov, with his speech impediment, could not have been greater. She found him, at first, a nuisance rather than a man to whom she could respond. But he was persistent: he would not let her say no. At her every performance, she saw him in the front row of the stalls with flowers. His initial poems to her are imploring, almost childish. But he had a new play in prospect, with a part for her in it. He was intelligent and ambitious. He was rising, likely to be increasingly successful. One night, probably in early 1941, she came to his flat.

And then, on 22nd June 1941, Hitler invaded Russia.

Simonov had known that war was coming sooner or later and had trained as a war correspondent. In 1939 he had briefly reported on the Russo–Japanese war in Mongolia. Now he was mobilised and ordered to report to a military newspaper at Brest, on the frontier. Valentina saw him off at the station – and told him for the first time that she loved him.

The troop train bore him westward towards, as he thought, the frontier. But by this time the blitzkrieg had already penetrated deep into Russia and the train never reached its destination. After a series of adventures, Simonov found his way back to Moscow with much excellent material and perceptive analysis of the situation at the front. This was favourably received at a time when communications between Moscow and the front were erratic. He was noticed at the top. For the rest of the War, he served as a war correspondent for Red Star, the Soviet army newspaper.

He was an aristocrat by birth. He had always felt an outsider in Soviet Russia and some of his close relatives had disappeared. But the invasion of his country changed everything. He knew now the direction his life must take. He felt himself to be a soldier, utterly and fearlessly devoted to expelling the invader and winning the War. And he was in the fortunate position that the weapon entrusted to him with which to fight Hitler was the one he knew better than anyone else to how to wield – his pen. His work as a war correspondent made its contribution. But some of his poems, in a country where everyone read and recited poetry, were even more important.

He had a week's break in Moscow, waiting for a vehicle to take him on a wide survey of the various fronts. His editor lent him his dacha outside the city so that he could have peace to write. One day that week, among much else, he wrote what became his best-known poem, 'Wait for Me'.

At first, he thought of 'Wait for Me' as a personal poem, for Valentina alone. But on his subsequent trip to the North, his companion got him to read it aloud wherever they went. He said the poem helped him to come to terms with separation from his wife. Soldiers agreed; they loved the poem and copied it out on scraps of paper to send home. Simonov came to realise that he had written something important.

He submitted it to *Red Star* (the Army daily) where it was rejected. But the *Pravda* offices were in the same building and he met the editor of *Pravda* in the corridor. Pospelov invited him into his office for a cup of tea and Simonov read 'Wait for Me' to him. After consulting a colleague, Pospelov said he would publish it.

Pravda was the national daily of the Soviet Union. He had reached the widest readership possible. The effect was immediate. In the words of a later editor of Simonov's poems:

> In February 1942, when the Germans were being driven back from Moscow, Pravda published a lyric which immediately won the hearts of our troops. It was "Wait for me." Soldiers cut it out of the paper, copied it out as they sat in the trenches, learned it by heart and sent it back in letters to wives and girl-friends; it was found in the breast pockets of the killed and wounded. In the history of Russian poetry it would be hard to find a poem which had such a wide general impact as Wait for me. It made the Soviet officer and Russian poet – Konstantin Simonov – world famous.

Alexei Surkov, Simonov's friend and colleague, related that 'in the first year of the War, it was hard to find anyone at the front who hadn't seen the *Pravda* edition which contained *Wait for me*'. On the home front, the impact of the poem was as great or greater. After the War, the wife of a soldier who had not returned wrote to Simonov:

> Do you realize what your poem meant to young wives like me who were left at home? We didn't believe in God, we didn't know how to pray, and we had such a need to say to someone 'Protect him, don't let him die.' And then your poem came. It was sent from the rear to the front and from the front to the rear. It gave hope to those who waited and to those for whom they waited. Every day, I looked in the postbox and whispered your words like a prayer, repeating 'Yes, my love, I shall wait, I know how to wait.'

When *With You and Without You*, a volume mainly of love poems which included 'Wait for Me' was published later in 1942, it was a best seller and sold out immediately.

Simonov commented bitterly after the War 'It was ironic that I, the poet, for whom no one waited, survived the War, whilst others, who had someone waiting, did not.' Valentina was not faithful to him. But she had made his name. Suddenly he was famous, his poem was on everybody's lips. At least three composers set it to music.

He continued his work as a war correspondent. It was normally a very dangerous job; but he was increasingly treated as a VIP and the commanders of the units he visited his took care to keep him from harm. He survived; and as the War went on, he sometimes even took Valentina with him.

Much of his best poetry had been written in the second half of 1941, when during a brief period, his belief in Valentina's love – his initial self-deception – sustained him, often in extreme danger. As 1942 progressed, he was less and less in love with Valentina; but he was less in danger and needed her less; for her part, she valued him the more because of his new national status. He wrote the screenplay for a film *Wait for Me*, in which she played the role of the girl who waited. But she was still unfaithful. The word spread that she was involved with Marshall Rokossovsky.

They married and he tried to convince himself that her infidelities need not prevent him from loving her, but he knew she would never love him in the way he needed. In a sense he now needed her love less, because his life was (in every other way) now more secure. They remained together (whilst often separated) throughout the War. She had his child. But after the War ended, they gradually drifted apart. Valentina fought a losing battle against alcoholism. It gradually destroyed her acting career, her marriage and finally her life. The final parting, when it came, was decisive:

> I just no longer love you, dear, and so
> I cannot write you one more line of verse.

They divorced and he married the widow of another young poet. The marriage seems to have been happy, although his new wife specifically discouraged him from writing poetry, particularly to or about her. Simonov became increasingly known primarily as a prose writer, dramatist, and editor. He never ceased to write about the War, although censorship sometimes prevented him from publishing everything he wrote. He died in 1979.

The love affair of the famous war poet and the star has remained endlessly fascinating to some Russians and articles still appear in the popular press. The actress Tatiana Kravchenko published a penetrating article in which she analysed the relationship from the woman's point of view:

> She had by nature and even to excess a woman's intuitive understanding of how to make herself loved: the more one gives, the more firmly one entangles. And he learned from her to give himself thoughtlessly, generously, demanding no guarantees, without bargaining, without counting the cost.

Perhaps this was true of their relationship during the brief period of their intimacy before the poet went off to the War. *Blindness*, a poem which Simonov published during the war but subsequently excluded from his collections, shows him in this state of mind. The War taught him, among other things, that this kind of relationship was not enough.

'I love you!' was probably written in the train for Brest, before he had realised quite what lay ahead of him in the War. Until that parting, Valentina had been for him a wonderful sensual experience, a mistress. At the moment of parting, he became aware of a need in him for something more. As he went off into an unknown and perilous future, he suddenly felt the need for the devotion, the loyalty and the love of a wife. Perhaps Valentina sensed this in him and played her part. Except in the heat of passion, she had never previously told him she loved him. And now she said it coolly, calmly, as if she meant it. And it to him it meant everything:

> That you could say what you said that evening,
> Seemed, till that evening, past belief!
> 'I love you! Love you!' Night; the station;
> Your little hands so cold with grief...

Supported by those few words (and perhaps some self-deception) he was able to gain strength to face the dangers and challenges that lay ahead.

When he came back, but had not yet faced up to the reality of their relationship, his belief in her love enabled him to write 'Wait for Me' and even, amid the dangers of the War, the two light-hearted poems 'Letters' and 'In Heaven'.

But he was only able to see her occasionally and it seems that others were not going to allow him to deceive himself: she had not been faithful to him. He was going to have to come to terms with her promiscuity. And all the time he was living the life of a war correspondent, always busy and intermittently in danger; he didn't feel able to tackle the risk of losing her completely.

In 'My Wife' he asks himself what it is that makes him want to be able to call her his wife. It's not that he wants the prestige of marriage with a celebrated star. Everyone knows about their relationship already. It's not that he wants to take her to meet his parents. And he comes to the conclusion that it is precisely her unreliability, her unpredictability, that makes him love her. And yet as a soldier who may not return, he needs to feel that she is waiting for him. It was an impossible situation – and one that, as he increasingly realised, was only to be resolved after the War.

In two poems, the fact that Valentina did not really belong to him was explicitly dramatised. Probably neither poem describes actual events. In 'At the Stage Door', a beautiful lyric in the Russian, he waits for her outside the theatre with two young fans – and she pays more attention to them than she does to him. He is able to imagine her without him. Her life, her career, will continue, the fans will still follow her and the snow will continue to fall, but he will not be there. In 'The Hostess', one of his most powerful poems, his presence is finally only that of a ghost. We are to imagine that the poet and his friends – presumably war correspondents like himself – gather regularly, when they can, in Valentina's flat. After they disperse, they go off to the various fronts and some of them are killed. Each time, fewer attend. The purpose of the poem is to reassure Valentina that she is right, while his friends are present, to accord him, the poet, exactly the same treatment as the others. She has become an ideal to them, a kind of icon: she gives them something which sustains them in battle; they need her. Until the party breaks up, the poet expects and receives no special treatment from her... But then what if he himself is among those who do not come back?

The soldier's need for the support and love of the woman who is waiting for him, who is faithful to him in his absence in war, is a theme to which Simonov, in these poems, constantly returns. Initially, the poems show it as an intense personal problem; later, as he objectified his emotions, he wrote about it in relation to the soldiers of the war in general. The later poems translated here were written after the success of 'Wait for Me', when Simonov was probably less often in physical danger but increasingly aware of the need to develop the theme of 'Wait for Me' in relation to others rather than himself. *Wives* makes it clear why this was important for the morale of the army:

> I've got to trust her. If I didn't,
> How could a man get through this hell?

In 'An Open Letter', he wrote just what was needed for morale – although the poem undoubtedly benefits also from intense personal feeling. It was based on a real event. On one of his journeys to the front, he was told that a young lieutenant had recently been killed. The day after he died, a letter arrived from his wife, in which she informed him that she was now living with another man. She asked him to cease 'pestering' her. His fellow officers had opened and read the letter, and it had made them very angry; they asked Simonov to write a suitable reply. He took the letter away with him and subsequently wrote this devastating letter in verse.

There was also, of course, another side to it. Men also can be unfaithful – especially soldiers and especially in time of war. Later, after the War, he wrote the moving 'The Colonel's Son' It seems to be a true story. He spent a great deal of time, after the War, in interviewing veterans, gathering material, mainly for his trilogy of war novels *The Living and the Dead*. One of those he interviewed was a nurse who had served at the front. Like many girls in her situation, she had found herself in a relationship with an officer. It lasted until the very end, when he died outside Berlin. She hadn't told him she was pregnant. After the War, she is bringing up their son alone, on a nurse's wages.

The War was the defining event of Simonov's life. He was probably never again so creative and fulfilled as he had been when the war was in its most dangerous phase; and all his later writings drew on his wartime experiences. In his introduction to a reading of his verse in New York in 1960, he said:

> I don't know how others may feel, but for me, human friendship is the most precious feeling on earth. That feeling has its greatest strength when people are under pressure; and in war, people are under great pressure.

'The House at Vyazma' presents this ideal. But the poem is an idealisation, probably not based on personal experience. Simonov's life, after his initial adventures in the first few weeks of the War, was never the comradely life of a soldier; it was the much more lonely life of an itinerant war correspondent. He was great poet and a great man; but also perhaps a lonely man, to the end.

Жди меня

Жди меня, и я вернусь.
Только очень жди,
Жди, когда наводят грусть
Желтые дожди,
Жди, когда снега метут,
Жди, когда жара,
Жди, когда других не ждут,
Позабыв вчера.
Жди, когда из дальних мест
Писем не придет,
Жди, когда уж надоест
Всем, кто вместе ждет.

Жди меня, и я вернусь,
Не желай добра
Всем, кто знает наизусть,
Что забыть пора.
Пусть поверят сын и мать
В то, что нет меня,
Пусть друзья устанут ждать,
Сядут у огня,
Выпьют горькое вино
На помин души...
Жди. И с ними заодно
Выпить не спеши.

Wait for Me

Wait for me and I'll come back!
Wait with all your might!
Wait when dreary yellow rains
Tell you nothing's right;
Wait when snow is falling fast;
Wait when summer's hot;
When no one waits for other men
And all the past's forgot!
Wait when those that wait with you
Are bored and tired and glum,
And when it seems, from far away,
No letters ever come!

Wait for me and I'll come back!
Wait in patience yet
Pay no heed when they repeat
That you should forget;
And when my mother and my son
Give up on me at last
And friends sit sadly round the fire
And talk about the past
And drink a bitter glass of wine
In memory of me –
Wait! No rush to drink with them!
Tell them to wait and see!

Жди меня, и я вернусь,
Всем смертям назло.
Кто не ждал меня, тот пусть
Скажет: – Повезло.
Не понять, не ждавшим им,
Как среди огня
Ожиданием своим
Ты спасла меня.
Как я выжил, будем знать
Только мы с тобой –
Просто ты умела ждать,
Как никто другой.

1941

Wait for me and I'll come back,
Escaping every fate!
'Just got lucky!' they will say,
Those that didn't wait.
They will never understand
How, amidst the strife,
By your waiting for me, dear,
You had saved my life!
Only you and I will know
How you got me through!
Simply – you knew how to wait!
No one else but you!

1941

Ты говорила мне «люблю»,
Но это по ночам, сквозь зубы.
А утром горькое «терплю»
Едва удерживали губы.

Я верил по ночам губам,
Рукам лукавым и горячим,
Но я не верил по ночам
Твоим ночным словам незрячим.

Я знал тебя, ты не лгала,
Ты полюбить меня хотела,
Ты только ночью лгать могла,
Когда душою правит тело.

Но утром, в трезвый час, когда
Душа опять сильна, как прежде,
Ты хоть бы раз сказала «да»
Мне, ожидавшему в надежде.

И вдруг война, отъезд, перрон,
Где и обняться-то нет места,
И дачный клязьминский вагон,
В котором ехать мне до Бреста.

'I love you!'

You've sometimes used the words 'I love you!'
But that was through your teeth, at night,
The truth was 'I put up with you'.
You almost said it in the light.

I could believe your lips in darkness,
The wicked magic of your bed,
But though the words you spoke were honest,
I did not credit what you said.

I knew you – you were not a liar;
You would have liked to be in love.
Only at night could you deceive me,
When body drives the soul above.

But in the morning, you were sober.
Your mind was now the guiding force;
And when I asked you if you loved me,
I think you once replied, 'of course'.

Then sudden war, the station platform,
Nowhere to kiss and to be kissed,
My seat in the suburban carriage
To take me far all the way to Brest.

Вдруг вечер без надежд на ночь,
На счастье, на тепло постели.
Как крик: ничем нельзя помочь!
Вкус поцелуя на шинели.

Чтоб с теми, в темноте, в хмелю,
Не спутал с прежними словами,
Ты вдруг сказала мне «люблю»
Почти спокойными губами.

Такой я раньше не видал
Тебя, до этих слов разлуки:
Люблю, люблю... ночной вокзал,
Холодные от горя руки.

1941

An evening without hope of loving;
No warmth, no happiness, no bliss;
And with a helpless sense of panic,
Upon my sleeve, I taste your kiss.

But so that I should know the difference
From drunken passion in my arms,
You suddenly said to me, 'I love you!'
Your lips that spoke were almost calm.

That you could say what you said that evening,
Seemed, till that evening, past belief!
'I love you! Love you!' Night; the station;
Your little hands so cold with grief...

1941

Если бог нас своим могуществом
После смерти отправит в рай,
Что мне делать с земным имуществом,
Если скажет он: выбирай?

Мне не надо в раю тоскующей,
Чтоб покорно за мною шла,
Я бы взял с собой в рай такую же,
Что на грешной земле жила –

Злую, ветреную, колючую,
Хоть ненадолго, да мою!
Ту, что нас на земле помучила
И не даст нам скучать в раю.

В рай, наверно, таких отчаянных
Мало кто приведёт с собой,
Будут праведники нечаянно
Там подглядывать за тобой.

Взял бы в рай с собой расстояния,
Чтобы мучиться от разлук,
Чтобы помнить при расставании
Боль сведённых на шее рук.

In Heaven

If God in his almighty power
Calls me to heaven when I die
And I am asked, as I go in,
What I shall choose to take inside,

I shall not want, in tedious heaven,
A girl who'd follow me around.
I'll take with me the very same
Who'd lived upon this sinful ground.

The awkward, willful one, the one
Who gives me (just for now) her love,
The one who drove me mad on earth
Will liven up my time above.

Not many people, probably,
Would bring a desperate soul like you.
The righteous, in astonishment,
Would gather round to peep at you.

I'd take with me the distances –
The agony of separation,
To call to mind when we're apart
The way you kissed me at the station

Взял бы в рай с собой всё опасности,
Чтоб вернее меня ждала,
Чтобы глаз своих синей ясности
Дома трусу не отдала.

Взял бы в рай с собой друга верного,
Чтобы было с кем пировать,
И врага, чтоб в минуту скверную
По-земному с ним враждовать.

Ни любви, ни тоски, ни жалости,
Даже курского соловья,
Никакой, самой малой малости
На земле бы не бросил я.

Даже смерть, если б было мыслимо,
Я б на землю не отпустил,
Всё, что к нам на земле причислено,
В рай с собою бы захватил.

И за эти земные корысти,
Удивлённо меня кляня,
Я уверен, что бог бы вскорости
Вновь на землю столкнул меня.

1941

I'd have to take the dangers too,
To keep you anxious, true and wise,
So that no coward can enjoy
The azure brilliance of your eyes.

I'd take to heaven a faithful friend
To drink a toast with and to share;
And I should take the enemy
To fight with – as we do down here..

Love and ennui and pity I'd take,
Even the nightingale in the wood –
Every tiniest detail of life
That we live on earth, I'd take – if I could.

Even death – if that could be –
I should not leave behind below.
All that is here our lot on earth
I'd choose to take with me – and so

God, in astonishment, would curse
The worldly loyalties of men,
And pretty soon, without a doubt,
Would pop me back on earth again

1941

Не сердитесь – к лучшему,
Что, себя не мучая,
Вам пишу от случая
До другого случая.

Письма пишут разные:
Слезные, болезные,
Иногда прекрасные,
Чаще – бесполезные.

В письмах все не скажется
И не все услышится,
В письмах все нам кажется,
Что не так напишется.

Коль вернусь – так суженых
Некогда отчитывать,
А убьют – так хуже нет
Письма перечитывать.

Чтобы вам не бедствовать,
Не возить их тачкою,
Будут путешествовать
С вами тонкой пачкою.

Letters

Don't be angry if I write
Only just from time to time,
Writing now, and then again,
Waiting till another time.

Letters vary such a lot –:
Some are sick and some are sad,
Brilliant just occasionally,
Far more often very bad.

Letters leave a lot unsaid,
Often are not understood,
Seem to mean more than they do,
Fail to mention what they should.

If I live, you won't have time
To tick me off when we are wed.
And if I die, there's nothing worse
Than reading letters from the dead.

When you travel, you will not
Heavy trolleys need to trundle.
They will fit into your bag,
Folded in a slender bundle.

А замужней станете,
Обо мне заплачете –
Их легко достанете
И легко припрячете.

От него, ревнивого,
Затворившись в комнате,
Вы меня, ленивого,
Добрым словом вспомните.

Скажете, что к лучшему,
Память вам не мучая,
Он писал от случая
До другого случая.

1941

When you're married, comes a time,
When you need a little cry –
You can quickly reach them down
And as swiftly put them by.

When you've locked the bedroom door,
Kept them from his jealous gaze,
Spare a kind and grateful thought
For your lover's lazy ways.

Say, 'it's better that he wrote
Only just from time to time,
Writing now, and then again,
Waiting till another time.'

1941

Я помню двух девочек, город ночной...
В ту зиму вы поздно спектакли кончали.
Две девочки ждали в подъезде со мной,
Чтоб вы, проходя, им два слова сказали.
Да, я провожал вас. И все-таки к ним,
Пожалуй, щедрей, чем ко мне, вы бывали.
Двух слов они ждали. А я б и одним
Был счастлив, когда б мне его вы сказали.

Я помню двух девочек; странно сейчас
Вдруг вспомнить две снежных фигурки у входа.
Подъезд театральный надолго погас.
Вам там не играть в зиму этого года.
Я очень далеко. Но, может, они
Вас в дальнем пути без меня провожают
И с кем-то другим в эти зимние дни,
Совсем как со мной, у подъезда скучают.

Я помню двух девочек. Может, живым
Я снова пройду вдоль заснеженных улиц
И, девочек встретив, поверю по ним,
Что в старый наш город вы тоже вернулись:
Боюсь, что мне незачем станет вас ждать,
Но будет все снежная, та же погода,
И девочки будут стоять и стоять,
Как вечные спутницы ваши, у входа...

1941

At the Stage Door

I remember two girls at the door in the night,
(Your shows ended later the year before last)
Two fans at the door of the theatre with me,
Who hoped for two words from your lips as you passed.
Yes, I was to go with you. And yet to them
I think you were kinder that night than to me.
They expected two words from you. I needed less –
For one word alone would have satisfied me.

I remember two girls; and tonight, it seems strange –
The thought of those two snowy forms at the door.
The lights of the theatre have long since gone out –
You won't be performing there now in the War
And I'm far away. Yet perhaps those two girls
On some distant journey still follow your fame
And now with some other man there in the snow
Are waiting without me, exactly the same.

I remember two girls.. and perhaps I shall live
To walk once again through the streets in the snow
And meeting the girls, shall discover you're back
To play in the town where I lived long ago.
I fear that I shan't have a reason to wait;
But the snow will continue to fall as before –
And the two little girls will wait on in the night
Eternal companions who stand by the door.

1941

A. Суркову

Ты помнишь, Алеша, дороги Смоленщины,
Как шли бесконечные, злые дожди,
Как кринки несли нам усталые женщины,
Прижав, как детей, от дождя их к груди,

Как слезы они вытирали украдкою,
Как вслед нам шептали:– Господь вас спаси!
И снова себя называли солдатками,
Как встарь повелось на великой Руси.

Слезами измеренный чаще, чем верстами,
Шел тракт, на пригорках скрываясь из глаз:
Деревни, деревни, деревни с погостами,
Как будто на них вся Россия сошлась,

Как будто за каждою русской околицей,
Крестом своих рук ограждая живых,
Всем миром сойдясь, наши прадеды молятся
За в бога не верящих внуков своих.

Ты знаешь, наверное, все-таки Родина –
Не дом городской, где я празднично жил,
А эти проселки, что дедами пройдены,
С простыми крестами их русских могил.

Smolenshchina

to Alexei Surkov

Remember, Alyosha, the roads of Smolenshchina,
Remember the rain and the mud and the pain,
The women, exhausted, who brought milk in pitchers,
And clasped them like babies at breast, from the rain.

The whispering words as we passed them – 'God bless you!'
The eyes where they secretly wiped away tears!
And how they all promised they would be 'soldatki',
The words of old Russia from earlier years.

The road disappearing past hills in the distance,
Its length that we measured with tears on the run.
And villages, villages, churches and churchyards,
As if all of Russia were gathered in one.

It seemed that in each Russian village we passed through,
The hands of our ancestors under the sod
Were making the sign of the cross and protecting
Their children, no longer believers in God.

You know, I believe that the Russia we fight for
Is not the dull town where I lived at a loss
But those country tracks that our ancestors followed,
The graves where they lie, with the old Russian cross

Не знаю, как ты, а меня с деревенскою
Дорожной тоской от села до села,
Со вдовьей слезою и с песнею женскою
Впервые война на проселках свела.

Ты помнишь, Алеша: изба под Борисовом,
По мертвому плачущий девичий крик,
Седая старуха в салопчике плисовом,
Весь в белом, как на смерть одетый, старик.

Ну что им сказать, чем утешить могли мы их?
Но, горе поняв своим бабьим чутьем,
Ты помнишь, старуха сказала: –Родимые,
Покуда идите, мы вас подождем.

'Мы вас подождем!' –говорили нам пажити.
'Мы вас подождем!' – говорили леса.
Ты знаешь, Алеша, ночами мне кажется,
Что следом за мной их идут голоса.

По русским обычаям, только пожарища
На русской земле раскидав позади,
На наших глазах умирали товарищи,
По-русски рубаху рванув на груди.

Нас пули с тобою пока еще милуют.
Но, трижды поверив, что жизнь уже вся,
Я все-таки горд был за самую милую,
За горькую землю, где я родился,

За то, что на ней умереть мне завещано,
Что русская мать нас на свет родила,
Что, в бой провожая нас, русская женщина
По-русски три раза меня обняла

1941

I feel that for me, it was countryside Russia
That first made me feel I must truly belong
To the tedious miles between village and village,
The tears of the widow, the women's sad song.

Remember, Alyosha, the hut at Borisov,
The cry of the girl as she mourned, and the sight
Of the grey-haired old woman, her velveteen jacket,
The old man, as if dressed for death, all in white!

And what could we say? With what words could we comfort them?
Yet seeming to gather the sense of our lack,
The old woman said, 'we shall wait for you, darlings!
Wherever you get to, we know you'll come back!'

'We know you'll come back!' said the fields and the pastures,
'We know you'll come back!' said the woods and the hill.
Alyosha, at nights I can hear them behind me.
Their voices are following after me still.

By old Russian practice, just fire and destruction
Are all we abandon behind us in war.
We see alongside us the deaths of our comrades,
By old Russian practice, the breast to the fore.

Alyosha, till now we've been spared by the bullets.
But when (for the third time) my life seemed to end,
I yet still felt proud of the dearest of countries,
The great bitter land I was born to defend.

I'm proud that the mother who bore us was Russian;
That Russian I'll fall as my ancestors fell;
That going to battle, the woman was Russian,
Who kissed me three times in a Russian farewell!

1941

Майор привез мальчишку на лафете.
Погибла мать. Сын не простился с ней.
За десять лет на том и этом свете
Ему зачтутся эти десять дней.

Его везли из крепости, из Бреста.
Был исцарапан пулями лафет.
Отцу казалось, что надежней места
Отныне в мире для ребенка нет.

Отец был ранен, и разбита пушка.
Привязанный к щиту, чтоб не упал,
Прижав к груди заснувшую игрушку,
Седой мальчишка на лафете спал.

Мы шли ему навстречу из России.
Проснувшись, он махал войскам рукой...
Ты говоришь, что есть еще другие,
Что я там был и мне пора домой...

Ты это горе знаешь понаслышке,
А нам оно оборвало сердца.
Кто раз увидел этого мальчишку,
Домой прийти не сможет до конца.

Я должен видеть теми же глазами,
Которыми я плакал там, в пыли,
Как тот мальчишка возвратится с нами
И поцелует горсть своей земли.

За все, чем мы с тобою дорожили,
Призвал нас к бою воинский закон.
Теперь мой дом не там, где прежде жили,
А там, где отнят у мальчишки он.

1941

The Child on the Gun-carriage

The major brought the boy out on the carriage;
His mother had been killed, no time for tears.
A child for whom the last ten days of battle
Had had the impact of as many years.

They brought him from the fortress, Brest-Litovsk,
Bullets had scarred the carriage and the gun;
His father had decided there was nowhere
A safer place where he could put his son.

The gun was shattered and his wounded father
Had tied him firmly to the shield, to keep
Him and his bedtime plaything on the carriage.
The grey-haired little boy was fast asleep.

We met him as we came to there from Russia;
He woke, and waved, as men came down the track.
You say that I should leave this job to others –
That I've been there and now I should come back.

You only know about all this from hearsay!
But we were there! It broke our hearts, my friend!
Whoever saw that little child as we did
Cannot come home again until the end.

I have to see, with those same eyes that saw him –
Those eyes that wept there, in the dust of war –
I have to see that child come back there with us,
And kiss the ground on which he lived before.

For everything which you and I have valued,
The law of war insists that we must fight!
Where I belong is not where we were living –
It's where that child has lost his home tonight.

1941

Да, я люблю тебя ещё сильней
За то, что редко счастья нам желали,
За то, что, раз назвав тебя своей,
Тебе всю жизнь об этом вспоминали.

За письма, о которых я молчал,
Где о тебе заботливо писали
Всё, что, к несчастью, я, слепой, не знал,
Но, к счастью их, все остальные знали.

Дай бог им счастья! А за слепоту
Спасибо той, что ослепить умела,
Спасибо за ночную красоту
Во власть слепому отданного тела.

Ты говорила: бедный мой, слепой,
И, азбуке слепых уча сначала,
Ведя меня в далёкий путь ночной,
Поводырём бывать не уставала.

Ты отказать слепому не могла
В том, что не смели зрячие, другие,
Ты целым миром для меня была.
А мир – на ощупь узнают слепые.

1941

Blindness

Oh Yes, it's true, I love you all the more
Because not many people link our names
And all the others, who have had your love,
Are still determined to assert their claims.

I've never mentioned to you all the letters
Which people very kindly write to me
To tell me things which everybody knows,
But which I, in my blindness, didn't see.

Good luck to them! But as for me, I thank
The one who blinded me. I bless the hour
I found the beauty born of darkness in
The body given to a blind man's power.

You said to me, 'because you cannot see,
I'll teach you things the blind alone can know.'
Through that dark journey, you have been my guide;
For you, it never was too far to go.

You are my world; you gave the world to me.
The blind alone can dare to see so much.
In blindness, I have learned to find by touch
What those with sight are not allowed to see.

1941

Мне хочется назвать тебя женой
За то, что так другие не назвали,
Что в старый дом мой сломанный войной,
Ты снова гостьей явишься едва ли.

За то, что я желал тебе и зла,
За то, что редко ты меня жалела,
За то, что просьб не ждя моих, пришла
Ко мне в ту ночь, когда сама хотела.

Мне хочется назвать тебя женой
Не для того, чтоб мир узнал об этом,
Не потому, что ты жила со мной,
По всем Московским сплетням и приметам...

Твоей я не тщеславлюсь красотой,
Ни громким именем, что ты носила,
С меня довольно нежной, тайной, той,
Что в дом ко мне неслышно приходила.

Сравнятся в славе смертью имена,
И красота, как станция, минует,
И, постарев, владелица одна
Себя к своим портретам приревнует.

Мне хочется назвать тебя женой
За то, что бесконечны дни разлуки,
Что слишком многим, кто сейчас со мной,
Должны глаза закрыть чужие руки.

My Wife

I want to say to you, 'you are my wife'
Because you were not called that by the rest;
Because in my old home, destroyed by war,
I don't suppose you'll ever be a guest.

Because I have not always wished you well,
Because I've had no sympathy from you,
Because one night, without my asking, you
Came to me just when you wanted to.

I want to say that you are now my wife,
Not just because I want the world to know
And not because, it seems, we live together –
Or all the Moscow rumours tell me so.

I do not boldly boast about your beauty,
Nor of the fame and fortune you have found.
Enough for me the gentle, secret woman
Who came into my house without a sound.

Death levels all the claims of worldly glory
And beauty's like a station that we pass;
And she who had it jealously compares it
With what she sees before her in the glass.

I want to say to you, 'you are my wife!'
Because the endless days of absence tear me,
Because I know a stranger's hand must close
The eyes of very many of those near me.

За то, что ты правдивою была,
Любить мне не давала обещанья
И в первый раз, что любишь, – солгала
В последний час солдатского прощанья.

Кем стала ты? Моей или чужой?
Отсюда сердцем мне не дотянуться...
Прости, что я зову тебя женой
По праву тех, кто может не вернуться

1941

Because you were so honest with me, darling,
And made no vows of loving evermore,
And only at the final hour of parting
Lied that you loved me, as I went to war.

Whose are you now? Are you still mine or no?
My heart cannot stretch out to what I lack...
Forgive me if I say you are my wife –
It is my privilege. I may not come back.

1941

Я, перебрав весь год, не вижу
Того счастливого числа,
Когда всего верней и ближе
Со мной ты связана была.

Я помню зал для репетиций
И свет, зажженный, как на грех,
И шепот твой, что не годится
Так делать на виду у всех.

Твой звездный плащ из старой драмы
И хлыст наездницы в руках,
И твой побег со сцены прямо
Ко мне на легких каблуках.

Нет, не тогда. Так, может, летом,
Когда, на сутки отпуск взяв,
Я был у ног твоих с рассветом,
Машину за ночь доконав.

Какой была ты сонной-сонной,
Вскочив с кровати босиком,
К моей шинели пропыленной
Как прижималась ты лицом!

When?

As I recall the year that's ending
I can't decide the happy time
When, more than any other moment,
I truly felt that you were mine.

Was it that night at your rehearsal?
The light that came on suddenly –
And your admonitory whisper
'You mustn't – everyone can see!'

Your starry robe for the old drama,
The riding whip held in your palms,
And how you ran to me so swiftly,
Straight from the stage into my arms...

Oh no, not then... Perhaps last summer,
I had a 24-hour pass
And reached you just as it was dawning
By all night driving on the gas.

And half awake and half still sleeping,
You jumped up barefoot from the bed
And tight against my dusty greatcoat
You pressed your sleepy little head.

Как бились жилки голубые
На шее под моей рукой!
В то утро, может быть, впервые
Ты показалась мне женой.

И все же не тогда, я знаю,
Ты самой близкой мне была.
Теперь я вспомнил: ночь глухая,
Обледенелая скала...

Майор, проверив по карманам,
В тыл приказал бумаг не брать;
Когда придется, безымянным
Разведчик должен умирать.

Мы к полночи дошли и ждали,
По грудь зарытые в снегу.
Огни далекие бежали
На том, на русском, берегу...

Теперь я сознаюсь в обмане:
Готовясь умереть в бою,
Я все-таки с собой в кармане
Нес фотографию твою.

Она под северным сияньем
В ту ночь казалась голубой,
Казалось, вот сейчас мы встанем
И об руку пойдем с тобой.

Казалось, в том же платье белом,
Как в летний день снята была,
Ты по камням оледенелым
Со мной невидимо прошла.

За смелость не прося прощенья,
Клянусь, что, если доживу,
Ту ночь я ночью обрученья
С тобою вместе назову.

1941

Upon your neck, your veins were beating;
My hand could feel the pulse of life!
That morning, more than any other,
It seemed to me you were my wife....

And yet I felt you once still closer.
One night you gave me strength to fight –
Now I remember – it was winter,
That icy cliff at dead of night.

The major, checking through our pockets,
Had said no documents must go.
The scout must have no name or number
If he should perish in the snow.

We reached the other side at midnight,
Deep in the snow prepared for war,
The light were twinkling in the distance
In Russia, on the other shore.

I now admit to a deception:
As I prepared (perhaps) to die,
I kept the picture in my pocket
You gave me when we said goodbye.

Seen by the northern light, your portrait
Seemed, in the darkness, almost blue.
I felt that when I must go forward,
Your hand in mine, you would go too.

Just as you were when it was taken,
Dressed in the same white summer frock,
Silent, unseen, you climbed beside me,
High on that cliff of of icy rock.

I ask no pardon for deciding
That (if I live) I swear we'll say
That was the night we shall remember.
That we shall call our wedding day.

1941

Хозяйка Дома

Подписан будет мир, и вдруг к тебе домой,
К двенадцати часам, шумя, смеясь, пророча,
Как в дни войны, придут слуга покорный твой
И все его друзья, кто будет жив к той ночи.
Хочу, чтоб ты и в эту ночь была
Опять той женщиной, вокруг которой
Мы изредка сходились у стола
Перед окном с бумажной синей шторой.
Басы зениток за окном слышны,
А радиола старый вальс играет,
И все в тебя немножко влюблены,
И половина завтра уезжает.
Уже шинель в руках, уж третий час,
И вдруг опять стихи тебе читают,
И одного из бывших в прошлый раз
С мужской ворчливой скорбью вспоминают.
Нет, я не ревновал в те вечера,
Лишь ты могла разгладить их морщины.
Так краток вечер, и – пора! Пора!
Трубят внизу военные машины.
С тобой наш молчаливый уговор –
Я выходил, как равный, в непогоду,
Пересекал со всеми зимний двор
И возвращался после их ухода.
И даже пусть догадливы друзья –
Так было лучше, это б нам мешало.
Ты в эти вечера была ничья.
Как ты права – что прав меня лишала!

The Hostess

When peace is signed, we'll gather at your door
At twelve o'clock at night, with noise and mirth,
Your humble servant, just as in the war,
And all his dearest friends – those that remain on earth.
That night I hope you'll be the same as when
We gathered round together where you sat
Beside the window with the pale blue blind
Around the table sometimes in your flat.
The anti-aircraft thuds a distant bass,
The record player wails an ancient sorrow,
The men are all enraptured by your face
And half of them go back to war tomorrow.
It's three o'clock, we're almost at the door,
But someone's reading verse before it ends
And one of those who came the time before
Must now be mourned for as men mourn their friends.
I wasn't jealous then or now – I know
That only you could smooth away their cares.
So short the evening and it's time to go!
The horns are sounding from the jeeps downstairs!
With you, I had a silent understanding –
I went with all the rest into the snow,
I walked with them across the winter landing –
And back again to see you when they go.
Perhaps the truth was not too hard to guess –
It's better thus, our love was in the way.
Those evenings, you belonged to none of us.
How right you were, to take my rights away!

Не мне судить, плоха ли, хороша,
Но в эти дни лишений и разлуки
В тебе жила та женская душа,
Тот нежный голос, те девичьи руки,
Которых так недоставало им,
Когда они под утро уезжали
Под Ржев, под Харьков, под Калугу, в Крым.
Им девушки платками не махали,
И трубы им не пели, и жена
Далеко где-то ничего не знала.
А утром неотступная война
Их вновь в свои объятья принимала.
В последний час перед отъездом ты
Для них вдруг становилась всем на свете,
Ты и не знала страшной высоты,
Куда взлетала ты в минуты эти.
Быть может, не любимая совсем,
Лишь для меня красавица и чудо,
Перед отъездом ты была им тем,
За что мужчины примут смерть повсюду –
Сияньем женским, девочкой, женой,
Невестой – всем, что уступить не в силах,
Мы умираем, заслонив собой
Вас, женщин, вас, беспомощных и милых.
Знакомый с детства простенький мотив,
Улыбка женщины – как много и как мало...
Как ты была права, что, проводив,
При всех мне только руку пожимала.

. . . .

It's not for me to judge how they should feel,
But in those days of parting and distress,
There lived in you that feminine ideal,
That gentle voice, those slender arms, that dress,
Which they so greatly lacked, as they went off
As go they must, come morning, to the front
To the Crimea, or Kaluga, or Rzhov.
No girls were there to wave their scarves to them;
No trumpets sounded for them; and their wives
Far away somewhere neither knew nor saw;
And in the morning they must give their lives
Into the implacable embrace of war.
That final hour before they went that night,
You all at once seemed to them all they had.
You never realised the frightful height
Which you had reached in them, for good or bad.
Perhaps they were not quite in love with you –
For me alone, most wonderful of wives –
And yet that evening, they all saw in you
That high ideal for which men give their lives –
That radiance of the child, the girl, the woman –
The bride – all that we simply can't surrender.
We go to death, protecting with our bodies
You, women, you – so helpless and so tender.
That image that we all have known since childhood –
A woman's smile – how much it is, how little!
How right you were that, as you parted from us,
You gave to all the same before we went to battle.

. . . .

Но вот наступит мир, и вдруг к тебе домой,
К двенадцати часам, шумя, смеясь, пророча,
Как в дни войны, придут слуга покорный твой
И все его друзья, кто будет жив к той ночи.
Они придут еще в шинелях и ремнях
И долго будут их снимать в передней –
Еще вчера война, еще всего на днях
Был ими похоронен тот, последний,
О ком ты спросишь, что ж он не пришел?
И сразу оборвутся разговоры,
И все заметят, как широк им стол,
И станут про себя считать приборы.
А ты, с тоской перехватив их взгляд,
За лишние приборы в оправданье,
Шепнешь: «Я думала, что кто-то из ребят
Издалека приедет с опозданьем...»
Но мы не станем спорить, мы смолчим,
Что все, кто жив, пришли, а те, что опоздали,
Так далеко уехали, что им
На эту землю уж поспеть едва ли.
Ну что же, сядем. Сколько нас всего?
Два, три, четыре... Стулья ближе сдвинем,
За тех, кто опоздал на торжество,
С хозяйкой дома первый тост поднимем.
Но если опоздать случится мне
И ты, меня коря за опозданье,
Услышишь вдруг, как кто-то в тишине
Шепнет, что бесполезно ожиданье,
Не отменяй с друзьями торжество.
Что из того, что я тебе всех ближе,
Что из того, что я любил, что из того,
Что глаз твоих я больше не увижу?
Мы собирались здесь, как равные, потом
Вдвоем – ты только мне была дана судьбою,

So peace will come, and we'll be at your door,
At twelve o'clock at night, with noise and mirth,
Your humble servant, just as in the war,
And all his dearest friends – those that remain on earth.
They come in belts and greatcoats and are slow
To take their things off and to come inside.
War was but yesterday – but days ago
They buried him – the latest one who died.
The one you ask about: 'Hasn't he come?'
And suddenly the conversation ceases
How wide, it seems, the table has become!
They silently begin to count the places.
And as you meet their glance, you'll feel you ought
To tell them why you've laid an extra plate.
You'll whisper softly, 'oh, I guess I thought
Someone might be delayed and get here late...'
We'll say no more to that – we know precisely –
Those who still live, have come, and those not in the hall
Have gone so far away that they're unlikely
To make it later on this earth at all.
So, let's sit down. How many do you think?
One, two, three, four – let's move the chairs up tight
To those who 'may come later' we shall drink
In the first toast we share with you tonight.
But what if it was me who was delayed?
And when I don't appear and you complain,
A whisper breaks the silence, half afraid
To tell you that you'll wait for me in vain?
Don't call it off – you mustn't spoil the evening!
What if for me you feel an extra pain?
What if I loved you? Put the thought aside
That I shall never see your eyes again.
Our rights in you were equal when we came here
Then later, you belonged alone to me,

Но здесь, за этим дружеским столом,
Мы были все равны перед тобою.
Потом ты можешь помнить обо мне,
Потом ты можешь плакать, если надо,
И, встав к окну в холодной простыне,
Просить у одиночества пощады.
Но здесь не смей слезами и тоской
По мне по одному лишать последней чести
Всех тех, кто вместе уезжал со мной
И кто со мною не вернулся вместе.
Поставь же нам стаканы заодно
Со всеми! Мы еще придем нежданно.
Пусть кто-нибудь живой нальет вино
Нам в наши молчаливые стаканы.
Еще вы трезвы. Не пришла пора
Нам приходить, но мы уже в дороге,
Уж била полночь... Пейте ж до утра!
Мы будем ждать рассвета на пороге.
Кто лгал, что я на праздник не пришел?
Мы здесь уже. Когда все будут пьяны,
Бесшумно к вам подсядем мы за стол
И сдвинем за живых бесшумные стаканы.

1942

But sitting all together around your table
We worshipped you in male equality.
Yes, later you can let yourself remember.
Later, if need be, will be time for tears,
When you can stand and shiver at the window,
And beg for mercy from the lonely years.
But now you must not spoil with tears and sorrow,
By grief for me deny the final right
To those who go with me to war tomorrow,
Or who, like me, did not return tonight.
Put out our glasses there with all the others!
And when you least expect us, we'll arrive!
Pour out the wine into our silent glasses –
That task must fall to someone who's alive!
You're sober yet, and so it's still too early
For us to join you; but we're on our way.
Midnight has struck. Drink on until the morning!
We'll wait here on the threshold till the day.
Who told a lie and said I wasn't coming?
Oh Yes, we're here! And when you're drunk all round,
We'll silently pull up our chairs to join you
And toast our living hosts without a sound...

1942

Когда на выжженном плато
Лежал я под стеной огня,
Я думал: слава богу, что
Ты так далеко от меня,
Что ты не слышишь этот гром,
Что ты не видишь этот ад,
Что где-то городе другом
Есть тихий дом и тихий сад,
Что вместо камня – там вода,
А вместо грома – кленов тень
И что со мною никогда
Ты не разделишь этот день.

Но стоит встретиться с тобой,
И я хочу, чтоб каждый день,
Чтоб каждый час и каждый бой
За мной ходила ты как тень.
Чтоб ты со мной делила хлеб,
Делила горести до слез,
Чтоб слепла ты, когда я слеп,
Чтоб мерзла ты, когда я мерз,
Чтоб гневом был твоим – мой гнев,
Мой голос – на твоих губах
Чтоб был, едва с моих слетев,

I Want You Here

With death an inch above my head
Upon the blackened ridge I lay
And I was grateful in my heart
That you were very far away.
And thunder was not in your ears,
And hell was not before your eyes,
And somewhere in a distant town,
A peaceful house and garden lies;
And water flows there to refresh,
And peaceful shade beneath a tree –
Yes, I was glad to tell myself
You could not share this day with me.

And yet I want you to be here,
Through every day and every night
And like a shadow, follow me
Through every battle that I fight.
I want you here to share my bread,
To share my grief, to share my tears,
To share my anger when I rage
And when I fear, to share my fears;
If I am frozen, you must freeze;
If I am blinded, you'll be blind;
My voice must be upon your lips,
My every thought be in your mind.

Чтоб не сказали мне друзья
Всё разделявшие в судьбе :
Она вдали, а рядом – я,
Что это женщина тебе ?
Ведь не она с тобой была
В тот день в атаке и пальбе.
Ведь не она тебя спасла,
Что это женщина тебе ?
Зачем теперь всё с ней да с ней,
Как будто в горе и в беде
Всех заменив тебе друзей,
Она с тобой была везде ?

Чтоб я друзьям ответить мог :
Да, ты не видел, как она
Лежала, съежившись в комок,
Там, где огонь был как стена,
Да, ты забыл, она была
Со мной три самых черных дня,
Она тебе там помогла
Когда ты вытащил меня,
И за спасение мое,
Когда я пил с тобой вдвоем,
Она – ты не видал ее –
Сидела третьей за столом.

1942

The friends with whom I share my fate
Must not say (as they seem to do)
'She's far away and I am here!
What can that woman mean to you?
'It wasn't her in the attack!
It wasn't her who got you through!
It wasn't her who saved your life!
What can that woman mean to you?
How can you say she's at your side?
How can her name be on your breath?
How can she take the place of friends
Who share with you this life, this death?'

I should be able to reply,
'Did you not see her as she lay
Curled up beside me on the ground
When death was but an inch away?
Have you forgotten, in the days
When things were blackest, she was there,
And when you came to save my life,
She helped you as you pulled me clear.
And when – perhaps you did not see –
I raised my grateful glass to you
To celebrate my near escape –
Beside us there – I saw her too.'

1942

Пусть прокляну впоследствии
Твои черты лица,
Любовь к тебе – как бедствие,
И нет ему конца.
Нет друга, нет товарища,
Чтоб среди бела дня
Из этого пожарища
Мог вытащить меня.
Отчаявшись в спасении
И бредя наяву,
Как при землетрясении
Я при тебе живу.
Когда ж от наваждения
Себя освобожу,
В ответ на осуждения
Я про себя скажу:
Зачем считать грехи её?
Ведь, не добра, не зла,
Не женщиной – стихиею
Вблизи она прошла.
И, грозный шаг заслыша, я
Пошёл грозу встречать,
Не став, как вы, под крышею
Её пережидать.

1942

The Storm

Well may I curse in years to come
The features of your face.
My love is like a cataclysm,
Transcending time and space.
There's not a friend or comrade dear
Who in the light of day
Could come into this flaming fire
And pull me clear away.
Despairing of escaping you
And raving like a fool,
As harnessed to an earthquake,
I live under your rule.
But when I come to free myself
From this hallucination,
I shall defend you when I hear
Their words of condemnation.
'Why do you number up her sins?
She's neither wrong nor right!
She's not a woman, she's a force,
A tempest in the night;
And feeling the approaching threat,
I went to meet the storm!
I did not stay, like you, indoors,
Where it was safe and warm.'

1942

В Заволожье

Не плачь! – Всё тот же поздный зной
Висит над желтыми степями.
Все так же беженцы толпой
Бредут; и дети за плечами..

Не плачь! Покуда мимо нас
Они идут из Сталинграда,
Идут, не подымая глаз,
От этих глаз не жди пощады.

Иди, сочувствием своим
У них не вымогая взгляда.
Иди туда, навстречу им –
Вот все, что от тебя им надо.

1942

Stalingrad

Don't weep! Above the yellow steppe
Still hangs the same late summer heat
And they, with children on their backs,
Come still, with tired and stumbling feet.

No tears! And as the crowd goes by
From Stalingrad to God knows where,
Don't try to catch their downcast eyes –
You cannot look for pity there!

Go on – don't strive to meet their gaze!
They need no sympathy, no shame!
All that they need from you is this –
You must go there, from whence they came!

1942

Открытое письмо

Женщине из г. Вичуга

Я вас обязан известить,
Что не дошло до адресата
Письмо, что в ящик опустить
Не постыдились вы когда-то.

Ваш муж не получил письма,
Он не был ранен словом пошлым,
Не вздрогнул, не сошел с ума,
Не проклял все, что было в прошлом.

Когда он поднимал бойцов
В атаку у руин вокзала,
Тупая грубость ваших слов
Его, по счастью, не терзала.

Когда шагал он тяжело,
Стянув кровавой тряпкой рану,
Письмо от вас еще все шло,
Еще, по счастью, было рано.

Когда на камни он упал
И смерть оборвала дыханье,
Он все еще не получал,
По счастью, вашего посланья.

An Open Letter

to a woman from Vichuga

I must inform you that the letter
Which you, at some time, recently,
Were not ashamed to send your husband,
Has failed to reach the addressee.

He was not wounded by your letter.
The coarse and vulgar things you said.
They have not made him lose his reason
Or curse the feelings that are dead.

And when he rose to lead his comrades
Against the ruins in the square
You cruel, blunt, unthinking letter
Was fortunately not yet there.

And when he staggered, badly wounded,
Bleeding and roughly bandaged, numb,
The letter you had sent to him
Had fortunately not yet come.

And when he fell down on the pavement
And dark and cold broke off his breath,
The letter that his wife had sent him
Was undelivered at his death.

Могу вам сообщить о том,
Что, завернувши в плащ-палатки,
Мы ночью в сквере городском
Его зарыли после схватки.

Стоит звезда из жести там
И рядом тополь – для приметы...
А впрочем, я забыл, что вам,
Наверно, безразлично это.

Письмо нам утром принесли...
Его, за смертью адресата,
Между собой мы вслух прочли –
Уж вы простите нам, солдатам.

Быть может, память коротка
У вас. По общему желанью,
От имени всего полка
Я вам напомню содержанье.

Вы написали, что уж год,
Как вы знакомы с новым мужем.
А старый, если и придет,
Вам будет все равно ненужен.

We took the town. I must inform you
That in the liberated square,
We wrapped him in a soldier's groundsheet
And buried him at nightfall there.

A tin star marks his grave location,
Next to a poplar, very tall.
But I forget – to you these details
Are of no interest at all.

Your letter came the morning after
And as the addressee was dead,
(I hope you will excuse us soldiers)
We read aloud what you had said.

It's possible you have forgotten
So by his comrades' general vote
I shall remind you of the contents.
Here is the gist of what you wrote:

You have, you say, another husband;
Have lived with him about a year.
And he himself would not be welcome
If he should ever reappear.

Что вы не знаете беды,
Живете хорошо. И кстати,
Теперь вам никакой нужды
Нет в лейтенантском аттестате.

Чтоб писем он от вас не ждал
И вас не утруждал бы снова...
Вот именно: «не утруждал»...
Вы побольней искали слова.

И все. И больше ничего.
Мы перечли их терпеливо,
Все те слова, что для него
В разлуки час в душе нашли вы.

«Не утруждай». «Муж». «Аттестат»...
Да где ж вы душу потеряли?
Ведь он же был солдат, солдат!
Ведь мы за вас с ним умирали.

Я не хочу судьею быть,
Не все разлуку побеждают,
Не все способны век любить –
К несчастью, в жизни все бывает.

Apparently you live in plenty;
You lack for nothing. By the way,
There's no more need for the allowance
Deducted from his soldier's pay.

And he should pester you no longer
And stop expecting you to write
That was the word you use – just 'pester'
You chose a word to make it hurt.

And that was all. And nothing more.
We read it patiently again –
The words which, in a soldier's absence,
You mustered to inspire your pen.

'Don't pester me.' 'Another Husband.'
What words to send when you're apart!
This man had gone to die for you!
Where had you lost your woman's heart?

I shall not be your judge. Not all
Can bear the strain of absence. No –
Not all, I know, can love for ever –
For love will come love will go.

Но как могли вы, не пойму,
Стать, не страшась, причиной смерти,
Так равнодушно вдруг чуму
На фронт отправить нам в конверте?

Ну хорошо, пусть не любим,
Пускай он больше вам ненужен,
Пусть жить вы будете с другим,
Бог с ним, там с мужем ли, не с мужем.

Но ведь солдат не виноват
В том, что он отпуска не знает,
Что третий год себя подряд,
Вас защищая, утруждает.

Что ж, написать вы не смогли
Пусть горьких слов, но благородных.
В своей душе их не нашли –
Так заняли бы где угодно.

В отчизне нашей, к счастью, есть
Немало женских душ высоких,
Они б вам оказали честь –
Вам написали б эти строки;

But still I cannot understand it
How you, without a thought or care,
Could send this virus in a letter
To spread the plague among us here.

I know that you don't love him. So
He isn't wanted any more.
Live with whichever man you choose to –
The latest, or the one before!

But God! It's not the soldier's fault
Defending you is 'such a bother'.
More than two years he's had no leave
And so you've left him for another!

Was it not possible at least
To break it gently to the man?
If you can't find the right expressions
Then get some help from one who can.

There are, thank God, still now in Russia,
Some kind and thoughtful women who
Would willingly have helped you write it
And chosen the right words for you.

Они б за вас слова нашли,
Чтоб облегчить тоску чужую.
От нас поклон им до земли,
Поклон за душу их большую

Не вам, а женщинам другим,
От нас отторженным войною,
О вас мы написать хотим,
Пусть знают вы тому виною,

Что их мужья на фронте, тут,
Подчас в душе борясь с собою,
С невольною тревогой ждут
Из дома писем перед боем.

На суд далеких жен своих
Мы вас пошлем. Вы клеветали
На них. Вы усомниться в них
Нам на минуту повод дали.

Пускай поставят вам в вину,
Что душу птичью вы скрывали,
Что вы за женщину, жену,
Себя так долго выдавали.

А бывший муж ваш – он убит.
Все хорошо. Живите с новым.
Уж мертвый вас не оскорбит
В письме давно ненужным словом.

Homage is due to these good women.
Like you, they have been left behind,
They would not hesitate to help you
To find the words to spare his mind.

I hope that they will read this verse
Those torn apart from us by war
Should know about the harm you're doing –
Not just unfaithfulness, but more.

You've sown a seed of doubt in us
And made their husbands think a little
And hesitate to open letters
Which come to them before a battle.

You shall be judged by distant wives
Whom you have slandered, made us doubt
And wonder, if we trust too much,
Unpleasant truths may soon come out.

And let them try and find you guilty
That for too long, you played a part –
The role of wife, the role of woman,
And hid your cold reptilian heart.

Well, now, your husband's killed. He's dead.
No problem! You have found a better!
The dead man won't annoy you now
With more of his unwanted letters.

Живите, не боясь вины,
Он не напишет, не ответит
И, в город возвратись с войны,
С другим вас под руку не встретит.

Лишь за одно еще простить
Придется вам его – за то, что,
Наверно, с месяц приносить
Еще вам будет письма почта.

Уж ничего не сделать тут –
Письмо медлительнее пули.
К вам письма в сентябре придут,
А он убит еще в июле.

О вас там каждая строка,
Вам это, верно, неприятно –
Так я от имени полка
Беру его слова обратно.

Примите же в конце от нас
Презренье наше на прощанье.
Не уважающие вас
Покойного однополчане

По поручению офицеров полка

К. Симонов

1943

Live without fear of shame or blame!
You'll get no pestering, no harm.
He won't come back, when the War's over,
And see you walking arm and arm.

You must forgive him one slight problem –
It's just that, for a month or more
It's possible the postal system
May bring his letters to your door.

A letter's slower than a bullet!
And nothing can be done; that's why
You'll get a letter in September
When he was killed in late July!

Each line he wrote in adoration,
Which I expect you'll find absurd;
So on behalf of all his comrades,
I formally take back his words

So, to conclude, the undersigned
Your husband's friends and comrades too,
Wish to express sincere contempt
For what you are and what you do.

On behalf of the officers of the regiment

K. Simonov

1943

Жены

Последний кончился огарок,
И по невидимой черте
Три красных точки трех цигарок
Безмолвно бродят в темноте.

О чем наш разговор солдатский?
О том, что нынче Новый год,
А света нет, и холод адский,
И снег, как каторжный, метет.

Один сказал: «Моя сегодня
Полы помоет, как при мне.
Потом детей, чтоб быть свободней,
Уложит. Сядет в тишине.

Ей сорок лет – мы с ней погодки.
Всплакнет ли, просто ли вздохнет,
Но уж, наверно, рюмкой водки
Меня по-русски помянет...»

Второй сказал: «Уж год с лихвою
С моей война нас развела.
Я, с молодой простясь женою,
Взял клятву, чтоб верна была.

Я клятве верю, коль не верить,
Как проживешь в таком аду?
Наверно, все глядит на двери,
Все ждет сегодня – вдруг приду...»

Wives

The stove has died right down to nothing,
It's midnight, and the only marks
Of light, are three small dots of red
Of cigarettes that break the dark.

What do we talk about, we soldiers?
There's New Year's Eve to celebrate
In bitter cold we sit in darkness
And snow falls on and on like Fate.

One says, 'she'll give the floor a mop,
Just like she did when I was there,
And then she'll settle down the children
And have some quiet in her chair.

We're forty – same age, both of us.
I guess she'll have a little cry
And then she'll have a shot of vodka
And toast her husband with a sigh.'

The second said, 'we're not long married.
I haven't seen her for a year.
I made her promise to be faithful
When we were parted by the War.

I've got to trust her. If I didn't,
How could a man get through this hell?
I like to think she kids herself
It's me, each time she hears the bell.'

А третий лишь вздохнул устало:
Он думал о своей – о той,
Что с лета прошлого молчала
За черной фронтовой чертой...

1943

The third just sighed and thought of her –
The wife that he had left behind.
He's had no letter since last summer.
She is behind the German lines...

1943

Дом в Вязьме

Я помню в Вязьме старый дом.
Одну лишь ночь мы жили в нём.

Мы ели то, что бог послал,
И пили, что шофёр достал.

Мы уезжали в бой чуть свет.
Кто был в ту ночь, иных уж нет.

Но знаю я, что в смертный час
За тем столом он вспомнил нас.

В ту ночь, готовясь умирать,
Навек забыли мы, как лгать,

Как изменять, как быть скупым,
Как над добром дрожать своим.

Хлеб пополам, кров пополам –
Так жизнь в ту ночь открылась нам.

Я помню в Вязьме старый дом.
В день мира прах его с трудом

Найдём средь выжженных печей
И обгорелых кирпичей,

The House at Vyazma

In Vyazma is an ancient house
Which once one night was home to us.

That night we ate whatever came,
The source of drink was much the same.

At dawn, we went away to fight
And one of us lived not till night.

But this I know, that as he died,
We and the house were in his mind.

That night, as we prepared to die
We had forgotten how to lie,

How to betray, how to be mean,
How to cling on to what is mine.

That night it was revealed to us
That life is sharing, bread and house.

In Vyazma is an ancient house
We'll search for it in days of peace

We'll find the traces of it there
Where stoves and bricks are burned and bare.

Но мы складчину соберём
И вновь построим этот дом,

С такой же печкой и столом
И накрест клееным стеклом.

Чтоб было в доме всё точь-в-точь
Как в ту нам памятную ночь.

И если кто-нибудь из нас
Рубашку другу не отдаст,

Хлеб не поделит пополам,
Солжёт, или изменит нам,

Иль, находясь в чинах больших,
Друзей забудет фронтовых,

Мы суд солдатский соберём
И в этот дом его сошлём.

Пусть посидит один в дому,
Как будто завтра в бой ему,

Как будто, если лжёт сейчас,
Он, может, лжёт в последний раз,

Как будто хлеба не даёт
Тому, кто к вечеру умрёт,

And putting all we have in one,
We'll build again that ancient home

With the same table, stove and pipe
And window stretched across with tape

In every detail just and right
As on that memorable night.

And if there's one who at the end
Won't give his shirt up to his friend,

Who will not share the bread he has
Who lies to us or who betrays,

Or reaching the exalted ranks
Of former friends no longer thinks,

We'll make a court to judge his case
And send him back into the house

There let him sit alone as if
Tomorrow battle comes and death,

And if tonight a lie has passed
His lips, it yet may be the last.

As if he will not share his bread
With one who shortly will lie dead,

И палец подаёт тому,
Кто завтра жизнь спасёт ему.

Пусть вместо нас лишь горький стыд
Ночь за столом с ним просидит.

Мы, встретясь, по его глазам
Прочтём: он был иль не был там.

Коль не был, значит, круг друзей,
На одного ещё тесней.

Но если был, мы ничего
Не спросим больше у него.

Он вновь по гроб нам будет мил,
Пусть честно скажет: Я там был.

1943

Or greet with cold and formal breath
The man who'll rescue him from death,

Instead of us, let bitter shame
Sit with him there in our old home.

And when we see him, we shall know
Whether he has been there or no.

And if he has not, then the mass
Of friends, will be by one the less.

But if he has, then not a thing
We'll say about it more to him.

Once more till death he will be dear,
If once he tells us, 'I was there.'

1943

Note: Tape was used to protect windows from blast-damage.
The X on every window became a symbol of the war.

Да, мы живём, не забывая
Что просто не пришел черед,
Что смерть, как чаша круговая,
Наш стол обходит круглый год.

Не потому тебе прощаю,
Что не умею помнить зла,
А потому, что круговая
Ко мне все ближе вдоль стола.

1945

The Cup of Death

The cup of death goes round the table
Each of us waits his turn to die.
We're always conscious that it's coming.
They don't know when, and nor do I.

If I am blind to how you treat me.
It's not because I cannot see.
It is because, around the table,
The cup comes round again towards me!

1945

До утра перед разлукой
Свадьба снилась мне твоя.
Паперть. Сон, должно быть, в руку:
Ты – невеста. Нищий – я.

Пусть случится всё, как снилось,
Только в жизни обещай –
Выходя, мне, сделай милость,
Милостыни не давай.

1945

The Wedding

In a dream, I saw a wedding
And I think the bride was you.
You the bride and I a beggar
At the porch – it may be true!

Let it happen as I dreamed it!
Only promise, as you stand
At the porch, to have the kindness –
Put no alms into my hand!

1945

Стекло тысячеверстной толщины
Разлука вставила в окно твоей квартиры,
И я смотрю, как из другого мира,
Мне голоса в ней больше не слышны.

Вот ты прошла, присела на окне,
Кому-то улыбнулась, встала снова,
Сказала что-то. Может, обо мне?
А что? Не слышу ничего, ни слова.

Какое невозможное страданье
Опять, уехав, быть глухонемым!
Но что, как вдруг дана лишь в оправданье
На этот раз разлука нам двоим?

Ты помнишь честный вечер объясненья,
Когда, казалось, смеем всё сказать.
И вдруг – стекло. И только губ движенье,
И даже стука сердца не слыхать.

1946

The Glass

With glass a thousand miles thick
Parting has glazed the windows of your flat;
And I look through, as from another world,
But not a sound is audible through that.

I see you pass and sit down by the window.
You smile at someone; you get up unheard.
You speak. Of what? Perhaps you speak of me?
No good! I cannot hear a single word!

How painful, how impossible it is –
That separation makes us deaf and dumb!
Or could it be that distance justifies
The actual gulf between us that has come?

Remember how we cleared the air that night?
It seemed, perhaps, a new and honest start!
And then – the glass. And just the moving lips.
And now I cannot even hear your heart!

1946

Бывает иногда мужчина –
Всех женщин безответный друг,
Друг бескорыстный, беспричинный,
На всякий случай, словно круг,
Висящий на стене каюты.
Весь век он старится и ждет,
Потом в последнюю минуту
Его швырнут – и он спасет.

Неосторожными руками
Меня повесив где-нибудь,
Не спутай. Я не круг. Я камень.
Со мною можно потонуть.

1946

The Lifebelt

You get from time to time a man
Who's every woman's silent friend –
A friend without ulterior aim,
A friend on whom she can depend.
He's like the lifebelt on the deck
Which hangs and waits, for years unheeded,
Until at last it saves a life,
That final moment when it's needed.

Your careless hands must never hang
Me somewhere handy to be found.
I'm not a lifebelt. I'm a stone.
Hold fast to me and you'll be drowned.

1946

Я схоронил любовь и сам себя обрёк
Быть памятником ей. Над свежею могилой
Сам на себе я вывел восемь строк,
Посмертно написав их через силу.

Как в марафонском беге, не дыша,
До самого конца любовь их долетела.
Но отлетела от любви душа,
А тело жить одно не захотело.

Как камень, я стою среди камней,
Прося лишь об одном: Не трогайте руками
И посторонних надписей на мне
Не делайте. Я всё-таки не камень.

1948

I Buried Love

I buried love and doomed myself to be
Its monument. Above the recent grave
Upon myself I carved a dozen lines,
Beyond my strength and posthumously brave.

Love, like a winner in the marathon,
Had reached the finish with his dying breath.
My love had lost the spirit and the soul
And body, lacking spirit, falls to death.

Firm as a stone, I stand amidst the graves
And all I ask is this – let me alone!
And untoward inscriptions upon me
Do not attempt! For I am not a stone...

1948

Я не могу писать тебе стихов
Ни той, что ты была, ни той, что стала.
И, очевидно, этих горьких слов
Обоим нам давно уж не хватало.

За всё добро – спасибо! Не считал
По мелочам, покуда были вместе,
Ни сколько взял его, ни сколько дал,
Хоть вряд ли задолжал тебе по чести.

А всё то зло, что на меня, как груз
Навалено твоей рукою было,
Оно моё! Я сам с ним разберусь,
Мне жизнь недаром шкуру им дубила.

Упрёки поздно на ветер бросать,
Не бойся разговоров до рассвета.
Я просто разлюбил тебя. И это
Мне не даёт стихов тебе писать

1954

I Cannot Write

I cannot write a single line of verse,
Not to the girl you were, nor to you now.
And after all the bitter words we've said
We've both got plenty left for one more row.

For what you gave when I was with you – thanks!
I never reckoned the precise degree
Of how much I received, how much I gave.
I'd be surprised if you gave more to me!

And as for all the evil, like a burden,
You laid on me, a heavy load of pain –
It's part of me and I can deal with it.
The scars remain indeed – but not in vain.

Don't fear that we shall talk till dawn and curse.
It's too late now for idle tales of woe.
I just no longer love you, dear, and so
I cannot write you one more line of verse...

1954

Сын

Был он немолодой, но бравый;
Шел под пули без долгих сборов,
Наводил мосты, переправы,
Ни на шаг от своих саперов;

И погиб под самым Берлином,
На последнем на поле минном,
Не простясь со своей подругой,
Не узнав, что родит ему сына.

И осталась жена в Тамбове.
И осталась в полку саперном
Та, что стала его любовью
В сорок первом, от горя черном;

Та, что думала без загада:
Как там, в будущем, с ней решится?
Но войну всю прошла с ним рядом,
Не пугаясь жизни лишиться...

Ничего от него не хотела,
Ни о чем для себя не просила,
Но, от пуль закрыв своим телом,
Из огня его выносила

И выхаживала ночами,
Не беря с него обещаний
Ни жениться, ни разводиться,
Ни писать для нее завещаний.

The Colonel's Son

Although he wasn't young, he was a soldier –
As steady under fire as any man;
Led on his sappers in their dangerous job
A field to clear of mines, a flood to span;

And when he died, it was before Berlin.
The final minefield was the fatal one.
He had no time to say goodbye to her
And never knew that he had got a son.

He was survived in Tambov by his widow
And in the regiment of engineers
He also left behind the one who'd loved him
Since 1941, that blackest year.

The one who sometimes wondered, without thinking,
What would become of her, after the War
But through the years of War's she stayed beside him,
Gave all she had and would have given more.

And for herself asked nothing, never wanted
Some token of his love, some small desire,
But shielding him from bullets with her body,
She dragged him, wounded, from the field of fire.

And nursed him through the nights and lay beside him
And asked from him no promise, never tried
To raise the issue of divorce and marriage
Or even for some money if he died.

И не так уж была красива,
Не приметна женскою статью.
Ну, да, видно, не в этом сила,
Он ее и не видел в платьях,

Больше все в сапогах кирзовых,
С санитарной сумкой, в пилотке,
На дорогах войны грозовых,
Где орудья бьют во всю глотку.

В чем ее красоту увидел?
В том ли, как вела себя смело?
Или в том, как людей жалела?
Или в том, как любить умела?

А что очень его любила,
Жизнь ему отдав без возврата –
Это так. Что было, то было...
Хотя он не скрыл, что женатый.

Получает жена полковника
Свою пенсию за покойника;
Старший сын работает сам уже,
Даже дочь уже год как замужем...

Но живёт ещё где-то женщина,
Что звалась фронтовой женой.
Не обещано, не завещано
Ничего только ей одной.

And yet it's true that she was not a beauty
Her figure nothing special, I confess,
That wasn't what he saw in her – remember
He'd never even seen her in a dress.

He saw her baggy-trousered, heavy booted,
Cap on her head, upon the roads of War,
Taking her first-aid bag where it was needed,
Her woman's voice drowned by the cannon's roar.

What did he see in her? Was it her kindness –
Her pity for the wounded? Or above
All that she showed she had a soldier's courage?
Or was it simply that she gave him love?

For certainly, with all her heart she loved him,
Although he didn't hide he had a wife.
What happened, happened. Nothing can be altered.
For him, she would have given up her life.

At home in Tambov now, the colonel's widow
Receives a colonel's pension since he died.
His eldest son is out at work; his daughter
A year or two ago, became a bride.

But somewhere now there also lives the woman
Who used to call herself his wartime wife.
Had nothing promised her, had nothing left her,
And all alone now leads a lonely life.

Только ей одной да мальчишке,
Что читает первые книжки,
Что с трудом одет без заплаток
На её, медсестры, зарплату.

Иногда об отце он слышит,
Что был добрый, храбрый, упрямый.
Но фамилии его не пишет
На тетрадках, купленных мамой.

Он имеет сестру и брата,
Ну, а что ему в том добра-то?
Пусть подарков ему не носят,
Только маму пусть не поносят.

Даже пусть она виновата
Перед кем-то, в чем-то, когда-то,
Но какой ханжа озабочен –
Надавать ребенку пощечин?

Сплетней душу ему не троньте!
Мальчик вправе спокойно знать,
Что отец его пал на фронте
И два раза ранена мать.

Есть над койкой его на коврике
Снимок одерской переправы,
Где с покойным отцом, полковником,
Мама рядом стоит по праву.

Не забывшая, незамужняя,
Никому другому не нужная,
Она молча несёт свою муку.
Поцелуй, как встретишь, ей руку!

1954

Not quite alone, she has their little boy:
He learns to read, he stumbles nursery verse.
She manages to clothe him; it's not easy
On just the basic wages of a nurse.

And sometimes now, she talks about his father:
How brave he was, how stubborn and how wise.
And yet he doesn't write his father's surname
Upon the school-books that his mother buys.

He has, of course, a sister and a brother,
But on his birthday, presents never come.
A pity that they don't have any contact.
At any rate, they don't insult his Mum.

Should she feel shame? What if she does feel guilty –
Feels somehow, some time, what she did was wrong.
But tell me this – what hypocrite would want it
That punishment should fall upon her son?

Let him have less embarrassment and gossip.
It's better for the child to be aware
His father died in battle; and his mother
Served at the front and was twice wounded there.

Above his little bed upon the wall
There hangs a picture from the final summer
The Oder crossing – and there stands his father
And on his father's right, there stands his mother.

She's still remembers and she hasn't married.
She bears her load of grief from day to day,
A woman no one needs and no one cares for –
Pay homage to her if you go her way!

1954

Поручик

Уж сотый день врезаются гранаты
В Малахов окровавленный курган,
И рыжие британские солдаты
Идут на штурм под хриплый барабан.

А крепость Петропавловск-на-Камчатке
Погружена в привычный мирный сон.
Хромой поручик, натянув перчатки,
С утра обходит местный гарнизон.

Седой солдат, откозыряв неловко,
Трет рукавом ленивые глаза,
И возле пушек бродит на веревке
Худая гарнизонная коза.

Ни писем, ни вестей. Как ни проси их,
Они забыли там, за семь морей,
Что здесь, на самом кончике России,
Живет поручик с ротой егерей...

Поручик, долго щурясь против света,
Смотрел на юг, на море, где вдали –
Неужто нынче будет эстафета?
Маячили в тумане корабли.

Он взял трубу. По зыби, то зеленой,
То белой от волнения, сюда,
Построившись кильватерной колонной,
Шли к берегу британские суда.

The Old Lieutenant

For three long months continues the bombardment.
The bloodstained Malakhov withstands it still.
The hoarse-voiced drum drives on the British redcoats.
Once more they throw themselves against the hill!

But by the far Pacific on Kamchatka
The fortress slumbers on in peace profound.
The lame lieutenant, garrison commander,
Pulls on his gloves and goes his daily round.

A grey old soldier, lazily saluting,
Shades with his sleeve his eyes against the sun;
The skinny goat belonging to the fortress
Is tethered with a rope beside the gun.

No news, no letters, no response to pleading –
They have forgotten, seven seas away,
That here upon the farthest point of Russia,
A company of men is in their pay.

But as he strained his eyes against the sunlight,
Far to the south across the sea, perhaps,
It seemed to the lieutenant they were coming –
There in the mist - he saw the shape of ships!

He seized the glass. Across the silent water,
Now green, now white with agitated foam,
In line ahead, the British ships were moving,
Advancing steadily towards his home.

Зачем пришли они из Альбиона?
Что нужно им? Донесся дальний гром,
И волны у подножья бастиона
Вскипели, обожженные ядром.

Полдня они палили наудачу,
Грозя весь город обратить в костер.
Держа в кармане требованье сдачи,
На бастион взошел парламентер.

Поручик, в хромоте своей увидя
Опасность для достоинства страны,
Надменно принимал британца, сидя
На лавочке у крепостной стены.

Что защищать? Заржавленные пушки,
Две улицы то в лужах, то в пыли,
Косые гарнизонные избушки,
Клочок не нужной никому земли?

Но все-таки ведь что-то есть такое,
Что жаль отдать британцу с корабля?
Он горсточку земли растер рукою:
Забытая, а все-таки земля.

Дырявые, обветренные флаги
Над крышами шумят среди ветвей...
– Нет, я не подпишу твоей бумаги,
Так и скажи Виктории своей!

What can have brought them here from far off Albion?
What do they want? A distant booming sound –
And suddenly, the sea below the bastion
Rose boiling with the impact of the round.

All afternoon, the guns fired on at random
And threatened soon to set the town aflame.
Then bearing a demand for their surrender,
Beneath a flag of truce, an envoy came.

The old lieutenant, feeling that his lameness
Might make the credit of his country fall,
Received the envoy haughtily and seated
Upon a bench beside the fortress wall.

What was there to defend? The rusty cannons,
Two dirty streets all overgrown with weeds,
The slant-roofed huts that served to house the soldiers,
A useless bit of land that no one needs!

But something told him he would not surrender.
He felt a chunk of earth beneath his hand.
He would not yield this place up to the sailor;
Perhaps forgotten, it was still his land!

The tattered weather-beaten flags still fluttered
Above the roof and up against the tree.
'Go tell your queen I shall not sign your paper!'
He answered the attacker from the sea.

. . . .

Уже давно британцев оттеснили,
На крышах залатали все листы,
Уже давно всех мертвых схоронили,
Поставили сосновые кресты,

Когда санкт-петербургские курьеры
Вдруг привезли, на год застряв в пути,
Приказ принять решительные меры
И гарнизон к присяге привести.

Для боевого действия к отряду
Был прислан в крепость новый капитан,
А старому поручику в награду
Был полный отпуск с пенсиею дан!

Он все ходил по крепости, бедняга,
Все медлил лезть на сходни корабля.
Холодная казенная бумага,
Нелепая любимая земля....

1939

The British, beaten off, had long departed,
The roofs repaired that stood beside the waves,
Some time had passed since all the dead were buried
And pinewood crosses placed upon their graves;

And then, delayed a year upon the voyage,
St Petersburg despatches came at length.
The orders were to take decisive measures:
The garrison must be brought up to strength.

A captain, fit to lead the force in battle,
Was posted there, where now he was to serve.
The old lieutenant's service was rewarded –
He was retired and placed on the reserve!

The poor old soldier walked about the fortress...
He knew the ship was ready to depart –
But in his mind, the cold official paper,
The useless bit of land that claimed his heart!

1939

Printed in Dunstable, United Kingdom

71686785R00165

Meet the Author

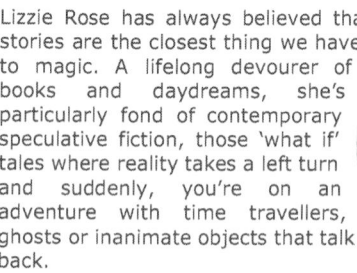

Lizzie Rose has always believed that stories are the closest thing we have to magic. A lifelong devourer of books and daydreams, she's particularly fond of contemporary speculative fiction, those 'what if' tales where reality takes a left turn and suddenly, you're on an adventure with time travellers, ghosts or inanimate objects that talk back.

After studying English Literature, Language, Mathematics, Psychology and Photography, Lizzie pursued teacher training to become a primary school teacher. She spent six years living her dream, teaching in Key Stage One classrooms, before transitioning to work with children with Special Educational Needs and Disabilities.

Working in a SEND school gave her not only patience but also an appreciation for how complex and wonderful human communication really is. Naturally, she decided to funnel all of that insight into writing stories for adults.

Currently, Lizzie is adding another feather to her academic cap: a Master's in Education, specialising in the use of Animal Assisted Intervention (translation: she gets to study how snails make everything better).

Online, Lizzie moonlights as TheHauntedBat - a Gothic fashion and homeware YouTuber/influencer whose aesthetic can best be described as "Victorian ghost, but make it cosy." Through her channel, she's connected with humans from all over the globe, many of whom are just as obsessed with bats, pumpkins, lace, and haunted teapots as she is.

At home in Hampshire, Lizzie and her partner Zoe share their lives with what can only be described as a small zoo. The current roster includes: a dog named Ernie, George the Bearded Dragon, Rupert the Axolotl, Stinkpot the Turtle, and Jack the Moorish Gecko and four and three-quarter cats (don't ask, it involves missing limbs). The feline line-up? Parsnip, Roast Potato, Tenderstem Broccoli, Bisto Gravy and Cheesy Leeks.

When not writing, Lizzie can usually be found road-tripping in Zoe's van, hoarding memories (and snacks), or obsessively defending her favourite number, which is, very specifically, 56.

If you'd like to send her feedback about the book (or simply argue about why 56 is clearly the superior number), you can reach her at: *threeleggedpress@yahoo.com*

Official Certificate of Birth

This certifies that **Frederick Norman Carter** was born on the **25th August 2028** at **09:59**, at **Queen Alexandra Hospital, Portsmouth**, weighing **7 pounds 6 ounces** and measuring **19.7 inches**. Witnessed and celebrated by loving parents: **Dr Danny Carter and Mrs Emily Carter**

"Every child begins the world anew, a fresh gift from fate."

What Must Be

What Must Be

Lizzie Rose

Published in Great Britain in 2025 by The Three-Legged Press,
Hampshire, England

First published in Great Britain in 2025 by The Three-Legged
Press

ISBN 978 1 9192706 0 9

The Three-Legged Press, First edition, 2025
threeleggedpress@yahoo.com

Cover design by Elizabeth Soal
Illustrations by Elizabeth Soal
Edited by Zoe Austin, Valerie Weston,
Agnes Soal and Karla Welch

To anyone who believes in fate - may the universe meet you halfway.

To My Love, who fills every chapter of my life with ecstasy.

To my parents, who showed me that while we cannot choose fate, we can choose love, courage, and strength along the way.

To Albus, my biggest boy. Your throne remains empty. If only I had known it was our last goodbye, I would have held on longer.

Reader Advisory:
This book contains themes and content that may be distressing to some readers, including **drug use, firearms, violence and other mature subject matter**. Reader discretion is advised.

Official Government
Book of Fate

This document constitutes the Official Government Book of Fate, issued under authority of the State. It is a personal and confidential record belonging solely to the individual named within.

The Book is the exclusive property of its rightful owner. Access, reading, or possession of another person's Book constitutes an unlawful act and may result in prosecution under applicable law.

The Book must not be copied, altered, defaced, or otherwise tampered with. Any attempt to modify or interfere with its contents is strictly prohibited. The contents of this Book represent the unalterable fate of the individual. Writing in, removing, or attempting to amend the Book in any form is prohibited and unlawful. Your Fate cannot be altered. Every life has a story, and every story has an ending.

The rightful owner shall receive this Book on or shortly after their eighteenth birthday. The owner may determine when, where, and how to read their Book. Receipt of this Book in error must be reported immediately to the nearest police authority.

The physical size or number of pages within the Book does not indicate the length of life of its owner.

If this Book is found by anyone other than its rightful owner, it must be delivered immediately to the nearest police authority. In the event of the death of the rightful owner, this Book must likewise be returned to the police without delay. Failure to comply with the provisions governing this Book may constitute a breach of law and will be dealt with accordingly.

Issued under the Government Authority.

Chapter 1

Frederick

Friday 2nd January 1976
Age 18
Fredrick's Family Home, Whitby, UK

*'You will hear the crack of the bullet first, and then
the impact - strange, dull, like pressure bursting
inside your chest. Warmth will begin to pour down
your back, and your breathing will become wet and
shallow. You will close your eyes and then feel a
warm hand holding yours. They will try to stop the
bleeding. You will die at 14:31. Age 67.'*

I suppose that's settled then, a quick death, clean and
almost merciful. What more could I ask for? My fate is
set now, etched, and certain. No need to stray from
the path, no false hope, no temptation of what-ifs.
Mother will be furious, of course. I promised her I
wouldn't read the whole thing, that I'd leave some
mystery in life. But I had to know.
Better to face the truth than spend a life peering into
shadows, questioning every decision and pondering
what the true meaning of my feelings are. At least now
I can live without the endless wondering.

I think of Jennifer. I'll have to end things with her soon before it carries on too far. When she turns eighteen and reads her Book, she'll understand why I couldn't stay. It'll sting, but there's no sense in building a future on borrowed time. At least now the decision of when and where has been made for me.

I can't help but feel a tinge of disappointment when I think about the life that I know I'll never have: the classic, idyllic nuclear family so many take for granted. I will never experience those simple, sacred moments that feel ritualistic in their joy: getting down on one knee, hearing a loved one say "yes," carrying a newborn home from the hospital, feeling the surge of pride and love that comes with holding a child. I'll miss the quiet milestones: birthdays, graduations, family dinners, grandchildren running through the house.

At least I'll have a dog to keep me company. Silver linings, as they say.

The thought slips apart when the radio beside me bursts into life again, crackling through the static. The announcer's voice cuts sharp and tinny, speaking of the gale still raging across the country. A crisp January morning, they call it - though the wind sounds anything but crisp, howling harder than it has all week. I picture the North Sea tossing against the coast, the kind of weather that would make even a fisherman seasick.

Mother's voice carries up the stairs, calling me down to blow out the candles on my birthday cake. Eighteen today. She's probably arranged the table just so, with her best floral tablecloth, the silver cutlery, and the good plates. She has set out her famous tinned-peach trifle, in that old green glass dish, which we only ever see on special occasions. She still sees me as her boy, her only child.

How am I meant to tell her that this will be my last birthday at home with her? That I will have to leave my job at my uncle's garage, a place I've known all my life?

I've made my choice, though in truth, it feels like it has been made for me. I'm joining the Army. I can already hear her voice telling me it's reckless and that I'm running from something. Maybe she's right. Maybe I am.

The candles flicker on top of the cake that she has baked for me. I smile, blow them out, play the dutiful son one more time. But soon enough she'll have to know, and it will be time for me to start living the life written out for me.

Chapter 2

Emily

Saturday 19th September 2020
Age 25
Emily's House, Portsmouth, UK

The moving boxes still sit in a haphazard pile in the corner of my bedroom, casting long, angular shadows across the floor, swallowing the faint glow of the streetlamp outside. Every time I glance at them, I feel the weight of unfinished tasks pressing down on me. It's a physical reminder of the life that I'm trying to piece together, slowly, one cardboard box at a time.

I moved in at the beginning of July, full of energy and good intentions, but now, a few weeks into the routine of September, progress feels like a distant memory, a discarded to-do list.

Last month I achieved so much. I unpacked, I organised, I made this new space mine. But now the rhythm of the school term has worn me down: virtual meet-the-teacher evenings, baseline Phonics and Maths assessments, last-minute tweaks to lesson plans. I barely have a moment to breathe.

I missed my old class, with all their quirks and our inside jokes. Relearning this new group is thrilling, yes, but exhausting. It's good to have some order restored after the chaos of lockdown. Still, every day feels like a delicate balancing act: nurturing, handwashing, instructing, guiding, more hand-washing - all while constantly recalibrating my teaching style for thirty tiny new personalities.

During the week I battle against the clock and my own fatigue. At school I don't have time to dwell on the messy corners of my life, the silence of my empty house, or the fact that at twenty-five I am living completely alone. I followed the path I'd always dreamed of, straight from university into teacher training, working tirelessly to become the best I could be.

I try to make learning fun while keeping firm boundaries. The children know where the limits are, but even within those limits they surprise me endlessly. When it's just me, the kids, and an off-the-wall answer to a question I didn't ask - that is what keeps me in this profession.

Every day I walk into my classroom knowing there is a sense of unconditional love from thirty little hearts and minds … maybe twenty-nine (Theo's not my biggest fan). It's a feeling no one could ever replicate.

This is enough. This fulfils me. This sustains me.

But then the day ends.

I lock the classroom door behind me, step into the empty corridors, and the quiet descends like a heavy curtain. By the time I reach my house, the silence is deafening.

No chatter, no laughter, no little feet scurrying around.

Just me.

The shadows of the boxes.

The ticking clocks.

The to-do lists.

It's in these moments, the ones when I'm finally free from the controlled chaos of my job, that the loneliness hits hardest. I am proud, fulfilled, and independent, yes, but I am also acutely aware of the stillness, the lack of human warmth and the absence of connection beyond my classroom walls.

I try to fill the silence with routines - cooking something that smells like home, TV playing in the background, a glass of wine - but no matter what I do, the quiet always finds its way back in.

At twenty-five I am technically an adult: fully self-sufficient, independent, autonomous and living the life that I have worked so hard to build. And yet some nights I feel only halfway grown-up: competent in the world, yet unmoored in my own house, constantly negotiating between independence and isolation, pride and the quiet ache for something more.

Tonight is no different from any other Saturday since COVID reshaped my social life. I had planned to be in bed by ten, a small anchor of control over my time. But here I am, the clock already stretched past midnight, slipping between cold sheets, the house around me dark and still. I've finished another season of The Office. Another empty bottle waits to go out for recycling. Another ghost of the nights I used to spend laughing with friends, now replaced by the hum of my own solitary company.

During my late-night doomscroll through TikTok, a ping from work jolts me. An email from Jane, my headteacher, interrupts my monotonous viewing. Why is she awake at this hour?

I pause, staring at the screen. It's the weekend - surely she has better things to do. Surely I have better things to do … but here I am, logging into my work emails.

The government has brought in the 'rule of six', and the logistics of squeezing all the parents into the school hall, for the beginning-of-year expansion plan meeting, are impossible.

Realistically, no more than six parents would have shown up anyway. But yes, Jane - of course I can set up a Zoom call. Another small inconvenience to squeeze into my life.

As I do every night, I reach for my Book of Fate, testing my willpower not to read further than today's entry. Just as my mum once did, and her mother before her, I read it dutifully, a daily ritual I've committed to. It's like flipping through the pages of my own diary, reliving each day by reading it instead of writing it. Some days the entries are long, winding paragraphs full of detail; others, like today, are mercifully brief.

"You will waste away another Saturday on the sofa, see no one, and respond to work emails."

It feels both accusatory and comforting, a blunt mirror held up to my life.

Yes, I am alone. Yes, the world outside my house is moving on without me.

But I am here, still present, still pushing through, still trying to reconcile the life I've built in accordance with my fate.

I hope a new chapter of this life will start soon.

GREEN & GROW

Chapter 3

Ben

Tuesday 21st November 1995
Age 18
Ben's Family Home, The Flat Above the Florist, Alton,
UK

I stared at the package on my bed, the padded brown envelope stark against the pale sheets. The government logo stamped across it felt like a seal of fate itself. Addressed to me, Mr. Benjamin Green, the letters were crisp, deliberate and impossibly final. My hand hovered over it for a moment, hesitant, as if touching it might summon consequences I couldn't yet imagine.

I picked up my Book of Fate. The weight of it pressed against my palms, heavier than any book should have been, heavier than any ordinary knowledge. The life I'd live, the choices I'd make, the regrets and triumphs, all contained within those pages. My future, literally in my hands, as tangible as the paper and ink beneath my fingertips.

I hadn't realised, not truly, what it would mean to hold my own story. I had the option to know everything: the twists I had yet to take, the mistakes I'd make, the lows and the hopefully grand highs. It was a responsibility that felt almost cruel.

—

I thought of Rose and the nights we had both spent together, laying beneath the flickering stars that had felt eternal. When the world asked nothing of us, not even our whispered secrets. The night I asked her to be mine, we made two promises:

First, that we would never let this love slip away, and second, we promised and we swore, that we would never read our Fate.

Why would we need to? Why would we ever dare? We wanted to live, to surprise ourselves, to stumble and soar without a guide.

And yet there I was. The decision I had once thought was so far away had found me. The envelope trembled slightly in my hands, and for the first time, I wondered if any story was really meant to remain unread.

The shrill ring of the landline sliced through my thoughts, pulling me back to the present. Startled, I dropped my Book onto the bed with a dull thud and headed for the kitchen.

I didn't need to think about the route I took, I had lived in this flat my whole life. Every step, every corner, every worn patch in the carpet was mapped into me. The place felt hollow with emptiness; Mum and Dad had insisted I take the day off from the florist, so it was just me up here, while they worked downstairs. Just me and the ringing phone.

I lifted the receiver. And then I heard her. Rose. Her voice burst down the line, bright and playful, like fingers running across piano keys. She was singing, deliberately out of tune, I could tell, just to make me laugh.

"Happy birthday to you, happy birthday to you, happy birthday to Bennnnnny, happy birthday to you."

She finished with a giggle that warmed the kitchen more than any sunlight could. For a moment, I forgot the book waiting on my bed, the weight of it and the answers it held.

She fired questions at me before I could even catch my breath. "Did you have your birthday-bacon-breakfast-bap yet?"
she teased, knowing full well it was the one tradition I never skipped.

"What did your Mum and Dad get you this year? Something good? Don't tell me it's another terrible jumper."
Her laughter spilled into my ears, wrapping around me like a familiar embrace. But then her voice changed. My world crashed back in. The brightness dimmed and the music faded. Softer, slower notes crept in, as though she had turned away from the phone or thought of something she wasn't sure she wanted to say.

"Benny... can I ask you something?"
I had known the question was coming, I had known it for years ... the inevitable moment.

"Did your Book arrive?" she asked.

"Yes." One word clipped and sharp. I didn't let it linger. If she could have heard the weight that had settled on my shoulders since receiving the package, the strain that every breath still carried, she might have pressed harder.

"Did you open it?" Her voice slowed, cautious, as if she was afraid of the answer.

"No." It was the truth, and it hid the war raging inside me, a constant pull, a voice whispering that all it would take was a single page turned to know everything.

She seemed satisfied, or at least willing to pretend to be. The brightness seeped back into her words. Her laugh returned, effortless and sweet, and I let it wash over me. My chest ached with it, the swell of something too big to name. Love? Hope? Fear?

I wondered if we could keep that feeling forever, if we could hold onto the promises we had made under those endless stars. Both promises.

—

22

The conversation rolled into our plans to meet later at the cinema to watch Golden Eye.

"It's Green, Ben Green," I murmured, earning another one of her giggles. She reminded me to wear the bomber jacket she had thrifted for me last week.

The call ended in a chorus of I love yous.

When the line clicked dead, silence rushed in again. Back in my room, I rifled through my drawers for a graphic T-shirt to wear under the jacket. But my eyes kept snagging on it.

The envelope. The Book. Its presence was suffocating, pressing from the corner of the bed like it knew I couldn't ignore it forever.

At the very least, I told myself, I should take it out. That wasn't the same as reading it. It was just … I couldn't exactly leave the whole envelope sitting on my bookshelf.

I peeled back the packaging, and my Book slid free.

My hands trembled as I cracked it open, not at today, not tomorrow, but somewhere safer. Fifty odd pages in. Just a glimpse. Just a taste.

My eyes fell on the words before I could stop them:

"You will stand at the side of the road, frozen. Blue lights flashing all around you. The red Ford Escort mangled, unrecognisable. A paramedic will place firm hands on your shoulders, turning you away. But it is too late. You have already seen them."

The words burned into me. My chest locked. The air thickened. I slammed the book shut so violently the sound echoed through the flat.

"No." My voice cracked. "No. No. No."

I shoved it deep into the wardrobe, burying it beneath clothes, boxes, anything I could find. Out of sight. Out of reach.

Rose was right. There was nothing good in knowing.
I pulled on my old favourite T-shirt, the Nirvana logo in cracked vinyl, fraying at the edges like a memory worn too thin.

Chapter 4

Frederick

Saturday 2nd January 1988
Age 30
Sergeants' Mess, Osnabrück, Germany

"Mornin', old man!" they shouted as I turned the corner, making me jump. My shoulder muscles tensed instinctively. I'd hoped I might slip through the day without too much fuss, but there was no such luck. The lads were already on my heels, grinning and firing off jibes.

"You'll be drawin' your pension soon, mate."

"Think you left your walking stick by your bed."

They never missed a chance. At thirty I really did feel ancient compared to these eighteen- and nineteen-year-olds, fresh out of training, all swagger and sharp edges.

I made my way to the cookhouse and poured myself a strong cup of tea, black as always, with no sugar. That, of course, only gave them more fuel - my "old man's brew," my routines that never changed. They ribbed me constantly, but there was no malice in it. It was how the Army worked, if they stopped taking the piss, that was when you started to worry.

After a while I stepped outside for a breath of fresh air and a moment of quiet. Birthdays always seemed to do something strange to me.

I wasn't a sentimental man by nature, but they always dragged my mind back home - to my mother's kitchen, to her tinned peach trifle, layers of sponge and custard that had seemed like the finest feast on earth. God, I'd have fought a hundred men for a bowl of her trifle this morning.

The air outside hit sharp and cold, the kind that burned your ears and made your eyes water. Germany in January always carried a damp chill straight through your clothes.

The snow around the block had already turned slushy and grey, mushed down by endless boots. It clung heavily to my soles as I trudged across the yard, every step dragging.

And still, for all the cold and the stick from the lads, I couldn't shake the thought: thirty years old today. Not young anymore, but not old either, somewhere in between, standing on the edge of it, almost halfway through my Fate.

A few of us piled into the NAAFI mid-morning, shaking the damp from our shoes. The place had a familiar fog of smells that never seemed to shift: bacon butties frying on the hotplate, cheap cigarettes hanging in the air, and the sharp tang of whatever aftershave the lads had splashed on. It was the smell of soldiering life, and somehow it now smelled like home.

We grabbed a spot near the window, the perfect place to watch who drifted in and out. Before I'd even sat properly, someone slid an envelope across the table. A card, thick, folded, and already grubby with fingerprints. Inside, it was signed by half the platoon. Not a heartfelt word to be found, of course, just scribbles and insults.

"Happy Retirement!" was scrawled across the top in thick black marker. Someone else had drawn a stick figure with a walking frame.

—

I couldn't help but laugh, properly laugh, because that was the Army way: no soft words, just the sort of banter that meant you belonged.

For a moment I let the happiness grip onto me. Surrounded by the lads, steam rising from the mugs, bacon sarnies rapidly disappearing, and that endless undercurrent of noise and laughter, I realised that, for all the jokes about being the old man, thirty didn't feel lonely. It felt like I had a family here, one held together by mud and sweat.

One of the lads insisted we headed into town for a few steins, and before long we were trampling the cobbled streets of Osnabrück, boots slipping on the wet stones. The German locals mostly ignored us, though a few rolled their eyes. British squaddies were never known for being quiet once the beer started flowing.

We found a little gasthaus just off the main square. Steins hit the table, schnitzels arrived on plates bigger than our heads, and we tucked in like we hadn't eaten in weeks.

By the time we marched back through the gates, the Sergeants' Mess was set up to surprise me. Balloons bobbed about, a banner across the wall screamed "30 AND KNACKERED," and the stereo was cranked high to proper tunes - Simple Minds, U2, a bit of Madness once the night really got going.

As midnight grew closer, I sat back with a pint, watching the lads sing along and stumble about, and it hit me - thirty didn't feel old at all. Not here. Not in this life. Surrounded by the Army, the banter, the noise, it felt right. Exactly where I was supposed to be. And maybe that was the point. My Book of Fate had said this was my path, and sitting here, pint in hand, I couldn't argue with it.

Chapter 5

Danny

Wednesday 3rd August 2016
Age 23
Poole General Hospital, Poole, UK

My 'Dogs Through History' calendar told me that on this day, in 1429, Christopher Columbus had begun his first transatlantic voyage. Right then, his expedition seemed easier than what I was about to face.

I caught sight of myself in the mirror hanging over the back of my bedroom door and groaned. In my rush this morning, I'd managed to button my shirt wonky, one side higher than the other, like I'd gotten dressed in the dark, after a few tequilas. Brilliant.

I took a few deep breaths, muttered something about pulling myself together, and fixed it. If I had survived five years of medical school fuelled by instant noodles and energy drinks, then I could survive Black Wednesday. Besides, half the other new junior doctors would be just as clueless, fumbling through the system for hours just to figure out how to prescribe paracetamol.

I gave myself a once-over, tugging off the label I'd somehow managed to leave on my new Levi's chinos. Classic.

———

Of course, my trusty burgundy stethoscope was slung around my neck. I'd been given it at the beginning of my first year of university, when it was basically just a fashion accessory. Now it suddenly felt heavier, like it knew I was meant to use it properly. No longer just a badge of honour but a tool I'd be reaching for constantly. And naturally, the first part of my rotation started in respiratory medicine - lungs, wheeze, phlegm and the whole symphony.

I gave the room a last once-over. Clothes slumped over the chair in a way that felt less artistic chaos and more this person has lost the will to fold. The bed was technically made, if you defined 'made' as 'a blanket lying somewhere in the vicinity'. Books, naturally, were scattered everywhere. Most of them were the serious-looking medical ones that I'd bought to appear impressive, which had now ended up more decorative than informative.

Wedged between Gray's Anatomy (the book, tragically, not the TV show) and some doorstop-sized Oxford Textbook of Medicine, I spotted it: my Book of Fate. The corners were bent, and the spine looked weary. Not from being lovingly read, but from years of noble service holding open doors, propping up wobbly shelves, and often acting as a coaster. Truly, literature at its finest.

I thought about picking it up. Maybe today was the kind of day I should read what Fate supposedly had in store for me. A glimpse into the chaos that lay ahead. But then again … where was the fun in that? Half the excitement of life was showing up completely unprepared and pretending you'd meant it that way.

I glanced at the mirror before heading out. Not exactly the polished, serious young doctor vibe I'd imagined. More like 'vaguely disguised as someone responsible'. But maybe that was okay.

After all, if I was going to spend the day trying not to kill anyone and looking like I knew where all the toilets were, I might as well do it authentically.

Handover was first, where everyone spoke in rapid-fire medical shorthand, while I stood there nodding, pretending to understand, like someone at a French film festival without subtitles.

I met the registrar (terrifyingly competent), the SHO (alarmingly awake for that hour), my fellow F1 (who looked just as confused as me, which was oddly reassuring), and the nursing team (aka the true bosses of the ward).

Within five minutes, I'd learned two things:

First, the nurses already knew exactly who was sickest and what they needed doing.

Second, if I stayed on their good side, I might actually survive and potentially get a biscuit along the way.

Ward round was like speed dating, except instead of "what's your star sign?" it was "why are you hypoxic?" The registrar swept through patients at lightning pace, while I desperately tried to scribble down acronyms I'd have to Google later. That day's star line-up: one pneumothorax, three with COPD, a sprinkling of pneumonia, and someone who insisted they were only breathless "when walking upstairs." Honestly, same mate.

My contribution so far had been enthusiastic nodding, winning a battle against the curtains, and not tripping over any walking frames. Success.

After ward round, the job list appeared. Yet it was less of a list and more of a magical scroll of doom which endlessly unfurled. Bloods (I only nicked myself once). Cannulas (why did arms suddenly become veinless when I was holding the needle?) Requesting scans (which mostly involved grovelling to radiology and pretending I understood the reason for the scan in the first place).

And then, the respiratory extras: oxygen monitoring, nebulisers, inhalers.

Basically, making sure everyone could still breathe while I was working out how to log onto the system.

So, there I was: first day, first shift, armed with a pen, a stethoscope, and sheer blind enthusiasm. I hadn't killed anyone … yet. I had only bled slightly on myself, and I was starting to suspect the real test of medicine wasn't knowledge, it was bladder control. I was beginning to feel like, maybe, just maybe I had this.

Until …

"You dropped this. Probably should take better care of it," a stern voice muttered. A nurse in a heavily pressed dark blue tunic forced something into my palm without breaking stride.

My ID badge.

Dr Danny Carter.

Those two little letters. Who knew they'd weigh more than the entire Oxford Handbook of Medicine? Last week I had just been Danny: a person who forgot to take the washing out of the machine for three days. Now I was "Doctor Carter" - keeper of lives, writer of illegible notes, guardian of the printer password.

I stared at the badge like it was a fake celebrity autograph. The photo was worse, in a mugshot style, like I'd just been caught stealing morphine. But there it was, now securely clipped to my shirt pocket.

Official. Permanent. Unavoidable.

Doctor.

Terrifying.

Chapter 6

Emily

Friday 23rd July 2021
Age 26
Emily's House, Portsmouth, UK

I wasn't entirely sure where this year had gone. Honestly, if you had asked me, I would have sworn it was only yesterday that I stood at the classroom door, welcoming the children inside and showing them where to put their stiff new bookbags.

And yet, somehow, in the space of ten months, those thirty faces had turned into thirty personalities I knew inside out. Thirty personalities who now felt alarmingly like my own family. Odd, isn't it? But here I am, attached to that classroom full of miniature humans. Each with their quirks, their favourite pencil colours, and their oddly passionate arguments about whether Father Christmas, the Tooth Fairy, or the Easter Bunny was the richest.

Even Theo, my most skeptical customer, had finally cracked by the end of the Spring Term. A small miracle, considering he spent the first half of the year staring at me as though I were a poorly written substitute teacher in a low-budget sitcom.

———

But there he was, last week, earnestly showing me his carefully written paragraph about Samuel Pepys' hidden cheese, and I nearly cried with pride. Or exhaustion. Or both.

While on my dreaded playground duty, one of my old Year 2s, now very much Year 6 material, cornered me in the playground and asked, "So, Miss Puddle, are you staying in Year 2 again next year? Why can't you move up to Year 6 with us?"

I stared up at him, gawky, half a head taller than me now, with those first unfortunate sprouts of acne making their debut across his forehead. I honestly struggled to compute that this was the same little boy I once had to peel, screaming and snotty, off his mother's leg at the school gate. He used to wail as though I'd said his packed lunch would now consist only of celery sticks; yet here he was today, talking back to me with the sort of confidence that only ten-year-olds and dodgy TV talent show judges possessed. It hit me, in that moment, that all those little building blocks I had been laying - teaching them how to write, how to add, how to remember the dreaded times tables - were the foundations these children would carry into every lesson after mine. I had planted the seeds, and now here they were proper beans. Well, beanpoles. But still. It made me a little misty-eyed if I thought about it for too long.

And then, inevitably, my mind wandered to the summer holiday ahead. Everyone says teachers have it easy with six weeks off. "Think of all the travel you can do!" they say.

"All the hobbies you can finally pick up!" Yes, well.

My grand itinerary consisted of the dentist, the optician, and my yearly guilt-ridden Tuesday morning pilgrimage to the eleven o'clock water aerobics class at the gym, where I would flail around in the shallow end, trying to justify the £28 I spent every month on my membership.

Exotic, no? I had also penciled in the thrilling adventure of reorganising the kitchen cupboards, which currently contained five boxes of lasagna sheets that I didn't recall ever buying.

It was, if I was honest, a slightly terrifying thought: all the structure and routine of school suddenly gone.

No timetable, no phonics, no thirty small people declaring to me every three minutes that they needed the toilet. Just me, my little house, and a very empty calendar.

I knew I would miss the chaos. I would miss the endless questions (like whether dinosaurs had birthdays), the hugs that left glitter stubbornly stuck to my cardigan for days, and the daily drawings that somehow managed to highlight every insecurity I never knew I had.

At the end of lunchtime, my saint of an LSA slid a neon-yellow bath bomb across the table like it was contraband. On top sat a tiny rubber duck, proudly cemented in place, with a tag that read: "We ducking did it!" And honestly, never had a duck spoken truer words.

We did it! We survived.

The meltdowns, the paint explosions, the mystery smells, the endless chorus of "Miss Puddle...", all conquered. If laughter really was the best medicine, then between the two of us we had basically overdosed.

The end of the day arrived as fast as the children had spotted the chocolate chip cookies I had sneakily brought in for their last day. Chaos erupted in the usual adorable blur of hands and crumbs, and I couldn't help but snigger at how quickly thirty tiny humans could zero in on sugar.

When three o'clock rolled in, the parents had thoughtfully brought me an array of gifts, including chocolate, stationery and wine - a generous reminder that that night, at least, a little liquid courage would be absolutely necessary to survive the leftover emotions of the day.

Before I could spiral completely into a blubbering sentimental mess, a gentle tap on my side pulled me back. I looked down to find Lucy peering up at me, her small face almost lost behind a ridiculous bouquet of flowers that was bigger than her.

She had chosen yellow gerberas, proudly explaining that "your favourite sunflowers at the shop 'avn't woken up yet." I couldn't help but smile at her earnest little voice and the way she clutched the stems as if they were treasure.

Her mum stood a little awkwardly behind her, giving a shy grin and murmuring her thanks for everything I had done for her child that year. Even though the social distancing rules had finally been lifted, she still hovered a meter away, as if the habit of caution had become permanent. But it was enough; the sincerity in her eyes, the small, grateful nod that spoke volumes, unmasked and unfiltered.

There was something comforting in that simple human connection after months of barriers, sanitizer, and invisible lines drawn in the air.

Lucy shuffled forward slightly, still holding the flowers like a shield, and I crouched down just enough to meet her at eye level. For a moment, the classroom, the chaos, the tiredness, and the loneliness, melted away.

After school, I planned an evening designed to keep my mind busy, anything to distract me from the looming silence that would inevitably greet me when I walked through my front door. I decided on dinner: a Chinese takeaway.

I stepped into the shop. "Your usual?" the lady behind the counter asked, already anticipating my order. I glanced around, cheeks burning with embarrassment, at the other customers waiting for their chicken balls to finish frying. Luckily, they were all slumped against the window seat, heads buried in their phones, completely oblivious to my mortification.

"Yes, please," I replied, and waited for my order: a Mixed Hors d'Oeuvres for two and crispy chilli beef - the true English-Chinese delicacy combo.

I glanced at the fortune cookie display, imagining the possibilities, but decided against temptation.

After all, my fortune could be read at any point without cracking a cookie in half.

Back home, I grabbed a fork and hauled the whole bag upstairs. I could pretend I was going to plate everything nicely, but let's be honest: that would have been a lie. I wasn't generating extra washing up just for appearances. I curled up on the bed, the first bite of crispy chilli beef hitting the perfect balance of sweet and spice, and I felt a little spark of joy.

I was greedy for choice when it came to wine, though the South African Shiraz was practically screaming my name from the gift bag I had dumped on the kitchen side.

A new book awaited me on the shelf ... well, newish. It had been sitting there for months, quietly judging me, side-eyeing my TikTok marathons and poor sleep schedule. Tonight, I finally gave in. I opened it, and it practically sighed with relief, ready to be swept away into a friends-to-lovers romance.

Soon, I melted into the bath, bubbles surrounding me like a fluffy, sudsy fortress. My belly was full of Chinese, my book propped on the edge, the Shiraz within arm's reach. I let the water and wine work their magic, imagining I was the heroine in my own novel - surrounded by the smell of roses and romance, rather than soy sauce and bath bomb.

The duck floated nearby, sternly observing my wine consumption, while the book leaned a little closer, almost whispering plot spoilers to me. For a little while, the real world disappeared entirely.

Finally, I hauled myself out of the bath and into bed, body warm and cozy, eyelids drooping. But before I switched off the light, I picked up my Book of Fate, as I did every night. I knew that day's entry was going to be emotional. Yet, I read along religiously. It recapped my day at school, mentioned a few of the gifts I had received ... and then:

"At China Chef, you will cross paths with - **The Love of Your Life** *- for the first time. You will look over, and your love story will begin. Once your usual order is collected, you will take it home, eat it in bed and have a bath."*

Wait. What? Who? How? *The Love of My Life*? When? Today?!

I sat bolt upright in bed. Who could it possibly be? The lovely eighty-year-old Chinese lady behind the counter? No. Could it be one of the phone-absorbed customers oblivious to the world? Perhaps.

I imagined it: the mysterious stranger knocking over a spring roll in slow motion, reaching for the last prawn cracker with a dramatic flourish. Or perhaps accidentally spilling soy sauce on his shirt and while I offered him a napkin with a shy, fumbled smile.

I stared at the page, half-amused, half-panicked.

I tucked the book under my pillow, letting the bubbles from the bath and the warmth of the Shiraz lull me to sleep, while somewhere in the back of my mind, I imagined that tomorrow I might just meet 'the love of my life' again, with a side of spring rolls, fortune cookie in hand, and perhaps a charming smile.

And if not? Well, at least I had wine, crispy chilli beef, and a rubber duck. That counted for something. Right?

Chapter 7

Taylor

Thursday 27th June 2002
Age 18
Unknown Flat, London, UK

Through bleary eyelids I woke to a TV blaring. Static, half the final round of a game show and half shouting adverts. Too loud for the morning ... if it even is morning. I wondered who had turned that TV on? Whose TV even was it?
I wasn't in my bed. Not even close. I was on the floor, the sticky carpet pressing patterns into my cheek and my tongue tasting like old pennies.
Come on, Taylor. Jesus Christ. How did you let this happen again? I was in another room I didn't recognise, with smoke-stained walls and old blankets disguised as curtains. There was another handful of strangers scattered like bodies after a battle.
The buzz from last night's hit had almost gone. Not gone enough to let me sleep, but not strong enough to hold me steady. Just that edge of nothingness scraping away inside me.
I wished I didn't, but I needed more. It's like a mosquito bite I couldn't scratch.
No, worse.

Like an itch inside the bone, right where no fingernail can reach. An urge I couldn't satisfy. A scream just below the skin.

I glanced sideways. A woman was sprawled next to me, mouth open, her breathing slow but shallow. Her hair was matted, and mascara was smeared across her cheeks like war paint. My eyes fell to her hand. Her ring-finger. A diamond, the glow from the TV caught in it.

And the first thought that came into my head? Pawnshop. How much could I get for it, how quickly could I trade it in for a hit?

Not: Who is she?

Not: Does she have kids, a husband, someone right now tearing the city apart looking for her?

No. Just the stone, the money, the high.

I hated myself for that. Hate that my brain makes that leap before anything human. Hate that the only thing I see in people anymore is what they can give me, or what I can take.

I shut my eyes tight until colours burst, then opened them again, trying to stretch my focus further than that ring. Further than her.

Across the room, I caught sight of a man slumped over a fold-out picnic table. His head bowed, chin resting on his chest. The needle still jutting out of his arm like some horrible flag, the tourniquet dangling loose. His skin is the colour of wax paper.

I stared at him. Is he breathing? I couldn't tell. Part of me wanted to crawl over, shake him, check. The other part of me didn't want to know the answer.

The pulse at the base of my skull hammered like a drum, steady and angry. A warning signal perhaps.

But what was it warning me about?

The man? Last night? Or is it warning me about myself - that I'm a passenger in my own body, blacking out entire chapters of my life and waking up to scenes like this, pieces missing and memory dissolved?

Every time I try to reach back, it's just ... blank. Like someone cut holes in my timeline. My life, my actual life, is gone, shredded, slipping away.

All I'm left with is this: the noise, the strangers, the TV screaming into the void, and the ache, always the ache, that wants more.

I tune into the blaring TV, though it takes a moment for my ears to catch up with my brain.

"John Entwistle, bass guitarist for the legendary rock band The Who, dies at fifty-seven."

The words spill out of the set like they're supposed to matter, like the world should stop because of them.

John Entwistle. The name means nothing to me. Just another musician gone. But *The Who* – that band name twangs at some cobwebbed corner of my brain.

I couldn't care less that some guy named John had died in a hotel somewhere, but I know who would have.

My Dad.

And suddenly I'm back there - backseat of the family car, seaside-bound. Windows wound down, the air salty and fast. Dad's hands drumming the steering wheel, grinning like he owned the road. He was always singing at the top of his lungs, and it was never quite in tune.

"All I did was have a bit too much to drink and I picked the wrong precinct, got picked up by the law and now I ain't got time to think." He'd sing, hammering the wheel right on the beat, and I'd laugh, pretending to hate it but secretly loving the way he knew every word.

That was my dad: loud, stubborn, alive.

The lyrics seem ironic now. Because me? All I have now is time to think. Time stretched thin and sharp, slicing at me. Time that feels more like punishment than a gift.

Dad would've cared that this musician called John had died. He'd probably rattle on with "they don't make music like that anymore, Tay," before turning the stereo up loud enough to rattle the windows.

I fished my Nokia out of my pocket, the plastic casing warm from my body heat. The screen flickered, battery flashing red in the corner like a warning light.

I scrolled through my contacts with that numb mechanical thumb. His name's still there. Always there. Just a press of a button away.

Maybe I should call him.

But as the thought formed, the phone gave up. The screen faded and the light died, and with it, the idea. The decision was made for me.

It's not like he'd pick up anyway.

I set the dead phone down beside me, face down on the carpet. The TV continued to shout, the strangers breathed, and all I could hear was the echo of my dad's voice singing over the sound of distant waves.

There was a thump.

A hollow clap against metal, followed by the flap snapping shut.

The letterbox. Post.

I froze, my eyes darted towards the doorway where the sound had echoed from. For a moment, I forgot to exhale.

What could it be? My brain started turning over the possibilities, frantic and foolishly. The sound was heavy, not just a flimsy envelope. Something thick, something that hit the floor with weight. A package.

Of course, my first thought was drugs. Maybe a delivery. Maybe escape wrapped in brown paper. For a second, I imagined it: some official-looking padded envelope with a neat red Royal Mail stamp in the corner. But inside? Grams of heroin, tidy little baggies, like they've suddenly decided to modernise distribution. First class tracked, signed for on delivery. "One signature for one salvation. Thank you very much."

It is so ridiculous that I almost laugh.

The Royal Mail doesn't just pop heroin through the door, do they?

… Do they?

My head ran away with the thought.

But no - that's not this world. Not with my luck.

So, what then? A bill? A gift from an elderly relative? A final demand? Pizza coupons? Maybe nothing. Most likely nothing.

And yet I couldn't stop thinking about it. My body twitched with the need to move, to get up, stumble through this stranger's house until I found the front door. It suddenly felt like the world might finally have sent me something other than silence, debt, and the endless itch of wanting more.

I decided that I needed to get it. To solve this mystery in my head.

I staggered through the doorway and into a narrow hallway. The carpet was worn flat in the middle, frayed at the edges, the smell of damp clung to the walls. And there it was - leaning against the door - a crisp brown envelope, the government logo stamped sharp across its face.

Could it be my Fate?

I blinked hard, trying to string dates together. What month was it? If my broken memory served me right, it was June. The 19th? The 20th? Shit. That meant it must be my birthday.

My Eighteenth.

This must be it then - my Book of Fate.

I tore the envelope open, the paper ripping ragged in my hands. It fluttered to the floor as I lumbered back into the living room, my chest tight. The woman on the sofa was still out cold, chest rising and falling, lips parted. Gently, I moved her arm aside so I could sit. She doesn't stir.

The book was thick, heavier than I imagined. The first page is all official jargon – bla-bla-bla, the legal spiel. 'Read it when you want' and so on.

I always thought I'd never even peek at mine. Why would I? You can't change fate. Better not to know.

But now it's in my hands. And I can't not look.

I tell myself I'll only skim it. Maybe up to the end of this year, just to see if this hell has an expiry date.

But once I started reading, I couldn't stop. The words dragged me under, page after page, my eyes racing faster as my stomach knotted tighter. The room around me melted away and smudged into nothing. It was just me and the book, devouring each other.

And as my fate darkened, so did my mind. The story before me felt distant, unfamiliar somehow, yet I kept reading, unwilling to believe that this story was truly mine. Surely it couldn't be. How could I let this all happen to me?

Every line cut deeper. Panic clawed up my throat. I needed to numb it. To blur it. To take the edge off.

I lurched forward towards the man still slumped at the fold-out table, the syringe dangling from his arm. I pulled it free. Then scrabbling through plastic bags on the floor, I began searching desperately. My hand closed around what I needed. Relief waiting.

The rest of what I read dissolved into a haze. Words blurred; chapters slipped from me. The story of someone I didn't even recognise faded.

My eyes snap open. Some time has passed. I don't know how much. The room is dimmer, the air is heavier. The woman is still on the sofa next to me.

But the book – what I think is my book - is gone.

Stolen. And I don't even have the energy to care.

Chapter 8

Ben

Thursday 3rd December 1998
Age 21
The Honeymoon Suite, Wisteria Hill Hotel, Alton, UK

Finally, I'm on my own for a bit. I've escaped up here to the Honeymoon Suite while everyone else is still downstairs, talking and drinking, probably not even noticing that I've snuck out.

My head is pounding from the noise and champagne, and I just needed five quiet minutes to breathe. Five quiet minutes to process what had just happened.

I look over to the ornate mirror, surrounded by slightly tacky silver accents. Still in my wedding tux, the waistcoat now creased, I glide my hand over my gel-stiffened hair. I look the same as this morning, but I don't feel the same. It's strange - one day you're just you, and then suddenly you're somebody's husband.

The whole ceremony feels like a film I just watched on fast-forward. Just a second ago I was standing at the altar, trying not to fidget, and then she walked in, and everything shifted.

I couldn't hear half the words, just the sound of my own heart banging in my chest.

The exchanging of rings, our big kiss - it's already blurring into snapshots. Lucky for me, the photographer took photos of every step - the genuine smiles on our faces made brighter by our mates making daft faces behind the camera.

But then there's Rose. The memory of her is clear as anything. The way her eyes locked onto mine like we were the only two people in the world. The way her hand trembled just slightly in mine, then steadied, as if we'd both found our balance the moment we were reunited. She laughed at something the officiant said, this quiet little laugh that only I seemed to catch, and it felt like the most beautiful secret.

How lucky I am? She's no longer just Rose, the girl I fell in love with, but my wife. My wife until death do us part.

Everything else will fade, I know - the chill in the air, the bustle of family, the clinking of glasses, the youth of our skin - but Rose, standing there in front of me, smiling like she does … that's a memory carved in stone.

How I wish Mum and Dad could have seen it. I knew they liked Rose, but I wish they'd had more time - more time to really know her, to know us, to see who I become when she's next to me.

The top table felt empty on my side. Of course, my sister was there, squeezing my hand under the tablecloth when the room grew too loud. Watching her laugh with the others, I caught little glimpses of Mum in her gestures, in the tilt of her head, in the way her smile softened at the edges.

Rose had placed a framed photo of Mum and Dad on the remembrance table, alongside others who couldn't be with us. The sign propped against the frames read: "We know you'd be here today if heaven wasn't so far away!"

I couldn't look at it for too long without my throat tightening, but I was grateful beyond words that she'd thought of it. That's Rose - always knowing what matters most. That's my wife.

Mrs Green.

It sounds good, doesn't it?

And I had Timothy by my side today. He has been my best friend forever, since those toddler group mornings when our mothers first introduced us. Not that we had any idea what was going on. Or the gravitas of that meeting.

Timothy was there today, steady as ever, a reminder that some bonds survive everything.

And then there were Rose's parents. Lucky doesn't even begin to cover it. From the moment I lost mine, they stepped in with kindness that asked for nothing in return. They helped with the funeral when I could barely survive, and ever since, they've treated me not like an outsider or an obligation, but as family. Today, watching them beam at Rose, and at me, I realised just how much I've gained, even in the shadow of what I've lost.

The reception has been brilliant so far. Speeches, dancing, everyone celebrating together. Our first dance to Aerosmith felt unreal, like it wasn't us but some couple in a shiny magazine.

Yet it was us.

I can hear the muffled bass through the floorboards and the occasional cheer, but up here it's just me and the hum of the heating.

Part of me doesn't want to go back down. I just want to sit in this silence and take in the fact that I'm twenty-one, it's December 1998, and I'm married.

I don't ever want to lose this feeling.

Chapter 9

Danny

Friday 30th October 2020
Age 27
GP Surgery, Gosport, UK

Coffee in hand, I'd thrown on my scrubs like an exhausted superhero who forgot their cape. Scrubs are easier to wash than my usual shirt and trousers, and yes - they're Marvel print (my childhood duvet reincarnated). And … perfect PPE, because nothing says "I fight viruses" like Iron Man.

My laptop bag is now officially my emotional support animal. Remote consulting is half medicine, half staring at a screen praying that the Wi-Fi doesn't betray me mid-diagnosis.

The waiting rooms look like the ghost of a health clinic past: a few chairs spaced like they're in witness protection, no magazines, no toys, no hope.

Everyone wears a mask and sanitises like they're preparing for a hand hygiene Olympics.

Most of the patients I see today will be pixels. Tiny, judgmental, COVID-suspecting pixels.

Ready to play …

"Who's in more pain at the end of the zoom call? Doctor or Patient"

Round One:

A 4-year-old has a fever. Swab booked. Safety advice issued to their mother. Pray for her. And for me.

She won this round. (Small human means maximum chaos!)

Round Two:

A man with COPD sounding like Darth Vader after a rough weekend. Is it COVID? Probably.

Is it an exacerbation? Possibly.

Am I going to lose my mind trying to explain this over the call? Definitely.

I won. (But only slightly.)

Round Three:

A lonely shielding patient who just wants human contact. Sorry mate, I come with bad Wi-Fi and intermittent eye contact.

Think this one is a tie. (Misery loves company.)

Meanwhile, I was documenting like a caffeinated cyborg: prescriptions are flying out, swabs are being booked, follow-ups scheduled, all whilst I am slowly morphing into the first verified case of 'square eyes'.

But it's not all bad ... some of it is really bad.

I stuff my laptop back in my bag (reuniting it with the alarming amount of empty crisp packets I've been accumulating).

On to the next part of my day. Patients. In person. Yuck.

Apparently it is now my job to look them in the eye and act like I know what I'm doing.

First up, a teenager with abdominal pain. Thanks to COVID, I can't just assume it's a tactical stomachache to dodge PE - now it's a whole diagnostic minefield.

Then there's a baby with a chesty cough, miniscule lungs rattling like a broken radiator, parents staring at me like I might magically fix it with one glance.

At the other end of life, an elderly man who's been quietly losing weight. No drama, just the kind of slow, unsettling story that makes your brain spin.

Each encounter is a performance: me, wriggling into PPE like a clumsy astronaut, fogging up my visor within seconds, then stripping it all off again only to repeat the whole circus with the next patient. In between, I'm scrubbing down the room with disinfectant wipes like I'm auditioning for some NHS-themed cleaning commercial (The glamour of medicine, right?)

All this whilst reassuring patients: "Yes, it's safe ... ish. Maybe."

Lunch was an opulent Tesco sandwich at my desk, accompanied by a leaning tower of hospital letters, pathology results, and enough COVID swab reports to carpet not just my room, but the entire M25.

The afternoon training arrives in the form of yet another remote teaching session. A barely distinguishable grid of equally pale, over-caffeinated trainees all solemnly discussing long COVID. No coffee break gossip about scandalous hook-ups, no awkward chair-scraping politics and worst of all, no free biscuits. Just me, my laptop, and rectangles of human misery. I nodded at the right times, while quietly wondering if my Wi-Fi router could get long COVID too and spare me.

The rest of the day blurs into the usual chaos: finish prescriptions, chase results (that were apparently filed to Narnia), dictate referrals to consultants (who won't read them), and hand over red-flag cases with all the enthusiasm of someone donating a kidney without anesthetic.

Finally, I escaped. I stepped into the dark October night, instantly feeling about ten years older and faintly radioactive. Powered by equal parts adrenaline, caffeine, rage, and Tesco meal deal.

I guess that student debt was well worth it, right?

As I began the drive back to my flat, I could't help but let my brain wander down the same tired road it always insists on taking. How on earth did we let the pandemic get this bad? I mean, we literally have Books of Fate.

Actual hand-delivered manuals of "here's what's going to happen, don't mess it up." And yet … somehow, we still managed to respond with the organisational skills of a drunk stag do in Benidorm.

You'd think, as a species, enough of us would read ahead. Just a couple of chapters, maybe even skimmed the blurb - but no. Instead, we stockpiled toilet roll like the virus was planning to attack from the rear.

Or perhaps some people were just too prepared.

I mean, I'm not one to judge. I still have my Fate, unread, wedged between my radiator and the wall, now upgraded from "book of my entire life's destiny" to "superior spider squasher." A noble purpose in my opinion.

And honestly, with everything we supposedly know - the predictions, the warnings, the graphs that look suspiciously like a child's drawing of a mountain range - there seems little point in me cracking mine open now. What's the worst it could say? "Spoiler: you'll still be exhausted, your coffee will still be lukewarm, the cases will continue to rise, and Boris will still be confused." Ground-breaking.

So no, I think. I won't be reading my Book of Fate tonight. It's far more useful where it is - flattening insects and reminding me that destiny is just as overrated as surgery Wi-Fi.

Danny's unread Book of Fate read:

Saturday 31st October 2020

"On Saturday you will switch on the TV and you will hear:

I am afraid that no responsible Prime Minister can ignore the message of those figures.
Doctors and nurses would be forced to choose which patients to treat, who would get oxygen and who wouldn't, who would live and who would die. The overrunning of the NHS would be a medical and moral disaster beyond the raw loss of life.
So now is the time to take action, because there is no alternative.
From Thursday until the start of December, you must stay at home.

You will use some crude expletives, and this will be the beginning of the second major UK lockdown. You are still exhausted, and you forget to drink your coffee."

Chapter 10

Frederick

Saturday 1st January 2000
Age 41
Sergeants' Mess, Aldershot, UK

I woke up this morning with a sore head, but I reckon half the battalion did too. The lads were celebrating hard last night, which is fair enough, it's not every day the whole world turns over into a new millennium. I knew that I would live to see the year 2000, but it still feels unreal. 2000.

Strange to think I was only 18 when I first marched into this life back in '76. Now I'm forty-one, a Warrant Officer, watching over a whole squadron. It feels like yesterday I was the one being shouted at for being late on parade after a night out.

From the moment the bar opened last night, the mess was packed. Cigarette smoke hung in the air, so thick it was like walking through fog, pint glasses stacked up in little pyramids on every table. Someone had raided the stores for streamers and bunting, Union Jack flags hung off the rafters, and a giant bit of cardboard nailed to the wall that read "Welcome to Y2K".

The jukebox couldn't keep up. Oasis, Robbie Williams, a bit of Blur, even the old rave stuff came out; lads bouncing up and down like they were all twenty again. Ties on foreheads, shirts hanging open, tacky 2000 glasses, arms round shoulders - the lot.

At one point a group of privates tried to teach the Regimental Sergeant Major how to do the Macarena. To his credit, he gave it a go.

When the clock struck midnight, we all went completely mad. Fireworks cracking off in the car park, everyone shouting Happy New Year!

I had lads I barely knew clinging to me like long-lost brothers.

Phones were ringing off the hook too. The queue at the payphone was half the corridor long, lads shouting down the receiver to wives, girlfriends and love interests. You couldn't hear yourself think, but you could feel it - that rare kind of joy where nobody cared what rank you wore or how many years you'd done. Just a roomful of soldiers, alive and together as the century turned.

By three in the morning the place was wrecked. Beer everywhere, chairs overturned, and some poor bugger fast asleep under the pool table with a party hat still on his head.

My head hammered as I drifted in and out of sleep last night, but it was a price worth paying. Nights like that don't come around often.

Still, by eight o'clock sharp I was in the Mess, tea in hand, making sure everyone was accounted for. Some of the young ones looked like death warmed up, and I had to bark at a couple just to remind them they're soldiers first and party animals second.

The Regiment is on higher readiness today with all this noise about computers crashing from 'Y2K'. Truth be told, most of us don't understand half of it. All these savvy experts warning everyone that the world's going to grind to a halt because the clocks might hiccup. It's the year 2000, surely technology is advanced enough by now to change four little numbers.

Still, orders are orders. Nothing's gone wrong so far, but we've been told to stay sharp just in case.

I've gone through the routine twice over already.

Guard rosters checked, vehicles checked, comms kit checked, all systems are stable. Everything in order.

It feels like any other day in uniform - discipline, repetition and keeping standards high even when it feels like busywork. That's the Army for you: doesn't matter if it's 1976 or the year 2000, the job's the job.

And yet, there's something captivating about standing here, boots planted on the floor, in a brand-new century. Twenty-four years of soldiering behind me, with six years still to go.

Tomorrow's my birthday. Another year older, though at my age it feels less like something to celebrate and more like something to nod at and carry on. I expect the usual ribbing from the lads, comments about my grey hairs, someone calling me "ancient" over breakfast. It's all part of the rhythm of Army life, the way we keep each other grounded.

I thought back to previous birthdays. The ones spent in Germany in the Cold War and Northern Ireland in the dark days. The festivities mixed with the endless exercises in the mud, weeks living out of a bergen, celebrated with mates made and thinking of the mates lost.

Truth be told, I don't want a fuss. After the way the millennium rolled in, I doubt any of us will have the energy for another big night anyway. My hope is the lads are still tired enough to keep things relaxed. Maybe a quiet pint, a handshake or two, and that'll be plenty.

A nice steady evening would be perfect.

Another candle on the cake or another mark on the calendar doesn't change much, but it does remind me I've made it this far.

I've carried more kit than I can count, more memories than I care to admit. The Army changes, the world changes, but we carry on and our Fate stays the same.

Tonight, if the clocks keep ticking and the kit keeps working, I'll raise a glass in the Mess. To the new century. To the lads still serving. To the ones who didn't make it this far. And to all that's waiting for us next - good and bad, we'll face it the way we always do. Together.

Chapter 11

Emily

Friday 3rd June 2022
Age 27
Eastney Beach, Southsea, UK

I had been on a pirate ship; the captain's gorgeous, strong wife was trying to break me out of some dingy cell below deck. We gazed into each other's eyes. They flickered shut as we had started leaning in like the final scene of a very questionable rom-com. Something had been about to happen, what, I couldn't quite say, but it had felt scandalous enough to make me worry I was about to get keelhauled into my own subconscious.

Naturally, that was when the BBC News app had twanged on my phone, yanking me straight out of my parallel-universe fantasy dream and back into my decidedly unsexy duvet cocoon. I groaned into the pillow like a ghost with a passion for haunting IKEA bedding, clinging desperately to the taste of salty air and the creak of the ship.

I had tried not to think too hard about what the dream meant - though let's be honest, the captain's wife wasn't exactly subtle in her advances.

I was sure I owned a book of dream analysis somewhere on my perfectly colour-coordinated shelves. I had never looked at it, but if I had, I was fairly certain the interpretation would've read: "You're suppressing things and need to get out more."

Dragging myself into the land of the living, I picked up my phone. The PTSD from the COVID years was still alive and well; every time the news app buzzed, my brain prepared for lockdown rules, toilet roll rationing, or a new strain named after an obscure Greek island. Instead, my eyes had landed on:

* Watch Live: The Queen's Platinum Jubilee Street Party – come and join the celebrations! *

As much as I respect Her Majesty's iconic matching hat-bag-dress combos, what had really got my pulse racing was the prospect of an extra bank holiday. A whole additional day of sanctioned laziness - courtesy of the Monarchy! Frankly, it was the most patriotic I had felt in years.

It had come at the right time too. It was nearing the end of the academic year and my energy levels had been dropping faster than Boris Johnson's popularity polls. I had said yes to far too many extras at school: taking on Geography lead (I have had a YouTube crash course in tectonic plates), starting a dance club (because I went to Zumba once), and digging the school's new wildlife pond (which looked less like Attenborough's late-night fantasy and more like a crime scene).

I mumbled a heartfelt thank you to good ol' Betty for her seventy years of service and the gift of an extra duvet day and rolled over, determined to drift back to my pirate dream. Longing to hear the waves and feel the salty breeze in my hair again.

Upon waking up, and not being at all embarrassed that I was only a few hours shy of missing today's sunset, I decided I probably should at least get twenty minutes of fresh air. Just enough time outside the house to convince my neighbours that I wasn't part of some experimental study on humans who only survive on Netflix and leftover Chinese takeaway.

All the thoughts of pirates had got me craving the beach. The idea of standing by the sea, hair whipping dramatically in the wind, staring out like some forlorn sailor's wife waiting for her man to return - yes, that appealed to me greatly.

Never mind the reality, which would likely involve a scratchy towel, gulls circling me, and sand somehow infiltrating places sand had no business being.

I packed my trusty rucksack with the essentials: a water bottle, two bags of crisps, a satsuma and a Wispa Gold. Breakfast, lunch, and dinner of champions. Nutritionists everywhere would be appalled, but honestly, what did they know about real survival?

Into the bag I also shoved my latest romcom paperback - this one featuring a rugged warrior and a well-to-do lady with a penchant for fainting at inopportune moments. I guessed that explained my dream perfectly then; my subconscious was basically turning into a Netflix algorithm of a spinster.

For good measure, I decided to bring along my Book of Fate, not that it would have much to report on today. "Woke up, ate crisps, nearly developed scurvy, fell asleep on the beach." Truly, the kind of stuff that belongs in the National Archives. Still, if destiny had anything exciting lined up for me, like an encounter with a real-life pirate with luscious curling locks, I wanted to be ready.

I slung the rucksack onto my shoulder, checked I had my phone (for emergency Instagram stories, obviously) and set off for the coast, prepared for an evening of high adventure or, failing that, pretending I knew how to skim stones.

Since most people had been up for eight hours already, using their bonus bank holiday time wisely, most people had already left, and the beach was now almost deserted. Lucky me.

I plonked myself down on a sand dune, munching through one of my packets of crisps with all the poise of a shipwreck survivor. While watching the sun begin to dip, painting the sea in those smug oranges and pinks, I had a thought: it wasn't all bad. I was lucky to live so close to a place like this, somewhere I could trick myself into thinking my life was poetic, rather than mainly admin.

I'd been packing up my rucksack when I caught a glimpse of my Book of Fate. Out of habit, I flipped it open to yesterday's entry and had read on from there. I had not been expecting much from today's entry, when suddenly my eyes had snagged on the words:

*"You will sleep in for an alarmingly long time. You will go to the beach to watch the sunset. You and **The Love of Your Life** - will both enjoy the peace and tranquility."*

My what? Me and my what?

I had whipped my head left, then right, looking next to me. There was no one. Nothing! Unless the seagull eyeing my crisps counted. Surely not.

What was I expecting anyway? A hot pirate with a mysterious eye patch? Come on Emily!

But still, my Book of Fate had never been wrong. Not once. Which meant the love of my life was here. Somewhere.

I stood up, brushing off the sand in a way that was meant to be nonchalant but mostly looked like I was swatting at invisible bees, and turned full circle.

There had been an old man fishing off a jetty nearby. He was far more interested in his line than me or the sunset. Nope.

Then I had clocked a woman parked up the hill, slumped against her car bonnet, eating what looked like a sandwich. Nope.

And then, I saw him. A figure further down the coastline, glowing faintly in the sunset haze. My stomach flipped. This had to be him. *The Love of My Life.*

I set off at a brisk walk. The walk turned into a jog. The jog turned into a full-blown Baywatch run (minus the slow-motion and with additional wheezing). I had to get closer, had to see him - this fated stranger who would apparently alter the entire course of my existence.

As the distance began to close my eyes adjusted to the evening light. Two people. Not one. And not just two people - two people holding hands. A man and a woman. And then I saw it. The undeniable bump.

She was pregnant.

I skidded to a graceless stop, half-bent over, panting like a Labrador that had chased the wrong ball.

Am I - was I - in love with someone else's husband? Was this really my destiny?

Oh, how on days like this I want to cheat, to flick ahead in my Book of Fate, just to see how the next page unraveled. But of course, I never do.

And so, I trudge back towards my crisps, muttering under my breath about how *The Love of My Life* had apparently been busy making babies with someone else. Typical.

Chapter 12

Taylor

Friday 12th November 2016
Age 32
Taylor's Flat, Plymouth, UK

Walking through the streets felt colder and sharper than usual. Even for November. Couples holding hands under umbrellas passed me, children splashed in puddles, and an old navy man sat hunched on the bench by the Hoe, staring out to sea like he's still waiting for his ship to return. Students drifted past, their late nights finally catching up with them, clutching their takeaway coffee cups like lifelines.

All their faces blur past, indifferent. They don't even meet my eye. Is it fear? Or maybe just people caught up in their own small storms, heads down, eyes fixed forward.

A rainbow of people has never looked quite so grey. Yet, it all feels like a sour reminder of a Fate I will never live.

I wander soggy streets, restless and continuously hunting for my next fix. I try to outrun the day, to silence the quiet gnawing ache inside.

Since losing my job at the corner shop last month, the days have stretched long and empty. I'd worked the night shift: stocking shelves, manning the till, mopping floors and cleaning doors. Small honest work.

But I lost it all for being late too many times.

I had slept too far into the evenings, my body heavy with the weight of the last hit and woke well into when my shift was meant to have begun. I knew they would have to let me go, I was more trouble than I was worth to them, but that didn't lessen the sting when they fired me.

I miss the job more than I expected.

I miss seeing my regulars. I miss the students piling in at two o'clock in the morning for a caffeine fix and plain pasta, eyes red from too many hours stuck to a screen. I miss the old woman who came in for her pint of milk at the same time every night, coins counted out with careful fingers, always a smile waiting just for me.

I miss the small rituals that steadied the hours.

How I wish I still had my Book of Fate now, just to re-read what I have forgotten. If I could have known the details, I'd have known it was my last shift. I would have said goodbye properly, maybe thanked those shoppers for bringing light to those grey nights.

Now I walk through Union Street, keeping my head down. I know the corners where the offers will come, where I will hear whispers in the rain.

I'm not cruel, not reckless, not some monster that people think of when they hear the word addict.

I'm kind enough to still hold doors open for strangers, soft enough to smile at kids chasing pigeons, all whilst being prodigiously tired. I feel that my Fate has been hard on me, and I am cruelly aware that kindness doesn't pay for beds or meals or the powder that keeps the ache at bay.

As I trudge closer to the harbor, I hear the waves slapping on stone. The wind is carrying the tang of salt and fryer grease from the chippy that never seems to close. I find myself wishing I could just sit, like the navy man, and watch the horizon instead of chasing shadows.

But wishes don't keep me warm, and the city isn't kind to people who pause too long. So, I keep walking, shoes soaked through, mind racing with the same thought.

I just need one more hit, just to get through the night. Back in the flat, the walls lean in close, stale with damp. Empty bottles, crumpled papers, worn clothes and festering takeaway cartons litter the floor.

Red envelopes shout at me from the kitchen side, my unpaid bills stacked like angry judges. I keep telling myself I'll deal with them tomorrow, but tomorrow never seems to come.

I stare at the wall, paint cracked and crumbling, and imagine their faces. My parents. Twenty years since I last saw them, but the memory hasn't softened. It's sharper now, crueler. The edges cut. My brother tried to fill the gap, tried to be everything I needed.

But how could I forgive him? He told them to go.

I know it's not fair, but grief doesn't care for fairness. To me, it's always been his fault.

The drugs offer a hollow consolation, dulling the pain but never erasing it. Just a thin veil draped over the anguish bubbling underneath.

On the table by the window sit the flowers I stole, their stems adrift in a pint glass. One pink rose, one iris - lonely companions in borrowed water. I hadn't wanted to steal them, but what choice did I have? No money, no kindness from strangers. Only me and the guilt of small crimes.

The iris already droops, its purple petals folding in on themselves, but I keep staring at the two flowers as if they carry some meaning. I suppose they do. Proof that I can still hold onto something fragile, some echo of them.

Evening arrives, and I'm left with lingering loneliness. As the streets outside darken, the city turns harsher and the memories sharper.

I lie back on the sagging sofa, pill bottles scattered on the floor beside me, praying that they will numb my expectations of seeing my parents again. Sometimes they visit me in my dreams, Dad turning the radio up, singing off-key, Mum laughing as she whisks ingredients together.

And sometimes they don't.

I tell myself I must stop expecting that they will just reach out. But the memories are too raw and my irrational hope is too strong.

So, I stop it all, every feeling.

The routine is mechanical, I reach for the small bag tucked under the sofa cushion, my hands trembling as I measure out my dose. This is a ritual carved into my bones: the tiny pinches, the sting, the rush.

For a moment the world softens, the ache dims, the grief fades into something manageable.

But today, the relief is fleeting. The memories press harder, louder, like they've learned how to break through even the fog I built around myself. And I realise, sitting in this room with its drooping flowers and its angry envelopes, that maybe no amount will ever be enough to silence my hope.

Chapter 13

Frederick

Monday 15th August 2006
Age 48
David's House, Farnborough, UK

After thirty years in the Army, I have officially retired. I'd read about this day in memoirs, motivational pamphlets and my Fate, but nothing could have prepared me for the strange weight of it. It's as if I've stepped off a train that's been hurtling at full speed for decades, onto a silent, deserted platform. The rails behind me, the world ahead, and only my own two feet to guide me.

Clearing out my locker and handing over my ID had been surreal. Thirty years condensed into a few signatures and a handshake. The lads gave the usual speeches. We drank more pints than I can remember and shared the standard "good luck mate".

Then I was out the gate.

Simple. Efficient. Army-style.

I woke up in the spare room at David's.

David has always been a practical sort, the sort of bloke who could fix a Land Rover with a roll of duct tape and a prayer, and still have time for a strong drink afterwards.

Even back in our army days, he had a calm sort of humour that cut through the chaos. Where the rest of us might have panicked over a last-minute change of orders, David just shrugged and said, "We'll sort it lads" and somehow, we always did.

David had left the Army five years prior to me, with a dream to take-up his new career in trucking. He swapped camouflage for hi-vis jackets and the constant noise of the barracks for the hum of a diesel engine. Trucking suited him - long hours on the road, thinking quietly, keeping his own rhythm. He talks about the open roads with the same fondness I once reserved for a well-run training exercise, like the miles are as much a part of him as his boots once were.

David's house reflects him perfectly. Not flashy, but solid. Practical furniture, minimal clutter, a garage full of tools that he actually uses and a garden that's more functional than ornamental. Nothing wasted, everything in its place.

He's the sort of man who knows the value of a spare key and a hot cup of tea after a long day. That he offered me his spare room without a second thought reminded me why I'd always trusted him.

I knew I would only be staying with him for a few months while the ponderous solicitors worked at their pace. Spending that time at David's felt like the perfect bridge between chapters of my life - neither an ending nor a beginning, just a steady, reassuring pause.

I'd forgotten how little fuss a true friend can make when you're in need, and how reassuring that is.

The house I'm buying is down in Portsmouth. It is close to the sea and very cheap for the area. Since Portsmouth is so linked the Navy, it is enough for me to feel comfortable with the unfamiliar.

Thanks to the money I inherited when my mother passed, combined with a little top-up from my carefully managed pension pot, I was able to get the house outright. A privilege I vow never to take for granted.

Owning something big, for the first time, feels like reclaiming a piece of myself I didn't even know I'd lost. After decades of moving every few years, the thought of a place that's truly mine is intoxicating. I look forward to it: sitting in the little garden with a cup of tea, a quiet street, space to put down roots … maybe make friends with the neighbours. I can't see it happening personally, but my Fate says it is so!

I started my first civilian day slowly, deliberately. Kettle on, black tea, no sugar, staring out the window. I am wearing a pair of jeans and a jumper instead of kit. No orders but a clear untested plan. I should feel free.

Truth be told, I felt almost adrift.

I unpacked the few boxes I had into the spare room. Clothes, books, photographs, medals. Little things that anchor a person, even if only in memory. Each item I handled seemed to echo decades of service, of routine of following orders without questioning. Now, holding them, I realised the novelty of choosing for myself - where to put a book, whether to hang a picture, whether to even unpack a box today.

By mid-morning, I felt restless. I went for a walk, letting the streets of David's neighbourhood wash over me. Some neighbours nodded politely; others pretended not to see me. Either way, I was happy to be out of the house.

I sat down on a patch of long grass for a few minutes, listening to the distant gulls and the faint roar of traffic. My mind wandered to the twenty or so years ahead. I felt the faint tug of my Fate, like an old friend nudging me forward.

The rhythm of civvy life was different - slower, quieter and almost polite. There are no shouting drills or call of reveille, the tension from urgent training schedules has disappeared. Just the mundane and comforting pace of a world that did not revolve around me.

Back at the house, I tackled small jobs. Tightened a loose cabinet handle. Fixed a leaking tap. Simple victories.

There are no medals awarded for this work, no cheers from the lads. But I felt a quiet satisfaction, an unfamiliar, domestic kind of pride.

Over the radio, I catch snippets of yet another headline - this time, a supposed major terrorist plot to target multiple transatlantic flights, prompting a temporary upgrade of the national threat level to critical.

My stomach tightens slightly, an almost reflexive response that surprises me. Decades in uniform have a way of embedding vigilance into your bones. Even though I'm officially retired, even though my ID badge is handed back and my kit packed away, part of me still sits on that invisible parade ground, ears tuned to danger, ready to move at a moment's notice.

I find myself scanning the room, imagining escape routes, visualizing how I might respond if the call ever came, if the quiet life I've just stepped into was suddenly shattered by chaos.

Chapter 14

Ben

Wednesday 5th December 2007
Age 30
St. Agnes' Primary School, Petersfield, UK

The badly decorated tree twinkles to the right of the stage, its baubles bunched almost exclusively around the bottom branches, where little hands could reach. The upper half sits bare except for a few stray strands of tinsel that had clearly been hurled upwards in hope rather than design. The fairy lights blink unevenly, one bulb refusing to cooperate, but the children who decorated it don't notice - their entire world is on the stage before them.

A dozen small faces scan the crowded hall, eyes darting over the rows of parents, each child desperate to catch sight of their own. A tentative wave here, a shy smile there, as nervous energy crackles across the line of performers. All around me parents lean forward, hearts practically spilling onto the polished hall floor.

I'm not a stranger to that feeling.

My gaze finds Harry and Quinn, standing so tiny against the enormous painted backdrop of Bethlehem. The scene reads more gaudy village fate than Holy Land, yet still just as glorious all the same. Above them, a glittering cardboard star dangles from the ceiling, swinging slightly on its string like a glittery disco ball.

Quinn looks angelic - quite literally. Rose poured hours into her costume, every feathered wing and loop of glittery tulle. The result is dazzling, though perhaps a little hazardous (her wings nearly toppled Angel Gabriel during the dance break!)

My five-year-old glows beneath the stage lights, a bundle of nerves and sparkle. Her big solo moment arrives, and she spins with all the grace her little legs can muster, circling in time to Twinkle Twinkle Little Star. My little angel. For a second my chest feels too small to contain my heart.

Harry, older by two years but suddenly looking so grown, waits at the side of the stage for his part.

He's a head taller than most of his classmates, his height made even more obvious by the crown perched proudly on his head. Rose had cut it from an old cereal box, painted it gold, and now it was gleaming like treasure under the lights. His tunic glitters with oversized stick-on jewels, the kind that spill out of Woolworths craft aisles, each one slightly crooked but stuck on with purpose. He is every inch a Wise Man.

I watch his small chest rise and fall as he gathers himself for his moment, eyes screwed shut, hands clenched around his plastic gift. The hall falls quiet.

With a giant breath, and the courage of a flower growing through concrete, he belts out his line, voice trembling but loud enough for all to hear:

"I give you myrrh!"

And the room erupts. A ripple of laughter rolls through the rows of mums and dads, not unkind but warm, affectionate, united in the magic of the moment. Harry's eyes flicker open, cheeks flushed crimson, but his chin tilts upwards in pride. His 'myrrh' thrust towards the cowering Mary and Joseph.

He knew he had done it.

All the practicing of "I give you myrrh" in the car had been well worth it.

No book, no sermon, no sage word of advice could ever prepare me for the tidal wave that hit me. A swell of pride so fierce it almost knocked me over, so pure it caught in my throat and stung at the corners of my eyes.

My two children, the two tiny stars of my universe, shining under hot stage lights and tinsel.

I look over at Rose sitting beside me, her fingers laced tightly around an already sodden handkerchief. She dabbed at her eyes, her love overflowing into tears. I wonder, not for the first time, what I had done to deserve this life. This fate. A warm home to return to at night, steady work to keep us comfortable, a wife who had stood by me through every turn, and now these two dazzling children up on stage. I am blessed with everything a man could ask for.

And yet... what was that feeling?

A strange hollow note in the middle of the symphony. Like something had shifted, some small piece missing that I couldn't quite name. Life was good, full even, but it did not feel as it once had. Perhaps that was simply the weight of time, pressing gently but insistently on my shoulders.

I was nudged out of the thought as Rose elbowed me, her eyes still fixed on the stage. She mouthed "photograph," her hand gesturing urgently toward the children. I grin, slipping my hand into my pocket and pulling out my new iPhone. For a moment I felt younger, cooler, as though the gleaming device was some badge of modernity that set me apart from the other dads fumbling with disposable Kodaks or bulky camcorders.

Had it cost me an arm and a leg? Yes.

Had I managed to time it perfectly with the Christmas price drop? Also, yes.

Had Rose scolded me for it, her tone that perfect mix of exasperation and affection? Of course.

But she had softened once she realised it could take calls, answer business emails, and most importantly, capture moments like this with just a tap.

I raised the phone, framing the shot so that both my little angel and my proud wise man fit inside the screen. Quinn with her enormous wings glittering under the lights, Harry with his cereal-box crown catching the glow like real gold.

I pressed the button a few times, the artificial click of the shutter sounding satisfyingly permanent. Now, instantly, I had them captured. And forever if I remembered to back them up. I made a mental note to email the best one to Rose's parents as soon as we got back to the flat.

Thinking of them tugged me further back still, to the days when my parents had been the ones sitting where I was now. Their faces tilted upwards, watching me and my sister sparkle under hot lights, cheeks red and sweaty. We had been the stars once - shepherds, angels, or the occasional farm animal pressed into service. I could still remember the itchy costumes, the sets that oozed the smell of poster paint and the nervous tremble in my chest before my cue. And somewhere in the crowd, my parents smiling proudly, much as I smiled now.

The memory wrapped itself around me, bittersweet, and for a moment I lingered in it.

Then movement at the front of the hall snapped me back. The teacher had leapt up, her arms flailing in grand, frantic gestures, furiously signing the actions to drag the children through the final verse of 'The Twelve Days of Christmas'. The room came alive with off-key voices, little hands waving awkwardly through turtle doves and leaping lords. My wandering thoughts scattered, replaced at once by laughter and warmth, and an almost unbearable pride that swelled in my chest until it hurt.

"And a partridge in a pear tree!" they bellowed, half the hall clapping along, the other half wiping their eyes. And in that school hall, with its lopsided tree and wobbly backdrops, I feel richer than any wise man bearing gold, frankincense, or myrrh.

Chapter 15

Danny

Friday 23rd July 2021
Age 27
GP Surgery, Gosport, UK

Scrubs aren't needed today; I wear smart chinos and a shirt, with a mask tucked into my pocket, just in case. I am feeling marginally more like the polished, respectable doctor my parents had always wanted - if you ignore the toothpaste stain down my sleeve and the fact my "smart" chinos definitely shrank in the wash and are now flirting with being capris. From a distance though, I reckon I could pass for competent.

I am missing my Iron Man scrubs however, my faithful sidekick throughout COVID. His laser beams that fought imaginary germs with me through anatomy lectures and long nights on call. Now it's just me, my biro, and a coffee that tastes like burnt despair. No superpowers in sight.

Arriving at the surgery, the waiting room feels almost normal again - normal being ten seats scattered like a half-hearted game of musical chairs. Posters shout at patients to cough into their elbows and wash their hands after every human interaction.

The morning meeting is mercifully short. The urgent cases are fewer now - only two post-COVID follow-ups and a lady who's convinced her cat might have diabetes and wants me to check (Spoiler: not my remit, though apparently, I'm everyone's vet now too.) The words "long COVID" get tossed around like confetti, and half the staff look like they've got it. Or maybe that's just what happens after one too many zoom calls.

Between patients, I call my shielding regulars. Mrs. Weston reports that she has become the Queen of Home Delivery, but misclicked and now owns forty-eight jars of gherkins. Mr. Dale proudly shows me his new blood pressure machine on Zoom, which honestly looks like something you'd use to launch a satellite. By the time he figured out how to press 'start', his blood pressure had doubled from sheer stress.

Routine care is back, though now that apparently means reassuring patients that a cough doesn't automatically mean a deadly virus and trying to comfort toddlers who scream like I've just stepped out of a slasher film every time they see my mask. Honestly, at least 70% of my job is nodding solemnly while people give me forensic-level detail about their neighbour's hedge ("it's too tall, doctor, it's affecting my vitamin D") or their dog's suspicious cough ("could it be COVID?").

The other 30% is me locked in a gladiatorial death match with the IT system, resetting the same log-in password so many times that I half expect to be arrested for hacking myself.

Still, there's a rhythm. Less chaos than hospital wards, fewer death-stares from consultants, and more tea breaks where there's at least a small chance someone's brought biscuits. I truly believe that biscuits have the greatest healing powers, even if it is a Rich Tea, the beige wallpaper of the biscuit world.

By mid-morning I acquire a medical student. Poor soul looks at me like I'm some wise guru, when in reality I've got crumbs wedged in the crevasses of my lanyard and a post-it note stuck to my shoe. I demonstrate the fine art of juggling remote and in-person consultations - which mostly means frantically clicking "unmute" on Zoom before the patient assumes I've died, and then running next door to poke someone with a tongue depressor.

We talk about 'patient-centered communication', which is medical code for nodding convincingly while someone lists every ache we've both had since 1997. I tell the student the golden rule: if you don't know what's wrong, tilt your head, frown sympathetically, and say, "that must be really frustrating." Works 90% of the time. The other 10% is just prescribing antibiotics.

Later, I see someone in the post-COVID clinic, still struggling with fatigue and breathlessness. I offer reassurance, pacing advice, and the usual spiel about "listening to your body" - which always feels ironic coming from me, since my own body has been running on caffeine, meal deals, and passive aggression since about 2012.

Lunch is, as always, the pinnacle of glamour: a sandwich inhaled at my desk while frantically trying to reply to emails, that all start with "just a quick one …" (spoiler: they're never quick). Half of the sandwich ends up in my keyboard, so in six months I'll probably grow a small colony of cress between the F and G keys. The afternoon plods on with the usual suspects:

A minor injury that somehow required three plasters and a TED Talk. A mental health check-in that left me wondering if I should be booked in next. And a chronic disease review where the highlight was discovering the patient's Fitbit knows more about their kidneys than I do!

Through it all, I imagine each patient in their homes, blissfully unaware, using their Books of Fate as paperweights while the chaos of life unfolds around them. "Could've prepared for this," I imagine it sighing. In addition to being a doctor, I now feel that I am a mandatory life-coach librarian for people who refuse to read the instructions for their own lives, preferring instead to drop their calamities on me one by one.

I swear, the universe is cruelly efficient at wasting my time.

It sometimes feels like they wait until I see them, like some medieval oracle, to explain that yes, sprained ankles and boiling pasta sauce catastrophes do, in fact, happen.

I probably should flick through my Fate soon, just to check my Fitbit hasn't failed me and I don't have a secret bout of gout brewing.

The pace of my work is generally steadier now though - and somewhere between the chaos and the crumbs, I realise my confidence has actually grown.

I can make decisions without immediately Googling "*how not to accidentally kill someone*" and, crucially, I've learned when to escalate or refer - mostly when I sense the patient is about to cry, faint, or tell me their rash has 'a personality'.

Lately I've been drawn to addictions work. There's something raw and real about it, maybe because I spend half my life pretending that I'm not addicted to the waiting room vending machine coffee. I wonder if perhaps Outreach could be the answer for my next career advancement?

Actually getting out into the community, meeting people where they are, instead of behind a desk.

I can already picture it: me, rocking up to some community centre with my trusty burgundy stethoscope, trying to make a difference while also trying not to trip over my own shoelaces.

After the clinics, I finished with admin: prescriptions, referrals, and recording outcomes. All the fun stuff!

Today's highlight was a teaching session on the new NICE guidelines for asthma management. 'Interactive', apparently. Which really means a consultant asks a question, everyone suddenly develops selective mutism, and I spend the whole-time avoiding eye contact like I'm back in Year 9 Maths. I did contribute once, mostly because my Wi-Fi lagged and I thought I was still on mute. Award-winning stuff.

I tried not to fall asleep, but honestly, the minute someone said, "stepwise management," my brain wandered off to a much happier dreamier place, pondering if there's more to life than this endless loop of clinics, guidelines, and lukewarm tea.

Here I am at twenty-seven … twenty-seven! And all I really know is work. Work and how to eat a sandwich one-handed while scanning through patient notes.

Sometimes I picture coming home to someone waiting for me. Someone I could share the daily nonsense with. Like the patient who described their wheeze as "a dying accordion". Or the patient who insisted that their insomnia was because the moon was "too judgmental". That it refused to shine on them properly, leaving them to lie awake in a dark, morally accusatory void, scrolling through conspiracy theories on their phone to calm their existential panic. Honestly, same.

Instead, I come home to an overflowing laundry basket and a fridge containing a single yoghurt that expired in September. Romantic!

I always thought maybe I'd meet someone through work - you know, the classic "two doctors reach for the same IV line and sparks fly" situation.

But apparently, when you spend all day sweating into PPE and smelling faintly of alcohol gel and despair, no one's queueing up to take you out for a drink.

Unless, of course, I lower my standards and start flirting with the photocopier, which, frankly, is the most consistent relationship I've got right now. At least it beeps at me.

Leaving the surgery, the streets feel busier, almost normal - or at least normal enough for 2021 - that I don't feel like I'm starring in some post-pandemic sequel, where everyone keeps two metres apart and nervously mutters "did you sanitise your hands?"

I reflect on how much has changed in a year: the chaos of the pandemic, the endless Zoom calls … that constant pressure somehow turned me into a clinician who can handle uncertainty.

I'm tired, yes, but there's a quiet sense of accomplishment, like I've survived the pandemonium and lived to tell the tale … with most of my sanity intact.

Independent GP, here I come! After a quick nap, probably.

Once home, I hunt for my Book of Fate.

Last time I saw it, it had been squashed under a precarious tower of medical journals - the perfect impromptu footstool for me to hang a picture frame high up.

I flip through the pages, searching for the correct year. And today's date? I've already written it what feels like sixty-four thousand times today.

23rd July 2021

> *"You will navigate the surgery in slightly-too-short chinos, juggling various patients, Zoom calls, and IT chaos while mentoring a student. For lunch, you will enjoy your usual meal deal."*

"The teaching session will leave you daydreaming about a world beyond clinics and guidelines. You will consider Outreach. Upon arriving home, you will order your regular from your favourite Chinese takeaway."

I chuckle. Oh yes, same old work - slightly ridiculous, slightly exhausting, and absolutely mine.

And yes, I'm getting a Chinese takeaway for dinner, because after all that chaos, I deserve it. Sweet and sour chicken balls with extra happiness on the side.

Somehow, even in the middle of all this mess, life still manages to be funny, shambolic and comforting - a little imperfect, and entirely, wonderfully me.

I can't help but wonder how long it will be before I get to share this commotion with someone else.

Or if I ever will.

Will anyone really love me alongside the endless piles of laundry, my non-existent sleep schedule, or my questionable obsession with naming my office stationery? Probably a niche market, but hey, stranger things have happened.

Perhaps I should flick forward in my Fate to see if it holds the answer. But where's the fun in that? Where's the drama, the thrill of pretending I'm not staring at a screen of other medics, wondering if she's out there?

The suspense is half the joy - and besides, I like imagining that somewhere, somehow, the universe is sniggering at me while I try to juggle life and medicine. It knowing that soon it will all make sense.

Chapter 16

Ben

Friday 7th December 2007
Age 30
Green and Grow Florist, Alton, UK

The shop is finally quiet. At last.
The door sign reads 'Closed' through the glass. The Christmas season is always absolute madness. Poinsettias are shoved into every corner, wreaths teetering against the walls, and the smell of pine and cinnamon hangs in the air so thick I can almost taste it.
I stayed late tonight. Just me and the fairy lights, flickering softly over the counter while I wrap bouquets and tie ribbons on wreaths for tomorrow's orders. The kind of late-night work where everything feels a little suspended in time, like the world outside has gone to bed and I'm the only one awake.
The kids are at the in-laws for the evening. Quinn, the stubborn little thing, is still refusing to take off her angel wings from her final nativity performance. She paraded around the living room earlier, twirling and making the halo wobble precariously, clearly convinced she was the star of the show - which, of course, she was in our minds.
Harry, the typical seven-year-old, is completely absorbed in his Nintendo DS, squealing with delight every time he makes Mario jump just right across the

screen. He keeps shouting instructions, as if his grandparents need to know exactly how to save the princess.

I could hear the faint sound of their laughter through the phone when I called earlier, and it makes me smile to think of how patient and kind Rose's parents are with them. They really do have a way of making the kids feel completely at home, fussing over them and letting them get away with just enough mischief to keep the evening lively. It's a relief knowing they're in such good hands.

Rose is out with her friends from college, probably gossiping about something utterly trivial, just like she always does. I can picture them all laughing, talking over one another, all the same little rituals that haven't changed since she met them back in '93. Even when I can't hear it, I can imagine her giggling at something she always found amusing, tucking a loose strand of hair behind her ear, and rolling her eyes at a friend's melodrama.

It's comforting, in a way, to know that some things never change - her laughter and the way she leans into her friends' stories.

I think about the debrief we'll have when she gets home. The way she'll replay, with her usual flair, all the best stories she's heard that evening, laughing at every detail. And then, in my own quieter way, I'll tell her about work, the small victories in the chaos, which she always somehow makes me feel proud of.

Orders tonight were very memorable, to say the least. There was a sympathy wreath for a goldfish funeral. Yes, a goldfish. Naturally, it had tiny holly sprigs tucked in for some Christmas cheer. I can only imagine what their kid will be asking Santa for this year!

Then a dozen roses with a note that said, "Sorry I ate the turkey, I didn't realise what it was for." I hope whoever receives it finds it as funny as I did.

One customer wanted a bouquet shaped like a miniature Christmas tree, complete with tiny baubles and a sparkly star on top. I'm not sure if it's genius or just mildly alarming, but I tied it up anyway. It's the most festive bouquet I've wrapped this season.

And, of course, an urgent request for mistletoe. No size specified, just "Make it jolly!"

Alone among this cheerful jumble of orders, I finally have a little space to let my thoughts wander.

I like to think Mum and Dad would be proud, watching from wherever they are. Green and Grow, the family business, still trudging on, still doing what it's always done. Orders are still piling in and, somehow, the tills haven't stopped ringing.

Mum and Dad used to bicker often at Christmas, owning a florist was never easy in December. But no order was ever too big, no bouquet ever too complicated. It was hard graft, and it's that same stubborn, determined sort of care that gave this place its reputation. Their strap line still clings to the window, peeling a little at the corners:

Green and Grow - Big or Small, We Deliver It All.

I sometimes imagine them grumbling at the paintwork, secretly smiling at what I've kept alive. Yet, I can't imagine running this business without the little modern conveniences I've picked up along the way. The order system lays out everything for me: when and how each bouquet needs to be prepared.

Harry keeps nagging me to make a MySpace page for the shop. I'm not convinced it'll bring in the right clientele. I doubt anyone ordering a funeral wreath is scrolling through profile pages late at night.

Still, I smile at his enthusiasm.

And, of course, my mind strays … to her. December is relentless that way.

I catch myself thinking of her, someone who once made this season feel like magic. The way she loved the frost on the windows, the twinkle of lights, how she'd hum to herself while untangling tinsel.

I wonder what she would make of my life now. The flat above the shop, still a family home. The kids, bouncing around with a mix of energy and disarray that she would have adored. The shop, alive and busy, carrying on relentlessly.

Sometimes, I can't help but imagine that maybe, just maybe, if she could see it all, she might have stayed. Maybe she'd have stayed if she'd known that this little life, I've built, wasn't half-bad.

I shake my head at myself, a little embarrassed by the daydream. It's silly, isn't it? Sitting here, surrounded by ribbons and pine needles, thinking of someone who's already left me.

Still, there's a quiet comfort in it. A warmth that lingers beneath the hum of the fairy lights and the soft rustle of paper as I finish wrapping the last bouquet. Christmas may be chaotic, and my heart may wander where it shouldn't, but at least for tonight the shop is mine, the memories are mine, and for a few precious hours, I can let myself imagine.

Chapter 17

Emily

Friday 19th August 2022
Age 27
Emily's House, Portsmouth, UK

Four weeks into the summer holidays and the days had started slipping through my fingers like sand. What had begun as an endless stretch of freedom was now sprinting towards September as if it had somewhere better to be. I could almost hear the school bells laughing at me from miles away.

I had been back to Eastney Beach six times already. Six. And each time, I carried the same ridiculous hope that I might bump into either *The Love of My Life* - or, if that was too much to ask, a hot pirate.

Alas, no such luck.

The beach was exactly as you'd expect heaving with happy families and children on what seemed like a mission to excavate the earth. Sandcastles loomed like miniature fortresses, and tiny hands dug trenches so ambitious I half expected them to break through the crust of the planet.

Parents lounged nearby, attempting to look relaxed while keeping one eye on their offspring, who had apparently forgotten the concept of 'personal space' entirely.

And me?

I wandered the shoreline, occasionally pretending to read my book but mostly scanning the horizon like some kind of hopeless romantic seagull.

Not a single *Love of My Life* moment appeared. No stolen glances over shared chips, no accidental hands brushing while buying my sixth Mr. Whippy. Just the odd toddler shrieking, occasionally at me, because I had clearly intruded upon their sandcastle empire.

Honestly, this entire holiday had been consistently devoid of any romance. Perhaps my true love was the man with the pregnant wife, a scenario so cruelly "Girl on the Train" that I had to pinch myself to make sure I wasn't imagining the whole thing. Perhaps this was life's way of reminding me that sometimes, the universe has a twisted sense of humour. I was forced to watch them live the life I had dreamed of, from a safe, tide-washed distance.

Today, however, I was not with the seagulls outside, pecking at the sand or squabbling over half-eaten chips. No, today I was in the middle of an epic marathon – but, not the kind that requires Lycra or dedication.

This was the marathon of scrolling, clicking, and reading. TikTok, Instagram, romance novels: my perfect recipe for losing entire days. Honestly, it was borderline heroic how much I could consume without leaving the sofa.

I had perfected the art of the wasteful day. I would scroll until something made me laugh so hard that I snorted. Then, when my brain begged for a pause, I

would reach for a romance novel - this one involving a love triangle so convoluted, I half suspected the author had a secret notebook of every awkward crush they'd ever had, combined with an alarming addiction to chocolate and melodrama.

Chapter after chapter, swoon after swoon, I would drift into a world of accidental kisses, stormy stares, and text messages that should have been sent hours ago.

Back to scrolling. Back to reading. Repeat until the sun dipped and I realized my dinner had been ignored in favour of watching more videos of animals doing suspiciously human things. Cats walking on mini treadmills like tiny furry athletes. Ducks dancing in puddles with more rhythm than I could ever muster. Corn Kid, the unstoppable joy machine, brightening my otherwise hopelessly single day. Louis Theroux rapping "Jiggle Jiggle," somehow simultaneously hilarious and profound. And, of course, more cats, because apparently, the internet runs on fur and the occasional deep emotional lesson disguised as a meme.

During part of the marathon scroll through Instagram, an image of my brother and his beautiful family suddenly popped up. All dressed to the nines, beaming on their holiday, in a location that I didn't even know he had booked to visit.

There they were, the perfect picture of sun, smiles, and coordinated outfits - like something out of a lifestyle magazine I would never be featured in. I felt that familiar tug of longing. I must reach out to him, try to arrange a meet-up. It had been far too long since we'd seen each other properly.

But that's the problem with these so-called "idyllic" teacher holidays. While I was blissfully free, everyone else, friends and family, were all still chained to their desks. Saving their precious days off for the cheapest, most strategically planned escapes in term time.

Meanwhile, here I was with no one to share my time with.

And so I stared at the photo for a moment longer, imagining catching up over hot chocolate or ice cream, or maybe just laughing over nothing in particular, and made a mental note:

Don't let it be too long. Send a message. Do something. Sometimes, social media isn't all noise - it's a reminder of the connections that truly matter.

I decided to text a friend from work. We see each other every day, so it's rare we actually hang out outside school, but I figured that by this point in the holiday, a little human interaction might be nice.

I texted Annie and asked if she fancied meeting at the café on the corner for tea and cake. Nothing too ambitious, just enough to break the cycle of doom scrolling and book-induced lethargy.

Her reply was ... unexpected.

> Not free Monday 😆 fancy watching Leicester vs Southampton down the Three-Legged Cat tomorrow? Group of friends joining too.
>
> 20:16

The Three-Legged Cat isn't exactly my usual haunt. I typically prefer establishments that smell more like books than beer, but it sounded infinitely better than spending another day in my own company with only my phone for conversation.

I felt a tiny thrill at the idea of leaving the house, of being part of something, even if it involved football, a sport I generally only care about when there's a national excuse to celebrate.

And then came the crucial question: what to wear.

I opened my wardrobe.

Should I resurrect the slightly snug t-shirt I bought for the Euro final last year? The one I had proudly worn while cheering for England before Italy crushed our collective dreams? Tempting. Nostalgic.

But probably not the best choice for blending into a pub crowd without looking like a desperate bandwagoner.

I held it up in front of the mirror anyway, just to be sure. "Do I look like someone who understands football?" I whispered to my reflection. My reflection didn't answer, which was hardly surprising.

In the end, I settled on something casual, approachable, and above all, not pyjamas. It felt like the perfect compromise between "I am socially competent" and "I may have spent the last two weeks scrolling through TikTok."

I fell asleep that night with a mild sense of excitement, imagining the pub, the laughter, the clink of glasses, the possibility of real-life conversation that didn't involve autocorrect fails or endless swiping. For the first night, in nine years, I forgot to read my Fate. Distracted by outfit dilemmas, pub menus, and elaborate mental plans to somehow appear effortlessly cool in front of Annie's friends.

There was something strangely sweet about it, this tiny step back into the world.

A gentle reminder that holidays weren't just for reading about stolen kisses and watching Corn Kid - they were for moments like this: unpredictable, slightly outside my comfort zone, and maybe, just maybe, the start of a story worth telling.

Chapter 18

Taylor

Thursday 16th February 2017
Age 32
Local Soup Kitchen, Havant, UK

The cold doesn't just bite, it gnaws. My teeth chatter before my body can catch up. I woke in a doorway off the high street, wrapped in a jacket someone left behind months ago. It smelled of damp, like it had absorbed every lonely night I'd survived and every ounce of warmth I'd ever craved. And still, it was not enough.

People passed by me with eyes averted, as though looking at me could infect them. I don't blame them. I'd avert my own eyes too if I saw me on this concrete step, hair matted and hands trembling. The children stare though, their curiosity is honest, unflinching. They look straight at me, like they can see through to the hollow I'm trying to hide. I wish I could explain that it's not a choice, that I didn't choose this doorway or this life. But my words don't matter to them - not yet.

My flat has gone. Gone like the weeks I let slip, gone like the money I didn't have, gone like the me that believed I could keep something for myself.

I had to toss most of the things I had collected over the years, I didn't have the strength to carry it all with me and didn't have the space to keep it in.

I kept a couple of shirts, a few spoons, some photos, and my needles, all of which I crammed into a battered rucksack. My life, compressed into a handful of things. I moved where the dealers went. Survival has a map, and it runs on needles and withdrawals. Sometimes I feel like I've lost more than I can name, but I keep moving anyway.

A drunk couple stumbled past and offered me a crumpled McDonalds bag filled with their left-over chips and a warm cup of coffee. My chest tightened. Kindness is almost unbearable. For one fragile second, I am not just a junkie, not just a shadow shuffling along the edge of the world. For one fragile second, this couple saw me as me - still human and still worthy of compassion. I wanted to talk to them, to tell them I am more than this, that I am still someone who remembers love, who remembers laughter. But they staggered away, leaving me with the warmth of the coffee and the cold knowledge that even fleeting recognition is precious. I guess beggars literally can't be choosers.

I sipped the drink slowly, letting it burn a small fire in my chest. And for a moment, I imagined there was someone who could understand me. Not my bad habits or the poor choices I've made. Just me.

Afterall, I'm still the same girl who believed she was worthy of being understood, even as the world around her told her she wasn't.

I closed my eyes against the cold, against the shame, against the craving, and I let myself hope - quietly, secretly, desperately.

I shuffled to the soup kitchen when it opened. My stomach already twisting and growling, stealing away the few chips I'd managed to eat earlier, almost as quickly as I'd swallowed them. Digestion has no mercy. Above the serving hatch, the decorations are still up from Valentine's Day.

Pink and red paper hearts drooped tiredly from bits of string, curling at the edges. An A4 poster of a cartoon cherub grinning down, saying, "You make miso happy," beside a neatly printed list of today's soup ingredients. I almost laughed. That little angel with its chubby cheeks had no idea how much joy a bowl of miso noodle soup could actually bring to someone like me.

It's my favourite soup they serve here. The warmth of the chillies hitting the back of my throat, the crunch of the water chestnuts, the noodles soft but still with enough bite to trick my brain into thinking I'm eating something fancy.

A culinary sensation if you ask me.

For a few moments, it sparks a part of my brain no drug ever quite reaches - the part that remembers what it's like to feel comfort without shame.

The soup sits heavily in my stomach, but not in a bad way. It anchors me. Reminds me that I exist, that I can be filled with something other than longing.

The volunteers move briskly behind the hatch, bowls clattering, spoons scraping. They don't stare, but they don't avoid my eyes either - which, honestly, is a kindness in itself. I've had enough of both extremes: the disgust that lingers too long and the deliberate blindness that cuts just as deep.

One of them, an older man with kind eyes, leans down a little when he hands me my bowl. He asks how I'm doing, voice low, like he wants to know and not just to tick a box. I glance up. He looks like he's had his own battles - the sort that leave dents in your spirit but somehow make your gaze softer, not harder.

For a moment I feel a pull towards him, like maybe he could understand what it's like to be at war. My throat tightens, but I can't let it all spill out there, in the queue, soup steaming in my hands. So, I mumble the classic: "Getting by."

It's a lie, of course.

I'm not getting by. I'm barely scraping together the threads of myself that are left. But I smile as I say it because I can't help myself. I've always been like that. Even in the middle of a spiral, I still want to make other people feel at ease. It's ridiculous really, the kind, sweet junkie, apologising for her own existence.

I couldn't help but wonder if my parents would help out in a soup kitchen like this. I could picture Mum with an apron tied tight, ladling out soup with her unstoppable chatter, making everyone feel like they'd been personally invited to her kitchen table. Dad would be behind her, sleeves rolled up, pretending he was in charge but really just doing the heavy lifting. They would love it, giving themselves away to the community, the way they always did. I question if they would they recognise me if they walked in right now? Or have I slipped too far from the daughter they used to know and love?

I try not to let the thought sit too long. It troubles me worse than hunger ever could.

My brother's number hums in the back of my mind like an unwanted ringtone. I know it by heart. I replay the digits in my head on nights I cannot sleep.

But I'm not ready to call. Not yet. I'm not sure if I'm waiting for him to apologise, or for me to forgive him, or just for a sign that we're still on the same planet. Forgiveness, it turns out, takes time, and maybe more courage than I've got today.

After I've eaten, I sit with the others, our bowls empty but our bodies reluctant to leave the warmth. Faces are drawn, eyes hollow, but there's something oddly comforting about it. Like we're all characters in the same play, stumbling through the same half-written script.

We trade rumours like currency: which churches don't ask too many questions, which hostels have space, which dealers might let you pay tomorrow if you look convincing enough. Survival is nothing more than patchwork - a quilt made of luck and lies you hope sound true.

By nightfall, I've scraped together enough for a small hit. Not much, but enough to blur the edges and dull the ache in my bones.

I tell myself it's just "to get through," the same way other people tell themselves they need a glass of wine to relax after work. Only my glass of wine comes with needles and embarrassment.

I curl up on a bench in the park, jacket pulled as tight as it will go, pretending it's a duvet. (If I close my eyes, I can almost convince myself I'm camping - minus the marshmallows, tent, or choice in the matter.) The cold seeps in anyway, creeping under my skin, but I try to hang onto the memory of earlier. The soup. The warmth of the chilli still burning faintly on my tongue, the understanding and kindness in the volunteers' eyes.

And I think - maybe tomorrow, if I can't find what I need on the streets to keep going - I'll go back for another bowl.

Sometimes it's enough, just knowing there's a place where you're not treated like a monster. Sometimes miso really does make you happy.

And maybe, just maybe, happiness is enough to try again tomorrow.

Chapter 19

Frederick

Thursday 16th February 2017
Age 59
Local Soup Kitchen, Havant, UK

I ladle out the soup in the way I was taught to dish rations thirty years ago: steady, no fuss, making sure everyone gets their fair share. Old habits die hard, even when the uniform is long gone. The kitchen is warm, clattering with spoons and chatter, though most of the faces in the line are tired and closed off. You learn not to push folk, just give them a hot meal and a bit of dignity.

There are decorations, I assume from Valentine's Day, still hanging above the hatch.

Someone's stuck a poster up with a cartoon cherub saying "You make miso happy". Ridiculous, but I don't mind. A bit of daftness never hurt anyone.

It makes me smile. The lads used to hang up worse in the block and call it festive.

Today it's miso noodle soup, the proper warming stuff. I can see it light up a few faces as soon as they catch the smell. One woman in particular - hair pulled into a greasy bun, eyes tired but sharp - looks at that bowl like it's gold. I know the look. I've seen blokes in the desert hold a water bottle the same way. Survival makes you grateful for small mercies.

When I hand her the soup, I lean down and ask, "how you doing?" Nothing dramatic, nothing staged. Just the sort of check-in I'd have wanted someone to give me, back when my own head wasn't right.

She glances up, startled almost, then mutters, "Getting by." We both know it's not true, but I don't press. I've learned the hard way, that sometimes just asking is enough. Sometimes it's the only kindness a person can carry without dropping it.

I watch her walk off, bowl steaming in her hands. There's a fragility to her, but also something stubborn, the way she squares her shoulders even with the world on her back. Reminds me of the boys I served with, the ones who'd crack a joke while their boots filled with water, just to keep the rest of us steady.

Behind the hatch, the volunteers rattle pans and keep the line moving. Some of them look away, embarrassed, others beam too wide, like cheerleaders at a funeral. I try to sit somewhere in the middle. See people, but don't stare them down. You can't fake respect, they'll smell it a mile off.

And truth be told, I get as much from this place as anyone in the queue. After the Army, civvy life felt like a freefall. No orders, no routine, just too much quiet and a looming Fate.

This kitchen gives me back a bit of structure.

When I see someone's face soften as that first spoonful warms their belly, well, it reminds me that even off the battlefield, you can still make a difference.

I hand out another bowl, nodding at the next person in line. The queue doesn't end, and neither does the need. But that's alright. We keep the pots full for as long as we can.

As I move around the hall, stacking chairs and wiping down tables, I call out softly to the last few stragglers, reminding them we were closing for the night.

Some ask where they might find shelter, and I give what guidance I can: a church here, a hostel there, or, failing that, the places I knew would at least keep the rain off their backs. I press my phone into a couple of hands, so they could try their luck with someone on the other end of the line.

In the far corner, one young woman wasn't stirring. She's bent over the table, her pen scratching feverishly across a scrap of paper. It was unusual - most came in looking only for warmth, food, or silence. Writing was rare. As I draw closer, she shields the page quickly, like a soldier caught with contraband. Her eyes met mine for a moment, and I knew better than to ask. I let her be.

When she finally slipped out into the night, I returned to her table. And there, left behind, was the page. A poem. Words etched in hurried strokes, but carrying a weight that stopped me in my tracks.

> Thank you for the steaming bowl,
> That stitched a tear within my soul.
> The fire of chilli, sharp and bright,
> Cut through the edges of the night.
> A chair, a moment, space to mend,
> The gift of warmth, the grace of friend.
> Your hours here, your quiet hand,
> Reach further than you understand.

I read it twice, then a third time, the room quiet but for the echo of chairs scraping across the floor. It struck me then, maybe this was the ghost of some old writer still lingering inside her, or perhaps the fragile beginning of a new one being born. Either way, it was proof that even here, in the weariness and shadows, words and hope can still take root.

—

I slipped the poem into my pocket, careful not to crease it too much, though the paper was already worn at the edges. It was as if it had been folded and unfolded a hundred times before she set the words down for good.

Once the kitchen was closed, I ambled to the bus stop. Walking through the drizzle, her beautiful words tugging at me with every step.

Chapter 20

Emily

Saturday 20th August 2022
Age 27
The Three-Legged Cat, Portsmouth, UK

When morning came, and I had overthought every single possible part of the day ahead: outfits, conversations, emergency escape routes. I honestly didn't really want to go by that point. But I convinced myself, with weak but serviceable logic, that the pub would surely be loud enough to hide in. No one really notices you in a pub during a football match, I reasoned, unless you accidentally cheer the wrong team.

Four outfit changes later, I finally settled on a casual denim skirt and a pink Western-themed graphic t-shirt. It felt like a safe middle ground: not too dressy, not too football-y. Crucially, it didn't announce allegiance to either Leicester or Southampton, because if I'm honest, I wasn't entirely sure which team I was meant to be supporting at this point anyway.

Walking through the heavy pub doors, I was immediately swallowed by a comforting darkness. Warm lamps glowed from the edges of the room, casting everything in a sepia tint. Little framed pictures of cats dotted the walls, which gave the place less of a raucous sports-bar vibe and more of a "grandmother with a slight gin problem" feel. I didn't dislike it.

I scanned the room for Annie.

The problem was, I had absolutely no idea what her friends looked like, or even how many of them there were. So, my chances of finding her was somewhere between slim and hopeless.

I couldn't see her anywhere, but I also wasn't about to hover awkwardly in the doorway like a lost supply teacher waiting for someone to let me into the staffroom. Still, I wanted to keep an eye on the entrance in case she arrived.

I made the only logical decision: sit at the bar. There was one stool left, perfectly positioned, though unfortunately located between two already occupied seats.

On one side, an entangled couple who were very much not here for the football (lucky them). On the other side, a person in a Western t-shirt of their own, the back of it proudly sporting the slogan: *"Save a Horse, Ride a Cowgirl."*

Well. That was fate if I'd ever seen it.

As if possessed by Chappell Roan herself, I slid onto the stool next to them, tipped an imaginary cowboy hat, and announced far too boldly, "Consider your horse saved."

What on earth was I doing? Who gave me permission to open my mouth like that? This was supposed to be my incognito evening, my blending-into-the-background mission. Instead, I had apparently entered some kind of roleplay saloon. A teacher on holiday, transformed by social anxiety, into a discount cowboy.

They turned their head slowly, like a gunslinger sizing up their opponent. For a terrifying second, I thought they were about to tell me to get lost, or worse, stare blankly until I melted into the sticky pub floor.

Then, to my immense relief, they cracked a grin.

"Well then," she said, raising her pint in a mock salute, "Guess the horse and I just hit the jackpot …"

I laughed a little too loudly - like, loud enough that the entangled couple beside me unclenched from each other for a moment to glare.

I tried to soften it with a more polite chuckle.

Smooth.

"Sorry," I muttered, attempting to sip the water I'd just ordered, forgetting that it was still full to the brim. Half of it went down my chin in what can only be described as the least seductive waterfall in history.

Cowgirl Shirt looked at me, amused. "You here for the match, then?"

This was a dangerous question.

I could lie and pick a team, though which one I wasn't sure? Leicester? Southampton? Was one of them wearing blue? Red? I couldn't remember. Knowing my luck, I'd choose the wrong side and end up on some viral video titled 'Local Teacher Starts Pub Riot.'

"Erm," I hedged. "I'm here for... moral support."

"Moral support?"

"Yes," I said, gaining confidence. "You know. I cheer when other people cheer. I boo when they boo. I clap when someone brings snacks. A very important role, really."

To my surprise, she laughed. A real laugh this time, not just polite. "Fair enough. That's more than half the crowd here, anyway."

My chest had started to do a strange fluttery thing - the thing it always did when engaging in the novels I devoured, wherein the main characters of a slow-burn romance finally brushed fingers across a table or accidentally knocked elbows.

There was something about her, maybe the fact that our matching Western-themed t-shirts made it look like we were part of some clandestine cowboy gang, made it easier, somehow. It broke the ice without a single awkward word.

The conversation flowed like a gentle river over rocks that could have been minefields of embarrassment.

Jokes about classic football hooligan behaviour mixed effortlessly with commentary remarks about the pub décor.

I kept telling myself it was harmless. Just chatting. Nothing more.

A casual evening.

Except it wasn't. Every time her eyes met mine, it felt like my body remembered a truth my brain had been carefully shelving for months, maybe years. I'd circled around it, masked it under "just friends" and "probably nothings," telling myself it was safer that way.

But sitting here, shoulder-to-shoulder, the match roaring and the pub vibrating with chants and laughter, I couldn't deny it anymore. I liked this. I liked her.

Annie greeted me as if nothing at all was happening, just a casual hello, while gesturing toward the rest of her friends. They were all gathered right in front of the big screen, the match now in full swing. "Come find me when you're ready", she said, like it was the simplest thing in the world, leaving me to wrestle quietly with my own nervous overthinking.

Before I could even consider if I was ready, Cowgirl Shirt leaned slightly closer, her shoulder brushing mine as she reached for her glass. Heat shot straight through me, in a way that was physically ridiculous but emotionally undeniable.

I knew instantly that I was now living out the same sort of slow-burn romance plot I'd find in the books I read, the one where people overthink every glance and gesture while simultaneously wanting to throw themselves at each other.

"Sorry," she murmured, her smile soft and slightly mischievous, like it wasn't really an accident at all.

My mouth went dry, a textbook case of "teacher-in-public behaving like a teenager with a crush." My brain wanted to say something witty. Something clever.

Instead, I think all I managed was an internal squeak.

Her smile widened, slow and knowing, and I swear my heart skipped. We kept talking, but it wasn't small talk anymore. It was warmer, gentler, soft around the edges like a blanket that smells faintly of home.

It was the kind of conversation where the world outside the pub, the match, the chaos of everything, faded into background noise.

At one point, she brushed her short messy hair back, and I realised I was staring, really staring.

Staring at the curve of her cheek, the single freckle on her neck, the way her teeth caught the light when she laughed, the crinkles at the corner of her eyes. I wanted to memorise all of her.

For the first time, noticing these things didn't scare me. It didn't make me nervous or guilty. It felt right. Comfortable, somehow, like I'd been holding my breath for years without realising it, and suddenly I could breathe again.

It was ridiculous. I knew it. And yet, I couldn't stop it. Every laugh, every glance, every incidental touch sent little sparks across my skin that I'd normally chalk up to caffeine or poor circulation. Tonight, though, I knew it was her.

By the time the final whistle blew, I couldn't even have told you who had won the match. Leicester? Southampton? The referee? Honestly, none of it mattered.

All I knew was that I wanted the night to stretch on forever, to linger in that strange, warm, fluttery bubble I had somehow found myself in, sitting next to her.

That feeling - the one where your heart rate decides it has its own nervous agenda and your brain keeps whispering, don't screw this up - was addictive.

I realized I hadn't once thought about fading into the background. I wasn't pretending to be someone else. I wasn't worried about looking awkward. I was just here.

And that, I decided, was far better than any perfectly executed outfit, any joke I had rehearsed in the mirror, or any imaginary plan to blend in.

I wanted to stay up all night talking to her, sharing stupid jokes, debating nonsense, laughing at the pub décor, or maybe just watching her sip a drink while I pretended to be casually interested in the match score.

I glanced over at Annie. She was many pints in, cheerfully chatting with another friend, utterly oblivious to the fact that I hadn't yet made it over to her table. Her carefree energy contrasted sharply with my internal monologue, which was currently a messy mix of "don't spill your drink, again" and "if you faint, at least do it gracefully."

But, honestly? I didn't care.

Not about Annie, not about the match, not even about looking like a slightly awkward adult still figuring out how to exist in public.

For once, I didn't care what Fate had scribbled out for me in its little book. I was taking control of my own story, and it felt exhilarating, ridiculous, terrifying, and wonderful all muddled together.

And then it hit me: I was going to ask for her number. I couldn't compute the thought of not seeing this woman again.

There would be no long-drawn-out sighs, no waiting for some magical sign from the universe.

I would do it.

Right here, right now.

Because for the first time in a long while, I wasn't hiding. I wasn't overthinking. I wasn't letting Fate dictate my life. I was simply... here.

And now, finally, I could ask for the number that might change everything.

Except, in classic me-fashion, I had to pause for one very important question first.

"Erm... what is your name again?" I asked.

Chapter 21

Danny

Monday 8th November 2021
Age 28
The Sailor's Rest, Hostel, Gosport, UK

Today felt different from the usual rhythm of general practice. Instead of heading to the surgery, I joined the local outreach team working with people facing addiction and homelessness.

I left my crisp white shirt on the hanger and swapped it for a knitted jumper and jeans, with trainers that had definitely seen better days. It felt a bit more like me.

I met early with some other medics at the Community Health Hub, loading up supplies. We packed naloxone kits, clean needles, wound dressings, leaflets on services, and, because the NHS runs on bureaucracy and biscuits, plenty of tea and custard creams. I of course personally tested the biscuits. For quality control. It was a tough job, but someone had to do it.

By mid-morning we were on the streets. There's an art to balancing a cup of lukewarm tea on a clipboard while trying to make notes. Offering help to someone who's probably seen more chaos in the last 24 hours than I've seen in my entire GP career. I handed out naloxone kits and chatted with people, occasionally remembering to breathe and not just nod like a confused bobblehead.

Somewhere between sharing a joke about the terrible state of the local bus service and gently reminding someone not to reuse a syringe, I realised that this - this messy, slightly frenzied, unpredictable work - was the kind of work that made me feel like I was actually doing something. It was not just checking boxes on a patient record or convincing a stressed-out parent that paracetamol really is enough for a minor fever.

And honestly, by the end of the morning, with my jumper smelling faintly of the street, my hair sticking out at impossible angles, and a bladder full of tea, I felt exhausted but in the best possible way. It was like I'd accidentally stumbled into the part of medicine that makes you feel human again.

Our next stop was a hostel. The staff there knew the residents well, and they introduced me to a few of them as if I were a bizarre new species they'd discovered in the wild.

I ended up sitting with a man in his forties who's been trying to cut down on alcohol. It was not the usual ten-minute consultation where you nod politely while secretly thinking about your lunch, but an actual conversation about cravings, sleep, and the loneliness that crawls under your skin.

I offered some practical advice, but mostly I just listened, which apparently counts as a revolutionary act in these parts. It struck me how much trust can grow simply by showing up, rather than expecting people to march into a clinic wearing clean socks and a perfect smile.

Then I met a woman in her late thirties. I asked her about her Book of Fate, half expecting her to have some neat plan for escaping the turmoil. She laughed, more bitter than amused. Her book was lost, stolen, sold, and probably turned into a coaster by now. Even she doesn't know what her next chapter looked like.

I noticed a raging skin infection creeping across her left arm. I dabbed some ointment on it while she talked about losing touch with her family, how the connections that should have been lifelines just frayed. I offered to help her call her family. "Maybe next time," she said, and I could tell that a small, almost imperceptible amount of hope flickered in her eyes.

I left the hostel feeling like I'd been part of a strange, messy, tiny miracle. And maybe, just maybe, my toothpaste-stained jumper had made me more approachable. Either that, or she just appreciated my stellar bedside manner.

Later, at the drop-in centre, I helped a nurse redress an infected ulcer on a young woman's leg. She was wary at first, eyes darting around the room, but they softened when I treated her with the same respect I would any patient in my clinic.

The team explained how outreach medicine is about consistency: showing up, offering small steps of care, and not judging. Not swooping in like some white-coated saviour, but turning up week after week, even when all you're doing is giving out paracetamol and plasters.

And then came my next patient. A man shuffled in, grinning through a mouth that was mostly gap rather than teeth, clutching a carrier bag full of what he proudly called "my medications." Inside was a jumble of blister packs, half-used inhalers, an unlabeled brown bottle of something vaguely herbal, and several packets of tablets - so old the foil had worn smooth and the print had completely rubbed off. I tried to look professional as I pulled each item out, while the nurse beside me silently mouthed good luck.

"So, tell me, what do you actually take every day?", I ask.

"Depends on what I find first." He chuckled insouciantly.

"… Right. We might need a system." I managed to get out.

Meanwhile, the kettle in the corner was clicking on and off with Converse enthusiasm and someone outside the door was swearing loudly at a vending machine that had eaten their KitKat. I couldn't decide whether to laugh or cry (or join them).

The drop-in isn't tidy. It's a graveyard of mismatched chairs, each one a different height, so you never know if you're about to sit like a normal human or disappear into a dental extraction position. There's a faint smell of burnt toast that no one has ever traced (I'm starting to suspect it's just part of the building's soul), and the posters on the walls are so old they probably count as historical documents.

But there's warmth. Someone always knows someone else's name, there's always tea - strong enough to dissolve a spoon if left unattended - and laughter that somehow manages to wriggle its way through the chaos like an uninvited but welcome guest.

By the end of the day, my stethoscope had vanished (later located on a teddy bear in the kids' corner, looking far more professional than me), my shoes reeked faintly of TCP, and my notebook was less 'medical log' and more 'manifesto of someone slowly losing the will to triage'.

But for all the mess, I felt like I'd done something worthwhile - not because I had cured anyone, but because I listened, didn't run away, and even managed to laugh.

In the afternoon we did a round through the town centre, checking in with rough sleepers. I handed out naloxone kits, did my best impression of a Blue Peter presenter while showing a man how to use one, and tried to look like I wasn't terrified I'd be asked to demonstrate on myself.

He told me his friend had overdosed two weeks ago and didn't survive. The weight of his grief sat between us like a third person, heavier than my medical bag, but somehow, he still thanked us for being there. As if my wobbly tutorial on needles had been any use against the sheer unfairness of it all.

I felt a mix of emotions. It was challenging, raw, and heart breaking, but also deeply worthwhile. And exhausting. And a little damp, because apparently every outreach shift involves some kind of drizzle, as though the British weather is in on the symbolism.

General practice has taught me to juggle chronic disease, mental health, and social issues in ten-minute slots. Outreach strips all that back: no computers, no receptionists, no passive-aggressive patient feedback forms. Just people. Humanity first, medicine second, snacks … somewhere between.

I don't know yet if this will become a regular part of my career, but today has reminded me why I wanted to be a doctor in the first place. Not the glossy TV-drama version with inspirational music swelling in the background. The real version: me squatting on a damp kerb, explaining an overdose kit to someone whose fate has been written by pain and bad luck. I realise that they probably trust me more than the average middle-class patient who once left me a one-star review because I didn't print their prescription quickly enough in advance of their holiday.

And then, of course, I feel the inevitable existential spiral: Where exactly is my life going? Is this it?

I wonder if I am destined to spend my days handing out naloxone kits and TCP wipes, building some kind of makeshift career - and family - among the very people society tries their hardest not to see?

It's an odd sort of kinship. Their disarray seeps into me, clinging like cigarette smoke, but so does their resilience - louder, sharper, more defiant than anything I've ever managed in my neat little respectable life.

And maybe, just maybe, being needed by them plugs the cavernous hole of my own loneliness. Because there's no room for self-pity when you're doling out plasters, paracetamol, and the occasional pep talk.

Cure their pain, ignore mine.

Doctor's orders.

Chapter 22

Frederick

Tuesday 2nd January 2018
Age 60
Frederick's Home, Portsmouth, UK

I woke a few minutes before six o'clock. Army habits die hard, and the discipline never quite left me. These days, routine was what kept me steady. Without it, the recent days might have blurred into nothing.
I filled the kettle, put it on, and waited for the familiar rattle of the boil. My tea was always strong, always black. No sugar. The toast went into the toaster, two slices which were always of the same brand. Simple things, predictable things.
When the toast popped, I carried my mug and plate to the kitchen counter. There sat the little block calendar, the one where you turned the cards over each morning. I flipped it as usual, not thinking, just another square of paper marking another day.
2nd January 2018.
The numbers hit harder than I expected. I had tried to forget. But there it was … my birthday.
My sixtieth birthday.
I stood there for a long moment, staring at it.
Sixty.

I had dreaded entering my sixties, though I never admitted it out loud. Men like me weren't meant to be sentimental, but I knew. I knew this would be the final decade marker of my life. Fate has told me every day that seventy wouldn't come for me.

My body already carried the scars and the wear. I had marched, run, fought, and carried more weight than I should have, in every sense of the word.

The kitchen felt too quiet. The tick of the clock, the hum of the fridge, the whisper of the kettle cooling. No one to say Happy Birthday. No one to bring me a card or raise a glass with. Just me, the calendar, my tea, and the toast cooling on the plate. How, on days like this, I missed the lads. The banter.

I told myself not to dwell. Soldiers didn't dwell. You carried on. You packed up the kit and you moved forward.

Looking around the room, my eyes fell upon the Alexa in the corner of the kitchen. A gift from David last Christmas, he had insisted I needed "a bit of modern company."

With great patience he had taught me how to use it. "Alexa, play *Start Me Up* please, and thank you!" or "Alexa, what can I make out of one egg, two bits of bacon, and milk, thank you?"

It had been a battle at first, my voice clipped and stiff, the commands precise, but David had smiled through it, encouraging me with endless patience.

I wondered, almost hesitantly, "Alexa... sing me Happy Birthday. Cheers."

The little device responded, and a slightly off-kilter version of Happy Birthday floated through the kitchen. The tune was a little odd, not quite like the versions you remembered from school or family parties. A little warped, a little robotic - but somehow, that made me smile. Chuckle, even.

I found myself leaning against the counter, tea forgotten for the moment, listening. The odd little melody made me think of all the birthdays that had come and gone without notice, and the ones that had been celebrated with merriment, too much drink, and not a shred of regret. And yet, here I am now, in this quiet kitchen, marking the day in a very different way. I made a mental note to call David later. Perhaps he would chuckle at the thought of his old army roommate standing in a kitchen, listening to a slightly off-key, robotic birthday song. I could almost hear his laugh, the one that had always made things feel lighter, even when life was heavy.

I went out into the garden, the cold nipping at my face, taking me right back to the early morning drills I used to do. I'd picked up a box of assorted bulbs from the reduced section of the supermarket. A small mission, but one hopefully worth the effort.

The back garden lay lifeless, a patchwork of brown shades, winter having stripped it bare. Yet in my mind's eye, I could already see the colours that might one day push through: daffodils in bright, sharp yellows, tulips standing tall in proud reds and deep purples, snowdrops like tiny white sentries bowing in the breeze. Planting this late in the season was a gamble, but one worth taking. Hope was always worth the effort.

Orders to the soil: nurture and grow. Carry out the plan.

I knelt on the hard ground, fingers working through the cold earth, planting each bulb with the precision of a man used to following and giving orders.

There was satisfaction in it.

A small operation, done well, quietly victorious.

Then came the sound of a garden gate creaking open.

The newly planted hedge between mine and my neighbouring garden was only a few feet tall, which made it impossible not to see my neighbour coming home. I nodded, a polite and disciplined gesture - acknowledgement, nothing more. He looked straight past me, deliberately ignoring my presence.

I decided to press the advantage. "I'm planting bulbs for Spring," I called out, voice steady, carrying the firmness of someone accustomed to being heard. "Got extras if you'd like some, mate."

A grumble of a no came back, followed by the unmistakable slam of a back door. Tough crowd.

I let out a quiet sigh, shook my head, and returned to the task. In the army, you learned quickly: some missions fail. You move on, you finish the job, and you take satisfaction where you can.

I returned to the house, fingers stiff and numb, thawing slowly in the warmth of my home. I reached for my Book of Fate, my old companion in all things uncertain.

Its cover was worn, corners dog-eared, pages yellowed with age and the spine cracked but protesting. Handling it felt familiar, like gripping the reins of a regiment I'd once commanded.

I flicked to today's date, careful not to damage the delicate pages further. Year, month, day.

And then it struck me, a fact I had tucked away in the back of my mind, forgotten but no less true, waiting for its moment to resurface in my sixtieth year.

"Today you will turn sixty. You will rehome a Border Collie from the local dog adoption centre. He will be called Gunner. He will provide you companionship for the rest of your life."

Gunner. The name alone brought a faint smile to my face. I had often thought about getting this dog while I was still serving.

The thought of a loyal companion at my side - someone who would never question, never complain, never fail you - had seemed as appealing then as it did now.

A fellow soldier, only four-legged, always ready for the next mission, always by my side.

I could almost see him now: alert, intelligent eyes, tail wagging, ears twitching to my every command.

A partner for walks, a sentinel at my side, a reminder that life had room for small joys even after decades of order, discipline, and duty.

I move over to the computer, fingers still defrosting, and switched it on. The hum of the machine fills the quiet room.

I open a browser and begin my search for the phone number of the local adoption centre, each keystroke deliberate and precise.

This is my mission now: find Gunner, bring him home, and start a new chapter.

Chapter 23

Ben

Friday 12th November 2010
Age 32
Green and Grow Florist, Alton, UK

I stumbled out of the taxi, the streetlamps flickered through the rain like reluctant fireflies. Timothy and I had been down the pub, nursing our own brand of heartbreak.

Sadness had found both Timothy and me this Friday night. His heart was freshly broken as his girl had walked out on him without warning. I wasn't immune either; the week itself carried a lingering haze of disenchantment, as it always did around the anniversary of my parents' death.

We sat. We drank. And drank some more. We sung along, off-key, inevitably, to a few overplayed hits: I Gotta Feeling, Boom Boom Pow, Tik Tok. Voices cracking as we slowed down to sing the more emotional renditions of Fireflies and Halo.

The sorrow was thick, sticky, and yet, as the night wore on, it began to dilute in alcohol and ridiculous lyrics.

By the time that the kind bar lady told us it was time to leave, we couldn't even remember what it was that had dragged us in there in the first place.

The taxi dropped us off and I reminded myself that I needed to pay Timothy for my half of the fare. But not right now.

My foot found the one puddle where the curb dipped, soaking my Converse through instantly. I stopped and looked across at the shop, its sign faint in the drizzle: Green and Grow.

The paint seemed weary, worn down by years of winter's relentless touch. I made a mental note to redecorate our shop in the Spring. When the ground dried, probably cracking the paint further, I'd patch it up.

I headed to the flat door beside the shop front, the one leading up the narrow staircase that ran parallel to the wall. My keys hovered in my hand, but as my fingers curled around the familiar shape, a thought struck me like a gust of wind through the corridor.

Her face appeared, unbidden, and suddenly eclipsed all other thoughts. Everything else - the puddle, the tired paint, the lingering alcohol - slipped away, and I found myself switching keys.

Not to the flat or to the staircase. Instead, I pushed the door to the florist shop open, bell chiming as I stumbled inside, leaving wet footprints on the internal mat.

The warmth hit me all at once: earthy, fragrant, the gentle disorder of plants thriving despite it all. Familiar. Home.

I stagger over to the shop laptop. The counter feels familiar under my hands, cluttered with offcuts and stray petals. I flip the lid open and hit the power button. Immediately, the fan whirs to life like it's trying to take off, heat puffing out in waves that warm my cold fingers. The Windows logo flickers across the screen, painfully bright in the dim shop light, and I watch it slowly grind its way to the start menu.

I type in the password.

> *PetalToTheMetal.123*

It makes me grin, imagining any hacker's despair.

The laptop accepts it without complaint, and I navigate to the internet.

The Wi-Fi lags, barely keeping up, stuttering through every click. My emails ping one after another, each notification a little spike of responsibility and chaos.

Orders. Orders. Orders.

A request for a funeral bouquet, two wedding arrangements, and ... a dog's birthday party. I stare at that last one for a moment, half expecting confetti to explode from the screen.

A Funeral, Two Weddings, And A Dog's Birthday Party. Sounds like some weird, overly sentimental 90s movie where everyone cries in turn, and somehow the Golden Retriever is the star.

I shake my head and smile. Just another day in the life of a florist.

I log into Facebook, having only recently signed up after Rose had shown me some of our old college friends on there. It felt like a yearbook that never ended, a place where everyone I had ever known could be summoned at the touch of a keyboard. Just typing a name into the search bar could reveal everything: relationship status, children, holidays, houses bought, careers, and even the mundane little updates you'd normally only catch in passing. The sheer scope of it made me dizzy, like holding the world in my hands, or at least the curated, filtered version of it.

A post from Rose appears first, pinned to the top of my feed. A photo of a glass of wine balanced on a box of chocolates, the caption reading:

> **Rose Green** is **Feeling Relaxed** 😌. Might actually make it through a whole movie without falling asleep... but probably not. #LazyFriday #MeTime #CouchPotato #KidsAsleep

My cursor hovers over the small blue thumbs-up, but I freeze. Clicking it felt dangerous, like an invitation for questions I wasn't ready to answer. Why was I on the laptop at this hour? Why was I scrolling through Facebook?

I pull my hand back, telling myself I was only here for a single search. Just one. Nothing more.

Hands trembling, heart hammering, I type her name into the search bar. I feel a gnawing mixture of guilt and urgency. It was wrong. I knew it. And yet I couldn't stop myself. I needed to know! Where was she living now? Did she have a new partner? Or any of the children she once dreamed about?

I could have just opened *her* Book of Fate. The book she had never collected from mine before she left me. It lies forgotten at the back of my wardrobe alongside mine. But that felt worse.

This … this was different. Just a search. Innocent.

The results load slowly, each profile a potential reality. Ireland, Canada, Australia. A whole globe of possible hers. And then England. Bingo.

My breath catches as I see her face.

Small in the profile box, smiling at the camera.

The same eyes. The same grin. I can almost hear her voice calling my name across the years, soft and familiar, tugging at some hidden corner of my heart.

The cursor hovers over her profile. One click, and I would cross the line. One click, and I would see her life. The life I had never gotten to be a part of, the life I had missed. My fingers itch, frozen over the trackpad.

Then the bell above the door clatters. The sudden noise jerking me violently out of my reverie. I snap the laptop shut and I look up to see Rose standing in the doorway of the florist, eyes wide, confused. The familiar warmth of the shop now feels heavy, constricting, as if the walls themselves knew what I had been doing.

My throat is dry, words sticking like wet petals in my mouth. "Rose … I – uh …" I lurched over the edge of the counter, trying to appear casual, though my soggy shoes betrayed me with a small squelch.

She raises an eyebrow, arms crossed, expression somewhere between suspicion and hurt. "What … were you doing?" she asks softly, but firmly, eyes flicking to the laptop now shut and silent.

"I … I was just … checking the emails. Orders," I blurt, fumbling to sound ordinary. "The, uh … the dog's birthday party one - you know, making sure everything's ready for tomorrow."

Rose's lips press together, a faint smile tugging at the corner of her mouth, but it didn't reach her eyes. "At … midnight?"

"Right," I said, gesturing vaguely at the screen. "Midnight emails … you know how it is." My voice cracked somewhere around the second syllable, and I cursed myself under my breath.

She shook her head, sighing softly. "Ben, you're hiding something."

I ran a hand through my damp hair, heart hammering. "I - no! I wasn't - It's nothing!" I add, too quickly, too desperately. "Just… just orders and stuff. Really."

Chapter 24

Emily

Monday 19th September 2022
Age 27
Emily's House, Portsmouth, UK

School had only just started back, and the rhythm of classroom life was finally smoothing out.

My new class? Absolute icons.

They've got a rare spark. Normally Year 2s laugh at poo jokes and fall apart if you say underpants in a lesson. But this lot? They actually get sarcasm.

They've started heckling me too. During handwriting, one girl leaned over and whispered, "Miss, why is your tummy bigger than yesterday? Is there a baby in it?" (No Maria, I just ate too much pasta for lunch!)

Another asked me how old I was. I told him, "Guess." He looked me dead in the eye and said, "Forty-six." I'm twenty-seven.

I nearly cancelled Golden Time.

Still, it's refreshing. For once it isn't just my LSA politely laughing at my lame remarks. Now I've got a full gaggle of seven-year-olds snorting into their sleeves as if I'm headlining a low-budget comedy club.

One boy even started clapping after I dropped the whiteboard pen lid three times in one lesson input, thinking it was part of my 'act'.

Today though I wasn't wrangling those little scallywags because we'd all been granted the holy grail: a day off. I sit on the sofa, curled under my recently purchased blanket, which is covered in tiny cartoon ghosts wearing cowboy hats and neckerchiefs.

How could I not buy it?

It looks like something a six-year-old would proudly bring in for Show and Tell Thursday, which, in fairness, is exactly my aesthetic right now.

Besides, it reminded me of her.

There isn't much else to do outside the house today. Shops are shut, businesses at a standstill, the whole country paused. It almost feels like lockdown again, except I'm not panic-buying whole chickens this time.

On the TV the steady beat of drums play, boots marching in sync, the wail of bagpipes blast though the speakers. London is draped in black for the Queen's funeral.

The kids, of course, had already given their takes on her death last week.

"So who's the king now? Charles? That's just silly, he's named after my dog."

"If the Queen has died, who's in charge of the corgis? Can we have them as class pets?"

And the dreaded: "Miss Puddle, what happens when you die? Do you become a butterfly?"

I'm not a huge royalist, but I did feel like I'd lost a distant great grandma. The sort who always smelled of lavender and gave you triangular homemade shortbread.

Watching the funeral procession and seeing so many famous faces flashing across the screen, felt surreal.

And then there's me: twenty-seven years old, wrapped in a ghost blanket, sipping tea and torn between sadness and the realisation that my pupils think I'm middle-aged. Half teacher, half pensioner.

I wonder if I should start knitting … or just accept my fate, as a woman who finds joy in both sarcasm from seven-year-olds and seasonal soft furnishings from TK Maxx.

Just then my phone vibrates against the arm of the sofa. Cowgirl Shirt.

The nickname affectionately saved to my contacts next to a smiling emoji wearing a sheriffs' hat.

Cowgirl Shirt
online

Howdy 👑 How are you? Have you got the day off today, assuming schools are shut too??
11:46

Yes, thank goodness!
Celebrating the death of Betty on the sofa 😌 Under a blanket with a cup of tea.
11:48 ✓✓

What a set-up 😌 She would be proud!!!
11:51

Though, I think she'd personally prefer to be down the Three-Legged Cat with a cheeky vodka red bull! 🍸
11:52

OH 💯 How are you celebrating?? Mourning? You off work?
11:52 ✓✓

Yep, and how I needed it today. I feel like a I'm close to joining Queenie underground! 😌 👻
11:52

Tired then 😌 😌 What do you normally get up to when you are off work? Other than pretending to watch football games... do you read much? 11:53 ✓✓

Erm... The odd audiobook here and there 😌 If that counts? I'm guessing you do 😌 seems like a teachery thing to do 😳

11:54

Ngl, I do read romance novels like they're going out of fashion 😌😌 and of course I read my Fate each night. Although, I've lapsed recently. 😐

11:56 ✓✓

Oh, how come? As in you read ahead each night?

11:56

NO! 😌 I just read back what I have done that day.

11:57 ✓✓

Like a dairy, but written for me. Hahaha. Have you read through yours? Don't tell me you know when you'll die already!!!!

11:59 ✓✓

No no no 😌 honestly, I barely read mine. Flick through it when curiosity wins!! But I think that comes from my parents. They never made much of a deal about theirs. 😌😌

12:01

Ah...

12:01 ✓✓

I think it would pain you to see what I am using my book for right now...

12:02

12:02

We carry on messaging long after we should've stopped. The clunky "getting-to-know-you" questions (favourite colour, weirdest pizza topping, who would win in a fight: a hundred ducks on horseback or one horse-sized duck) shifted into something heavier. Childhood dreams, childhood traumas, all spilled out between emojis and perfectly timed GIFs.

I drift around the house as we talk. First curled up on the sofa, then perched on the kitchen counter, then stretched out in the bath, phone held above the bubbles. Finally, I collapse into bed, still typing, still laughing, still confessing things I hadn't told anyone in years.

The little clock at the top of my screen keeps ticking forward, smugly reminding me how bad of an idea this was. Midnight. Then one o'clock. Two o'clock. By three my eyes stung, and my thumbs were basically on autopilot. I knew I'd hate myself when my alarm went off in four measly hours.

But honestly? I didn't care.

Sleep is overrated when the conversation makes you forget what time it is.

I like talking to her more than I like sleeping. And given my love affair with naps, that was saying something.

And then it happened:

> Em, I just wondered if, and it's totally ok if not, but would you want to maybe go on a date some time? It's ok if you're not feeling it … it's just I really enjoy talking to you. 😄😊   03:56

I rewrote my reply seven times, each draft circling back to the same thing: a huge, undeniable yes.

If I'd bothered to check my Book of Fate that night, I'd have seen it spelled out clearly, no mystery at all:

*"You will message her all day, while the Queen's funeral plays on in the background. The conversation will stretch into the early hours, and end with - **The Love of Your Life** - finally asking you out on a date. You will say yes and agree on a date in October."*

And for once, Fate wasn't being cryptic. It was spot on.

Chapter 25

Taylor

Thursday 20th June 2018
Age 34
Cardiology Ward, Basingstoke and North Hampshire
Hospital, Basingstoke, UK

I've lost count of how long I've been here. It feels like forever. Not that that's a bad thing. I'm grateful for a comfortable bed and warm meals three times a day. Honestly, I feel like I'm living it up in the Hamptons compared to the anarchy outside.

The machine I'm hooked up to beeps again, the one that tells them I'm still alive and reminds me that I made it. I'm surviving.

My favourite nurse, Miracle, came round first thing, like clockwork: cuff on, thermometer in my ear, finger clipped. I don't fight it now, just hold my arm out obediently.

She always says good morning like she means it. Not the flat, automatic kind of greeting, Miracle's has a little sunshine in it.

Breakfast arrived and it's the usual toast with a little jar of strawberry jam. Toast is a luxury you really miss when your toaster gets thrown out on the street with you (same with a mattress!)

I ate it slowly, savouring every bite, because once I'm out, I know the toast and jam mornings will be gone again.

The doctors arrive in a little parade at the end of my bed, more of them than usual today. They introduce themselves one by one - even the student doctor who looks like they should just be leaving secondary school. The consultant, with grey hair and caring eyes, sat on the edge of the chair next to the bed, rather than looming over me. He asked how I'm feeling, not just my body, but my head too.

"We know this isn't easy," he says, and for once I believe it's not just a line.

They described things in plain English instead of medical code. They told me my heart is under strain, but it's holding up. They explained about the antibiotics pumping into me and reassured me that the infection is improving. They clarified what the methadone program could offer me and about options for when I leave.

The consultant queried if I'd got anyone on the outside that I could lean on. I shook my head and they didn't look away or hide from my answer.

The student doctor piped up, asking if I've managed to eat okay, and she smiled when I told her I'd polished off the toast and jam.

When they finished examining me, they didn't just walk away mid-sentence. They asked if I had any questions about my recovery. I don't, not really, but I said thanks anyway. The consultant patted my arm before he went. It's small, but it felt like something.

After they left, I stared at the ceiling again, but this time not because I was feeling ignored, but because I was letting what they said sink in. For once, I didn't feel like a case file. I felt like a patient. Maybe even like a person.

By mid-morning they needed to take bloods again.

The student doctor from earlier came back. I hadn't expected her to be the one to take my blood today; usually jobs like this get passed to nurses or phlebotomists. But she pulled up a chair and spoke to me like I mattered.

Even though I've had blood taken more times than I can count, she still went through every step, explaining it as though it were new.

She showed me the tourniquet, pulling it tight around my arm, and for a second, I wanted to laugh. That rubber strap has been as much a part of my life as a lighter or a spoon. Yet she held it up like it was something extraordinary, almost ceremonial, as if I didn't already know its bite.

She frowned a little, searching for a vein. My arms are a graveyard of collapsed vessels, old scars and puncture marks. "Just the small ones left," I muttered, almost apologetic. She didn't judge, didn't sigh in frustration the way others sometimes do, just nodded and kept looking, patient and careful. Finally, she found one that hadn't given up on me yet.

I felt the sharp yet familiar sting of the needle. She then clipped the vials on neatly, steady hands drawing the blood through the line. I watched the deep red travel down, filling each bottle in turn. She held them up against the light, checking them like they were precious. To her, maybe they were, little testaments of what's still working inside of me.

Between bottles she asked if I had anyone visiting today. When I told her most of the people that I used to call friends were nothing but bad news, she didn't press or judge, just nodded like she understood.

The whole thing took only minutes, but it felt longer, gentler somehow. She wasn't rough or rushed, didn't treat me like a difficult case. Just a person. When she was done, she taped a small ball of cotton-wool onto the fresh puncture site, as if without it I would have bled out.

She then asked if I was comfortable, like she genuinely cared about the answer.

Such a small thing, but it made me feel like more than a bed number. For once, the taking of blood didn't feel like another reminder of what I've done to myself, it felt like care.

Lunch came round quicker than I expected. A kind man wheeled the trolley in, balancing trays like it was second nature. His English wasn't perfect, but he smiled at everyone in a language which we all understood. To me he felt like some kind of food angel, quietly keeping our tummies full and our bodies going while our minds and hearts were failing us.

I'd ordered sausage and mash. The potato was a little lumpy, a touch dry, pressed into a neat round scoop. But I liked it.

It took me straight back to childhood, sitting around the table after school while Mum dished up dinner. She always asked, "One scoop or two?" in this sing-song voice, pretending she was the lady at the seaside ice-cream stall. My brother and I used to giggle every time, and then ultimately argue over who got the bigger portion.

For a moment, I could almost taste that memory more than the food on the tray in front of me.

If Mum and Dad knew I was here, they'd come in a heartbeat. They'd bring sandwiches from home, magazines, packets of crisps and maybe some grapes. They'd set up camp by my bed, only moving when visiting hours ended or the parking ticket ran too high. I could see them in my head so clearly. Mum smoothing down the blanket, Dad cracking terrible jokes just to fill the silence.

And that's what I ache for now. Not for the rush, not for the hit. For that simple comfort of family chatter, the kind I hear drifting from other beds when husbands, wives, and children come to visit.

We would talk about traffic, the latest news, shopping lists. Ordinary things that I used to roll my eyes at. I never thought I'd crave the mundane, but I did. My heart stung with it, sharp and heavy all at once.

Between watching the ward drift by and finishing another well-thumbed paperback, Miracle came back … this time bearing drugs. Just not the ones I had previously been after.

She reconnected the antibiotic IV line to the cannula in my arm with the same ease she does everything, like she's done it a thousand times before (she probably has).

As the drip started, she told me about the weather outside: clear skies, warm sun, the kind of day you don't believe exists when you're trapped in here. She laughed about her kids, how they're desperate for beach trips once the school holidays start. For a moment, it felt like she was pulling me out through the window with her words, letting me borrow her life just long enough to remember the world beyond these walls and my addiction.

Not long after, other medications came round. My methadone dose was finally sorted, and the bitterness on my tongue was almost a relief. It felt like a sign that my body might stop clawing at itself one day.

The ache in my arm from the cannula nagged at me, the plastic digging against skin that's already known too many punctures, but I didn't complain.

I watched the ward like a play. Nurses shuffling papers, porters rattling trays, doctors speaking in soft huddles. The book trolley creaked past, a treasure chest on wheels. Free books - dog-eared, stamped, swapped a hundred times over.

I had taken one yesterday, but as I turned the pages, I couldn't stop thinking about my own lost Book of Fate. I only read it once before it was taken, but the words clung to me in fragments. I wish I had it here. I wish I could flip ahead and see when this all ends. When my infection clears, when I'm meant to forgive my brother, when finally, I will see Mum and Dad again.

Other patients reminded me I'm not alone. One was shouting into her phone, voice rising and falling in waves. Another, sobbed into her blanket, muffled but loud enough to hear through the thin curtains. Yet, at that point in the day, I just wanted it to be me and the ceiling tiles. I'd counted them so many times I knew the patterns by heart. I wondered how many more nights I'd lie in this bed with those squares for company. I used them to distract me from the question of what happens to me on the day I walk out.

Will I go back to the chaos waiting for me, or is there still some other path hidden away, one I cannot yet see?

For now, I just hope the infection clears. That the antibiotics drip enough life back into me to survive another week.

My birthday is coming up, and part of me secretly hopes I'll still be here. Not because I love hospitals, but because at least here there are people to notice. To smile, to say "Happy Birthday". To make it feel, if only for a day, like I belong to the world again.

Chapter 26

Danny

Saturday 20th August 2022
Age 28
The Three-Legged Cat, Portsmouth, UK

"Consider your horse saved," a voice said.

I didn't even register it at first. Then, she slid onto the stool next to me, tipping some imaginary hat like she was the star of a budget-conscious Western film.

Ah, I got it. She was referencing the slogan on my t-shirt. Smooth. I liked it. Very suave.

Then I noticed her pink Western-themed t-shirt. At that moment, I had two competing thoughts: some people would call this fate (colliding in some kind of cowboy-themed Twilight Zone!) And the others: that's what you get for updating your wardrobe with Asda's latest couture drop.

Spectacular.

Then she laughed. Hard. I mean, the kind of laugh that makes the people around you turn and stare. Because, really, who decides mid-football match to roleplay a saloon scene in a pub?

To be so simultaneously terrifyingly bold and inexplicably charming really caught my interest.

She tried to sip her water (and failed astonishingly). Half of it ended up dribbling down her chin, which I was unsure whether was her plan, or if she was just auditioning for a wet t-shirt contest. Either way, I was watching with full attention.

I was hooked.

Then came the football question. She hedged her bets like the fate of the entire universe rested on her shoulders. "Moral support," she said.

Moral support.

I almost rolled my eyes. She clearly hadn't come for football. She'd come because someone had guilt-tripped her into it. Invited, coerced, blackmailed, who knows. Take your pick.

I was here with my brothers, both glued to the screen, screaming like they were trying to be heard in the stadium itself. I, however, had come on a flimsy pretense of 'time away from work'. Which really translated to 'practicing being a human with hobbies that don't involve needles or blood pressure cuffs'.

The truth? Football and I had a casual fling at best.

I can follow the rules, nod at the right moments, even fake outrage at a referee if pressed - but my heart? My heart belongs to rugby. Rugby is grit, glory, actual violence in shorts. Basically, NHS job security on a pitch.

Football? Football is... fine. Like dry toast.

It'll do the job, but don't ask me to get too excited about it.

Since she had arrived next to me this whole afternoon had become much more interesting.

We talked. I don't even remember about what exactly. Cowboys, cats on the walls, the horror of football hooligans (including my brothers!) She was infuriatingly endearing. Fidgeting, stuttering, spilling water, laughing too loud. Her nervous energy felt contagious.

I noticed the little details. Her hair was pulled into a messy bun with strands rebelliously escaping from the sides. The tiny sunflower earrings dangling from each of her ears looked like they had front-row tickets to watch my fascination for her grow.

Silver rings stacked on her fingers, each one different, (none of them practical) all tapping against her glass anxiously. And then I noticed the most important detail of all: no wedding ring. My inner narrator practically did a drumroll at that one. (Important observations, obviously.)

A glinting nose ring gave her that edge, the kind that said, "I own at least one leather jacket and I look better in it than you ever will."

She had that air of someone life had definitely tested, but who still strutted through the pub like the sticky carpet was red and velvet!

Her friend arrived between us, fluttering around like a hummingbird on espresso, and I felt a pang.

Would this mystery woman vanish now? Would she disappear back into the real world, leaving me with only this absurd encounter and a small puddle of water on the bar?

I tried to keep my composure, but let's be real - I was twenty-eight, a fully grown doctor (sort-of), and she had me completely unhinged with just a t-shirt, a messy bun, and a laugh.

And here's the kicker - I wasn't even sure if she liked women.

Me? I'd known since I was little.

The signs were all there. I was fascinated by certain actresses in a way that was definitely not about their acting skills. Constantly asking myself, "Do I want to be her, or do I want to be with her?" (Spoiler: usually both.) And let's not forget the teenage years, hiding under my duvet at two o'clock in the morning, with my portable DVD player, binging The L Word like it was some kind of sacred text.

I wasn't confused. Just quietly gay.

Now, here I was, years later, flustered, giddy, and wondering if I should start humming the L Word theme tune like some kind of secret gay mating call.

And then, she actually asked for *my* number. After the water spills, awkward laughs, and frantic overthinking, she wanted my number.

My number.

I raised an eyebrow, smirked, and thought: Finally.

Some excitement in this otherwise mind-numbingly beige Thursday night.

This otherwise mind-numbingly beige life.

Honestly, I didn't know what this was - romantic comedy? fever dream? mild concussion? I just knew it was fun. And for once, I didn't hate being dragged into someone else's definition of 'a good night out'. Purgatory with lager.

I made a new contact on my phone, because apparently that's what we do now instead of awkwardly scribbling numbers on napkins like in the films.

Eleven digits later, it hit me: I didn't even know her name.

A minor detail, but I was already half-planning our hypothetical wedding guest list, so really, it felt important.

I looked up, ready to ask, only to find her looking back at me with the same sheepish, deer-in-the-headlights expression.

Same brain space. Same 'who even are you?' look.

"Erm… what is your name again?" she asked, voice wobbling like she'd just been caught cheating on an exam.

"Danny," I said, trying to sound cooler than I felt. (Spoiler: I failed.) "And yours?"

"Em. Emily… Em." She stammered, tripping over her own name like it was the hardest word in the English language.

And that was it.

Danny and Em. Like some sort of tragic indie band, or a dodgy 2000s rom-com I definitely would have stayed up past midnight to watch (instead of studying for my university exams).

Chapter 27

Ben

Friday 25th June 2015
Age 37
Sainsbury's Supermarket, Alton, UK

Friday nights were always chaos.

Rose, of course, insisted that I lock-up the shop early and pick up the kids from school. "Family night," she said with that infuriatingly bright smile, the one that could make a grown man feel like a villain for daring to resist.

Family nights, as I had come to know them, were a kind of enforced torment. At thirteen and fifteen, Harry and Quinn were in that sweet spot where every behaviour was either mortifying or strategically aimed at pushing my patience off a cliff. And yet here we were, all of us trudging through Sainsbury's, a reluctant parade marching behind Rose's relentless cheer.

Harry was already pleading for pizza, arms flailing like a tiny conductor orchestrating the world's most tragic symphony.

Quinn was campaigning, equally loudly, for nuggets - preferably the turkey kind, shaped like dinosaurs, because why not add archaeology to the bedlam?

Rose was doing her diplomatic dance in the middle, trying to broker peace, prevent nuclear-grade tantrums, and somehow maintain the illusion of normalcy - all while making sure no one cast a judgmental glance our way.

I pushed the trolley along quietly, the floral scent of my day still clinging stubbornly to my shirt, letting the storm of demands, negotiations, and teenage melodrama wash over me.

There was a strange kind of calm in it, like floating in the eye of a hurricane. Everyone wanted something, everyone had an opinion, but none of it was really aimed at me. I just existed there, a silent observer in my own Friday night circus.

I caught Rose's eye and gave the smallest of smirks. It was worth it, I thought, just for her.

As we turned the aisle, nothing could have prepared me for who I saw.

It was her.

There she was.

By the fresh pasta section, crouching to read the labels, the same tilt of her head, the same dark hair tied back. The cacophony of my kids, their shouting combined with the clatter of the shop, faded into nothing. All I could see was her.

I slowed, pretending to examine the jars of sauce.

Rose was scolding Harry for tearing open a packet of breadsticks, Quinn bouncing impatiently on her toes. They didn't notice my gaze, didn't notice the way my chest tightened, like someone had just slammed the shop door on my lungs.

I told myself not to be stupid. Don't look, don't stare. But when she straightened up, half-turning her face toward me, my heart went rigid.

I'm sure it's her. It has to be her.

I wanted to walk over, to say something, anything - but not with the kids trailing behind, not with Rose's suspicious eyes probably already on me somewhere.

What excuse could I give? My wife already thinks I'm distant, distracted. To chase after another woman, through these polished aisles, would only confirm the fears I've tried so hard to hide.

"Next aisle Benny, we need aisle seven" Rose chimed, yanking my attention away.

I turned the corner towards the next aisle, trying to summon every ounce of peripheral vision just to catch one last glimpse of her before she vanished from my life again. And there she was, walking away, calm and unaware, like she belonged to some other world.

My thoughts spun uncontrollably between the vitamin tablets and shower gels of aisle seven. I willed myself to focus on my family. My wife.

I looked at Rose.

Her beautiful smile. Her bewildering eyes. Her hands.

Holding … what?

A box?

A pregnancy test. What!

"I think I'm a little too young to be menopausal, Benny," she said, her voice light and teasing. "But this would explain a few things!"

A baby.

We had wanted a third for years, but fate never seemed to be on our side. We'd assumed it wasn't meant to be. How I wished, in that instant, that I had my Book in hand, ready to tell me the right words, the right way to respond.

"Well … that would change things," I managed.

Chapter 28

Frederick

Thursday 3rd January 2020
Age 62
Braemar Dog Park, Portsmouth, UK

At six o'clock this morning I woke like clockwork, with the usual stiffness in my legs. Joints clicking like old rifle bolts. Nothing new. Years of Army life drilled routine into me, and my body still struggles to understand there is no call for such early mornings now.

Kettle on, tea strong, and Gunner's breakfast sorted first. Always his before mine. He sat there watching me with those shining eyes of his, tail thumping against the cupboard. He overflowed with not only intelligence but more energy than a fresh recruit on his first day of training. His coat thick and shiny, black with a splash of white across his chest, and paws like he's dipped them in milk. The kind of dog that makes you feel like you're the one being taken for a walk.

After breakfast, Gunner wouldn't stop pawing at me, until I finally gave in. I tugged on my worn coat and scuffed boots, and we made our way to Braemar Dog Park.

The air was damp, the sort that bites the back of your throat. Portsmouth always carries a trace of salt in the air, even when you're nowhere near the sea.

The ground crunched underfoot with frost, every blade of grass stiff and silver.

We were halfway across the field when it happened. I threw the ball - the green one with the teeth marks chewed into it - his favourite and mine.

Out of nowhere, a little Cavalier King Charles Spaniel, tricolour in his markings and legs half the length of Gunner's, came darting across. Both made for the ball. Gunner reached it first, of course, but he stopped short when the Cavalier skidded up beside him, as if he wasn't quite sure of the rules anymore.

That's when I saw her, the lady I had been waiting a lifetime to meet. The dog's owner. A lady, maybe a little younger than me, though not by much. Her woolen hat was pulled low and her cheeks were flush against the cold. She laughed when Ernie (the Cavalier) tried to wrestle the ball out of Gunner's mouth. The boldness of such a small dog.

We got talking. The way you do when you can't avoid it. About the dogs at first, Ernie's age, Gunner's tricks and about the park itself. And then talking led to walking.

Initially she drifted ahead of me, leaving me feeling like a bit of a shadow. Old habits die hard. I was trained to follow, not push forward. But then she eased her stride to match mine, letting the conversation stretch on until names were exchanged (though I already knew hers from my Book of Fate). A small detail, yet somehow significant.

Barbara. It's not a name you hear often anymore, but it suited her, completely gentle and full of warmth.

We spoke about how the trees looked skeletal this time of year, their leaves long composted into the soil.

Barbara noticed the ducks gathering by the pond, wings tucked in, noisy as a platoon on payday. We chuckled at how they didn't seem to care about the cold.

I pointed out a robin, a bold little fellow hopping along a branch. Barbara smiled and said, "You know what they say - when a robin appears, a loved one is near." It was something my mother used to tell me too, and though I never admitted it aloud, I'd always been secretly fond of the thought.

We walked the paths together. Gunner kept circling, checking on me every so often, ears twitching like he was making sure I was all right. In complete contrast Ernie trotted happily between us, curly ears bouncing, clearly confident in his place.

She told me she used to bring Ernie here most mornings before work, and now she was retired she kept the habit as a way of holding onto routine. I nodded at that. Routine has kept me alive more than once.

I told her Gunner was a rescue, came to me almost two years ago to the day. A fine lad. She smiled a proper smile, not the polite kind you flash to a stranger you'll never see again.

We talked about the Christmas just past. She said it was quiet, just her and her sister with a small roast. I told her mine was much the same, only with Gunner for company and the usual Christmas repeats on the telly.

Conversation moved onto New Year's Eve. She didn't much like fireworks, worried about Ernie trembling under the table. Luckily a few pops and bangs never seemed to faze Gunner.

I told her about my recent birthday celebrations spent with David, conversation quickly moving to fond memories of my Army days.

Ordinary things, but the kind that feel heavier when you've not spoken to someone properly in a while. It felt nice. It felt good.

Time past quickly. Faster than it should have. I don't usually notice, not these days. Most mornings stretch long and empty. But with her, the minutes seemed to disappear. One minute we were tossing the ball again, laughing at Ernie's stubborn little growl, and the next she was glancing at her watch, saying she ought to be getting back.

This caused an unaccustomed feeling. An unfamiliar twist in the gut. Something I wasn't ready for.

I realised I didn't want her to go.

Silly thing, really. I'm sixty-two. I'd only been in love once and my Fate had told me it would never happen again and therefore it never mattered. The Army didn't leave much room for that anyway. I had casual flings, women who liked the uniform for a while, but nothing of importance. Standing there in the cold, watching her call Ernie to heel, clipping his lead back on, my heart wanted the morning to stretch a little longer.

Of course, I know the end of this story and I knew my Fate. People don't just stumble into your life at my age, not in any lasting way.

I guess it will take more than Fate for this to develop any further past strangers. She's got her world and I've got mine, and worlds like that don't tend to join up neatly. I knew I would catch a glimpse of Barbara in the park again, just when I couldn't remember without cross referencing with my Book.

Still. For an hour, I wasn't just 'one man and his dog'. For an hour, it felt like I was part of something again, bigger than just my Fate.

Chapter 29

Emily

Friday 21st October 2022
Age 27
Emily's House, Portsmouth, UK

The house had been turned upside down and then righted again. Every cranny had been scrubbed; every surface wiped until it gleamed like an Ofsted inspection was due any minute. Even my bookshelves, normally a colour-coordinated shrine to organised chaos, had been tamed as if I was auditioning for one of those BookTok accounts I mock, but also religiously stalk.

I told myself I was assuming nothing. Well... not nothing. Enough to know that the zebra-print bedding I'd chosen when I was fifteen wasn't exactly the kind of impression that whispered 'sophisticated adult woman you might want to kiss.' It screamed more 'woman who peaked during her GCSEs and has been sleeping in the relic ever since.'

So, I swapped it out for my brand-new Asda set, patterned with pumpkins and bats. Hardly seductive either, but at least it said 'seasonal fun' instead of 'teenage zoo exhibit.' I figured, worst case scenario, Danny would be so spooked she might faint straight onto the bed and, voilà, date success.

Danny and I had arranged to meet at mine. After dragging myself through the first half of Autumn Term and her slog of long days doing outreach, neither of us could face another date drowned out by pub chatter or the fake enthusiasm of a restaurant.

Being somewhere familiar, somewhere we could literally kick off our shoes and relax, felt perfect for our first proper date.

Unlike every other one of my recent first dates, exclusively sourced from the mysterious lands of dating apps, I didn't have to worry that she might turn out to be a forty-five-year-old man who lived in his mum's basement. I'd already met Danny through actual real life, which these days felt almost exotic.

We'd said eleven, but in true queer fashion neither of us were ready on time. By half eleven, we both admitted defeat and bumped it to one. Perfect for me, since at eleven-thirty I was still trying to rinse conditioner out of my hair, looking blotchy and damp. I hadn't even started on makeup yet, and there were at least three more doomed outfit changes in my near future.

Eventually, I settled on a flowy black skirt and my trusty Halloween t-shirt adorned with a ghost wearing a floral sheet. It was giving 'millennial witch chic'. Seasonal, playful, a bit cheesy and authentically me really.

I even curled my hair, which felt a bit extravagant for a Friday night in. My makeup went on, not too heavy, just a swipe of my signature glitter eyeshadow. Because honestly, glitter is the one thing my Year 2's and I see eye-to-eye on.

For a finishing touch, I hooked on my earrings shaped like tiny cowboy hats (for obvious reasons).

By the time the doorbell rang, my stomach was an absolute jumble of nerves and butterflies, but beneath it all was a fizzing excitement I hadn't felt in years.

For once, I wasn't dreading a first date. For once, it actually felt like it might be fun.

There she was: Danny. My date. My doctor. Well, not my doctor, thank God, that would've been weird, but a doctor. Which, somehow, made her look even more competent and put-together in comparison to the glittery chaos standing opposite her.

She was wearing a dark maroon open shirt, layered over a white t-shirt, clean jeans and trainers that had clearly seen more action than my gym membership. Her hair was in an artful state of messy: halfway between I've been running around all day saving lives and I just rolled out of bed like this.

She looked casual. Effortlessly cool. Exactly the opposite of me, standing there like a millennial witch who had taken three outfit changes and a nervous breakdown to achieve this level of casual.

"Hi," she said, smiling in a way that hit me square in the chest. Calm and steady, unlike my heart rate.

"Hey," I squeaked, and immediately wanted to be buried alive under my pumpkin duvet.

She stepped inside, taking her shoes off at the door (a good sign, I told myself - respectful, domestic, possible long-term girlfriend material). I tried to look unflustered, which for me translated to wildly over-explaining.

"Sorry it's just my house is so tidy because I went on this cleaning frenzy, don't worry, I don't normally live like Kim Woodburn's overachieving cousin. The bedding, it's new, because I thought the old one was too … stripy."

She laughed, thank God.

"I didn't realise I was here on some kind of health and safety inspection," she sniggered.

"You're a doctor," I blurted. "Being inspected by you just feels inevitable."

"Well, I could give you a full report here in the doorway, but I think I'd rather give a summary over dinner." She said with a flirty smirk.

I gave her an awkward tour of the house, pointing out the downstairs and upstairs toilets, the spare room, and oddly, the empty bedside cabinet next to the side of the bed that wasn't mine. Why I even felt the need to show her that, I had no idea. Did I think it screamed caring host? Maybe. Did it just scream overly anxious teacher who lives alone and dissects everything? Definitely.

Danny didn't make me feel ridiculous for my rambling tour. She just smiled, nodded, and commented on how nice everything looked and how rainbow-y my shelves were.

Her eyes drifted over the spines until one caught her attention: my time-travel romance about a woman who falls for an alien on the London Underground. Entirely realistic, of course.

When she finished the blurb, her expression tightened with quiet concern.

"I mean, really," I said, "who hasn't accidentally kissed a space creature somewhere between Piccadilly and King's Cross?"

We both burst out laughing, the kind of laugh that makes your stomach twist into tiny, happy knots.

We collapsed onto the sofa, her naturally settling on the opposite side to the one I usually sank into. Cushions formed a polite buffer between us at first. But, as we talked, like we did every day on the phone (just without the constant eye strain), I noticed the cushions slowly migrating to the edges, making room as we inched closer together. My heart thumped, erratic and out of control.

She said something, I honestly can't remember what, but the next thing I knew, she leaned in and kissed me. Just like that. No warning, no preamble.

My brain short-circuited somewhere between "is this actually happening" and "do I remember how to breathe?"

All at once, every ridiculous quote in my romance novels suddenly made sense: sparks flying, planets aligning. Somehow, in my little living room, a time-traveling alien on the London Underground seemed like a completely reasonable plot twist.

Eventually, I pulled back, eyes struggling to refocus.

Danny grinned, that knowing, mischievous grin that made me forget my own name.

"Erm … dinner," I stuttered, my voice far higher than intended. "What's for dinner? Your favourite? Should I … cook something? Or order? Or - "

Danny raised an eyebrow. "You're asking me that now?"

"Yes!" I admitted, flailing slightly. "Because now that we're kissing, we clearly need a sustenance plan. Priorities, you know?"

She laughed, warm and low, like a blanket you want to wrap around yourself. "Fine," she said, tilting her head.

After a lot of indecision, and a brief, highly serious debate about what the alien and time-traveller would have picked, we settled on a Chinese takeaway. Both discovering in the process that we had the exact same favourite shop.

I placed the order, my hands shaking slightly as I entered the number, looking at the menu on the fridge as if it wasn't saved in my phone's favourites.

Soon enough, we were tucking into sweet and sour chicken balls and crispy seaweed, chopsticks poised like tiny weapons, sauce-covered plates balancing precariously on our knees.

Between bites, we traded stories: disastrous school moments, outreach horror stories, the ridiculous things kids say that make you question your life choices.

Somehow, having a lap meal in my living room felt far more intimate than any candlelit restaurant I'd ever endured.

After the last spring roll was shared and the sun had now completely set, I gathered every shred of courage I could find. "So … um … do you want to stay the night?"

Danny looked at me, slow grin spreading across her face. "Yeah," she said. Then, ever practical, she added, "But do I need to move my car? I left it on the road outside, in front of your neighbour's house."

I waved a dismissive hand, trying to act cool, but probably looking like I was mid undiagnosed tremor. "He won't mind," I said confidently. "Honestly, it's just a charming old man living next door. Besides, he's far too kind to mind. He'd probably offer to wash it for you if he noticed."

Danny gave a small nod of acknowledgment to my reply, satisfied that her car would be safe. After a pause that felt just a little too long, she smiled and, thankfully, confirmed that she would like to stay the night.

She leaned in closer. "It feels like fate, that we met in that pub Em." She smiled wistfully.

All I could manage was a dry chuckle and, "I wouldn't know, I haven't read mine since!"

Chapter 30

Ben

Wednesday 13th February 2016
Age 38
Green and Grow Florist, Alton, UK

The bell above the shop door hadn't stopped ringing all day, a constant chime that was beginning to sound more like an alarm than a welcome. Customers streamed in one after another, cheeks pink from the February chill. It was the day before Valentine's and thus the busiest day of our year. The floor around me was littered with thorns, petals, scraps of ribbon, and cellophane slivers. The air smelled thick of roses - red, pink, even the odd peach or white one, though red was always most popular for this time of year.

We sold roses by the dozen, mostly, though some customers came in asking for one single, perfect bloom, as though it carried more romance that way. Others demanded great, extravagant bouquets; arms' worth of velvety crimson heads with gypsophila clouding around them like mist.

A woman came in with two orders, one bouquet of red roses for her husband and another for her dad, who she said had been on his own since her mum passed. For him, she chose a mix of bright chrysanthemums, something cheerful and full of life. "He'll never expect flowers on Valentine's," she said with a grin, "but it'll

make his day." I wrapped each bouquet in different paper, one bold and romantic, the other warm and earnest, and she left the shop looking lighter herself, as though the giving was half the gift.

Another customer, a young boy, no older than Harry, bought tulips, saying his boyfriend "wasn't really a rose person." I tied the stems together with a satin ribbon and smiled, because secretly, tulips are my favourite choice for Valentine's Day too.

Every year I send tulips to Rose, with a note that says in one way or another: I already have my Rose, the only one I'll ever need close.

It would have been easier to manage all these orders if Rose were still behind the counter with me, fielding the endless questions and demands. She always had a knack for charming even the most impossible customers, her hands as quick at arranging as her tongue was at softening a complaint.

But now, with her pregnancy so far along, I was afraid to even ask her to fetch a spool of ribbon, let alone help tie a bow.

She sat in the little chair behind the desk for an hour or two in the mornings, just to keep me company, but I could see the effort in her face, the way she rested one hand on her belly as if steadying the life inside. Who was I to complain about sore feet and a cramped back, when she was carrying an entire future, an entire fate?

Still, I was desperate to know, was it a son or a daughter? What kind of little person was already making themselves known in kicks and turns beneath her skin? The naming had become a game between us in the evenings, running through lists, vetoing each other's suggestions, laughing over old-fashioned relics and impossible spellings.

More than once, I caught myself drifting towards the wardrobe to where my Book of Fate was tucked away. Just one peek, one page turned a month ahead, and I

could know. The temptation burned in me, but so did the memory of the last pregnancies. Of the joy when our two older children were born, and the wonder of discovering them in their own time. Maybe it was better, I told myself, to wait.

I thought about how much had changed over the years. When Harry was born, we had barely finished celebrating our first wedding anniversary, still fumbling our way through the grown-up responsibilities of running the shop and keeping the flat in order. Since then, fashions in flowers and ribbons had shifted, and the styles of wrapping had come and gone, but Valentine's always brought the same whirlwind of chaos – and parenthood, no matter how many times we stepped into it, always carried the same thrill of wonder.

I thought about Rose and our little family as I packed up the endless stream of online orders, each bouquet another reminder of how far we'd come. I thought about every Valentine's Day that I'd ever sent flowers to Rose. I thought about the Valentine's still to come, the day when I'd help our children pick out bunches and cards for their significant others.

One by one I worked through the orders, wrapping, trimming, tying, until I saw it.

Her name.

Not just her name, but her address too, typed clean and clear on the order form.

For a moment I just stared, heart hammering faster than the poor shop bell had all day. I'd sworn I'd stopped looking for her after that chance sighting in Sainsbury's, and then ultimately the discovery of my third child. That should have been enough to close the book, to shove all those memories back into the dusty cupboard of my mind.

Yes, she had crept into my thoughts now and again over the years, but I'd learnt to shake her off, the way you swat away a persistent fly: irritating, distracting, but not worth your energy.

Except now she was here, staring up at me in twelve-point font, daring me not to notice.

Of course, it wasn't the rarest name in the world. There could be another one of her, couldn't there?

Could be. Probably was. Hopefully was.

… But what were the odds?

Maybe whoever ordered these flowers for her had no idea of her connection to this shop. To me. Surely, they wouldn't have picked here of all places. Unless Fate was having one of its little laughs again.

The address was local, close enough that I could deliver them myself. The thought started burning in my chest as I began wondering if anything would flicker in her eyes if she saw me.

As I packed each stem into the bouquet, bright and vibrant, I found myself replaying the old reel of our last few months together. The things I did, the things I didn't, the words I said too sharply, and the ones I never said at all.

By the time I tucked the final rose in, I was practically conducting a tragic opera in my head, every thorn a reminder of some misstep.

And then came the gift tag.

Three little words printed in neat script, carrying more weight than the ribbon and card alone could hold, the unspoken truth sealed beneath the words:

Sent with love
xxx

Chapter 31

Danny

Saturday 22nd October 2022
Age 28
Emily's House, Portsmouth, UK

I woke to the rain tap-dancing against the window, the kind of British drizzle which gets cast as a 'pathetic fallacy' in school English essays, but in real life just ruins your fringe.

I turned over and realised I wasn't wrapped up in my usual, slightly-questionably-clean sheets. No. This was different. This was a whole pumpkin patch of fresh cotton, crisp and new.

And then it hit me. Oh shit. I'm in Em's bed.

My brain, ever the diligent observer, began its morning round of checks: rapid heartbeat? Tick. Sweating palms? Tick. Stupid grin plastered across my face? Tick. Sense of humour intact? Debatable.

She was beside me, half-buried under the covers, hair pointing north, south, east, west and into a whole other alternate dimension. Honestly, she looked like a science experiment gone slightly wrong. Utterly impressive!

My instincts abruptly kicked in. First instinct: poke her. Second instinct: don't poke her. But my third instinct, the one that always wins, whispered: This is your life now. Go for it. So, I poked her.

"Hey," I said, my voice still gravelly from sleep and slightly channeling a hungover jazz singer.

She groaned, a sound somewhere between a sneeze, a yawn, and possibly a marriage proposal. "Mmmfff …"

"Yep," I nodded solemnly, "I agree completely."

Her eyes opened just enough to see me grinning like a lunatic, and she broke into a smile so wide I almost dissolved into the mattress. "You're insane," she croaked.

"Would you like a professional opinion on that?" I shot back, "Your diagnosis is correct and unfortunately it is highly contagious."

I flung my arms out dramatically, staring at the ceiling like I was starring in a Sunday afternoon period drama. Inside, though, I was giddy. I got to wake up next to her. Is this real life? Should I ask a colleague to check me for delirium?

Should I consider checking her for delirium?

"So," I announced, in my very best serious-doctor voice, "we survived the night. Any lingering side effects? Sweating? Palpitations? Overwhelming urge to get a pet together?"

She squinted at me as if I was a particularly odd patient who'd just confessed to eating crayons. "You are ridiculous."

And yet, she laughed. A laugh that fizzed straight through me, lighting me up brighter than the bedside lamp I may or may not have broken last night (long story, that's not so romantic).

She rolled onto her side, tucking her body against mine, our legs entwined together and suddenly the whole room felt warmer.

Honestly, she radiated more heat than an NHS waiting room in July, and within seconds I was both swooning and calculating the odds of survival without hydration. Still, I didn't move. If this was how I was going to die, suffocated in her pumpkin duvet, cooked medium-rare by her body temperature, I figured it was a respectable death. Maybe even a little romantic.

We started talking about yesterday. How easy it had been. How it felt like we'd skipped the awkward early chapters and leapt straight into the comfortable middle. It was so absurdly right that even I, Dr Skeptical, didn't question it.

Eventually, she stretched and slipped out of bed. "Tea," she announced. "And biscuits. We need a proper debrief. NHS standard protocol, right?"

I watched her go, trying not to look too dreamy, and failing completely.

From downstairs came the sounds of her kettle rattling, spoons clinking, cupboards opening and closing with unnecessary drama. And I thought: I want this. Again and again. Every Saturday morning until we're old and grey (as well as arguing about digestive biscuits versus hobnobs).

For the first time in years, I hadn't checked my work chat or emails. So, no endless passive-aggressive messages about patient follow-ups. No one asking if ibuprofen could cure their existential dread. And honestly? I didn't care. Let the NHS crumble without me for a morning. I was far too busy feeling deliriously happy and stealing someone else's duvet.

She came back up with two steaming mugs, hair wrangled into the same messy bun as when we had first met in the Three-Legged Cat. She was drowning in a Scooby-Doo t-shirt at least two sizes too big, and somehow, she'd never looked better.

'Keep calm and pretend it's half-term', the mug that she set down on my bedside table read. (Yes, I had already claimed it as mine!)

She placed her mug down on her own side, amidst the chaos: glasses, tangled jewellery, a few random crystals and her Book of Fate. Serving proudly as a coaster, just as mine often had. I stared at it, tempted. What if we peeked ahead, flipped to the page that told us where this was all going? Would it say forever? Or would this just be a passing phase?

But then I looked at her flushed cheeks, giggling at her own half-baked jokes, and I knew. I didn't need a book to tell me.

The future was already sitting here, in bed, dunking biscuits into tea, hair a disaster, and somehow making me feel happier than I'd ever been.

Chapter 32

Frederick

Thursday 17th January 2020
Age 62
Frederick's Home, Portsmouth, UK

Gunner and I had made it our ritual, every Thursday, same time, same path. Trudging through the park with the quiet hope of spotting Barbara. I wasn't sure why I kept coming here. My Fate had never promised a love story, and yet, I wanted to explore this new character. I sought the comfort of her presence, the feeling of time bending when she was near, the conversations that felt like stepping into another life entirely.

Most Thursdays were shadowed in disappointment. She wasn't there. We walked anyway, for the sake of routine, but the spark was dimmer - both in Gunner's tail wag and in my own stride.

But this Thursday felt different. The air carried a faint promise, a hint of warmth that made me straighten my shoulders and feel that familiar pull in my chest. And there she was.

I spotted Ernie first, darting across the field, ears flapping in the wind, short legs moving like pistons. His joy was obvious and contagious. And then I saw her.

Barbara, moving behind him with effortless grace, the lead clipped around her waist and a ball thrower in her hand.

I tried to keep my composure. After sixty-two years, and many of those spent in the Army, I knew how to mask excitement. But as soon as our eyes met, all pretence fell away. My boots carried me across the field faster than my mind could catch up.

"Barbara," I said, voice low but carrying, trying to sound as steady as a sergeant giving orders.

She looked up, with the smile I had previously noticed, quiet and warm. "Well, look who it is. My Thursday Soldier," she teased, and for a fleeting second, I felt caught off guard from the happiness.

Gunner bounded ahead, tail wagging, and Ernie chased him, little legs kicking up tufts of grass. Two dogs, two worlds of energy, and somewhere in the middle, a retired army vet trying not to trip over his own laboured breath.

I drew in the scent of wet grass and the sharp, bracing edge of autumn, and found my voice catching. "I ... I wasn't sure you'd be here today," I stammered,

then added, almost sheepishly, "I've been keeping an eye out for you ever since we last met."

"My daughter has been visiting over the last few weeks, wouldn't let me out of her sight. Said I was 'too sprightly' to be left alone." Barbara rolled her eyes with mock exasperation, though I caught the flicker of pride beneath it.

We started walking together, as natural as if we'd arranged it. The gravel crunched under foot. She asked me how I'd been keeping, and this time I gave her the truth. The truth was, retirement had recently felt too quiet, even with Gunner as company. Too much clock-watching, too much listening to the silence in a mind that once held marching orders.

"I just ... I'm sorry. I feel like I'm being terrible company," I apologised.

"You know," she said, tapping the ball thrower against her hip, "you are better company than you think."

"Better than Ernie?" I asked, light-heartedly.

She gave me a look that could outmanoeuvre any formation I'd drilled into over the years. "Almost."

We both laughed, and for a moment I let myself imagine what it might be like if Fate was wrong. If maybe, just maybe, it had left a page blank for us to write ourselves.

We walked and talked until our legs ached and the dogs began to lag behind, tongues lolling and tails drooping.

"We must do this again," she said, her voice soft but insistent, and I nodded, feeling a surge of warmth that had nothing to do with the autumn sun.

Leaving the park, I carried a quiet excitement in my chest, the kind that soldiers feel before a long march - not fear, but anticipation.

On the bus home, my thoughts kept drifting back to Barbara. For the first time, I found myself wrestling with a strange tension between the Fate I knew and the Fate I secretly wished for. Could I have misread it? Missed some crucial detail? Perhaps a few pages had stuck together, or ink had faded.

I burst through my front door. I leave my coat and Gunner's lead draped carelessly over the back of the kitchen chair; an uncharacteristic display of disorder that felt almost rebellious.

I scan the shelves for my Book of Fate, my fingers trace down its worn spine. It had been some time since I last consulted it, and yet I am approaching it now with the careful attention of a soldier inspecting orders before a mission.

I opened it to the year, the month, and flicked through January.

There is a brief mention of a new friend called Barbara. But there is no hint of love.

Only a warning of something much scarier than love ... a looming worldwide pandemic.

A strange phenomenon related to an unknown virus.

I swallow hard and let the words settle over me. I feel almost lucky that I had checked and reminded myself of what was to come.

It was time to hunker down, to shield myself and stay safe. I would survive, of course, but it would be hard.

No bus journeys. No park walks. No Barbara ... well not until closer to my final page.

I tell myself not to overthink it, not to fall into sadness. Now, the mission was different: it was about safety, discipline and endurance.

I exhale and, with the same calm precision I once used to plan operations, address the small but pressing necessities of civilian life.

"Alexa, add toilet roll to the shopping list."

Chapter 33

Taylor

Thursday 3rd January 2019
Age 34
Horizon Health Rehabilitation Centre, Guildford, UK

Today had felt different. I didn't wake up tremoring with the familiar clawing shakes in my stomach. Instead, I had woken up with that strange, heavy mixture of anticipation and fear. I knew that today I would walk into rehab.

I had left the hospital around four months ago. They had offered me so much help and guidance, things I hadn't even known I needed.

There had been relief when they told me I was fit for discharge, but it had been tangled with dread. Dread that I was returning to the cold, indifferent world outside.

For now, I had finally been granted a space in temporary accommodation. Four thin walls, a bed that wasn't mine and a key that felt more borrowed than owned. It was shelter, yes, but it never quite silenced the fear of how fragile it all was, how easily it could be taken away. And with it came the anxiety that, again, I would fade into the background, suddenly invisible, my eyes avoiding contact, my voice barely above a whisper.

But here I was, taking a step towards change, change that I hoped would be for good.

165

The rehab building looked less like a clinic and more like an old school. Brick walls, heavy wooden doors and the faint smell of disinfectant lingering in the air.

My bag felt almost too light as I carried it, almost like I hadn't brought myself with me at all. And maybe that was true. There wasn't much left.

Inside, I kept the few fragments of myself I could carry. There were a few photos of my family, a tether to a time when I had been loved and safe. I packed my only spare pair of socks and a fleece jumper, for this winter had been bitter. I had also tucked in a ragged paperback that I had taken from the hospital. It was a thriller novel with a note scrawled inside the cover: "Never surrender, refuse to yield, keep fighting and always stand firm." I knew I shouldn't have taken it, but that note had felt like it had been written for me alone. Somehow, in that random, small act of kindness, I had found the courage to arrive at this doorway.

Lastly, I had dropped in my lucky spoon and lighter, in the hope that these would be taken and therefore I could not use them.

Upon arriving at reception, they asked me to sit in a waiting area first.

A woman behind the desk spoke softly, explaining the forms. She asked for my name, date of birth, and when I had last used. I had mumbled my answers, cheeks burning with embarrassment, whilst my hands trembled over the clipboard.

Another staff member had come over to me a short while later, a man named John. He didn't judge, didn't flinch at my quivering hands. He just ticked boxes, asked if I had any medical problems, allergies or prior rehab experiences. I nodded, shook my head, and said the right things in the right places, feeling fragile under the weight of it all.

They had taken my bag and rifled through it in front of me. No needles, no bottles, no sharp things, no secrets - just the clothing, the photos, the novel, my spoon and my lighter. They handed the book back, the photos tucked safely inside, and locked everything else away. I wondered if they would give all of it back.

Next came the physical check. Blood pressure, pulse, height and weight. They noted the track marks on my arms, the bruises fading into my skin.

The nurse asked when I had last eaten properly. I laughed, though it cracked in my throat. The last time I had eaten three square meals a day had been in the hospital. I have since longed for toast with jam or even a dry scoop of mashed potato.

After the check, it was time for a talk.

A counsellor walks with me to a quiet room and asks me to explain why I am here. My throat goes dry.

I want to say, "Because I'm tired of being cold and hungry. Because I'm tired of chasing something that never fills the hole. Because I am finally ready to forgive." But all I can manage is, "I can't do this anymore."

She had nods as if she has heard it a hundred times before, yet somehow, she still makes me feel like she believed me.

"Do you have anyone we can contact for you? Someone we could add to the visitor list?" she asks.

"Just my brother," I murmur.

"Perfect. Great stuff. We'll just need his name and address."

"Address is Green and Grow, Alton," I recall, my fingers brush the photos sticking out of the novel for courage.

"And name?" She presses.

I remember the warmth he has always offered, even when I have been too lost to feel it, and the long, winding path to forgiveness I was still learning to walk.

"Benjamin Green."

Chapter 34

Ben

Thursday 12th November 2018
Age 40
Green and Grow Florist, Alton, UK

The shop had been quieter than I expected for this close to December, though the online orders were still coming in steadily. The counter was crowded with orders for Christmas bouquets, wreaths, and sprigs of holly and mistletoe. I busied myself with the flowers, trimming the stems, refreshing the buckets, doing anything to keep my hands moving, anything to stop my thoughts from circling back.

But of course, today of all days, there was no escaping them.

It had been years, but the anniversary of my parents' death still haunted me. I remembered the crunch, the flashing blue lights, the silence that followed. Mum and Dad gone in an instant, leaving me with a void that I'd never been able to fill. I had to go back to the flat and comfort her, my little sister, be the brave older brother, answer the questions I didn't know the answers to.

Every year I stood here, arranging blooms, wishing they could see me now. Wishing they could see how the business had flourished, how their legacy lived on in the shop's walls.

The bell over the door jingled just after six, just as the shop was about to close.

I looked up, half-expecting the usual: some agitated husband buying roses on the way home, as if it were a chore.

But it wasn't.

A woman stepped inside, wrapped in a heavy coat, hesitant as though the warmth of the shop might burn her if she stepped too far in.

Her eyes moved slowly over the buckets, scanning stems and petals with a strange mix of caution and certainty, until finally she approached the counter.

Her fingers fumbled with the coins she laid down, pale and trembling against the wood. Her voice, when it came, was soft and almost apologetic.

"Could I have one pink rose, please? And one purple iris."

For a moment, the world tilted.

My breath stuck in my throat.

Pink roses - Mum's favourite. Purple irises - Dad's. Nobody knew that.

Nobody but us.

I stared at her, unable to move.

The eyes. The mouth. Older, yes, tired and weathered by years I couldn't even begin to imagine, but familiar in a way that made my stomach lurch. She looked at me with polite impatience.

But I knew. God help me, I knew.

All those late nights spent dreaming I would see her again, searching for her online, the possible sightings, the hints of her exitance – none of them could have prepared me for this.

She smiled faintly at me and it was like watching a ghost draw breath again.

"Taylor," I whispered, my voice raw.

Her head lifted. "Ben," she said. Just my name. Soft. Fragile. Like it had been caught in her mouth all these years.

The flowers slipped from my hands, scattering across the counter. I vaulted over it, and before I even knew what I was doing, I pulled her into my arms.

We clung to each other, desperate, shaking. Her body felt so small, so breakable, bones sharp beneath the bulk of her coat. I could have crushed her if I wasn't careful.

I pulled back only enough to see her face. The lines etched into her skin; the wear of years hard-lived mixed with the stubborn glint of the sister I remembered.

Tears blurred my vision, and I saw hers spilling too. Words tumbled between us, jumbled, rushed.

Decades of silence was broken in minutes, desperate to bridge the years we had lost.

She told me about her addictions, her years of running from place to place, running from herself. Nights she didn't think she would wake from. Mornings she wished she hadn't.

Crashing on sofas, wandering towns, losing and finding and losing again. She told me about the hospital stay, the slow, painful climb back to something that felt almost human, and now, the fragile safety of the temporary accommodation she'd been given.

Her voice cracked when she asked about Rose. About my wife.

"She's... she's still just as perfect as the day I married her," I managed, my throat tight. "She's been my rock. Kept the shop alive when I couldn't. Kept me alive, truth be told."

Taylor's eyes softened, as tears shone on her cheeks. "And did you have kids?" she asked, her voice trembling with both hope and fear, as though she wasn't sure she deserved to hear the answer.

"We have three children", I said proudly.

"Three!" she chimed.

"Harry's the eldest, eighteen now. He's right in the middle of deciding on universities, weighing up history courses. He's got that same spark of curiosity Dad had, always asking questions, always wanting to know what came before and why."

"Eighteen! and …"

"Quinn! She's … er sixteen! And she is our firecracker. Full of life, just like Rose. She's studying art at college, and she's got such a gift, Tay. I think she's going to make something remarkable of herself," I said, marvelling at her potential.

"An artist, she didn't get that from you!"

"Well … no," I sniggered. "And then there's Sky. Just two years old, our whirlwind, our little surprise. You can't pin her down for more than a minute. What gets me most is how her brother and sister adore her. They protect her, play with her, fold her into everything they do. It's like she was always meant to be here. They're my world, Tay … they're everything. Everything."

She closed her eyes, inhaling like she was trying to take them into her lungs, into her bloodstream.

"They sound beautiful, Ben. I can't believe I missed all of this. I can't believe I let it happen."

"They'd love you," I said quickly, fiercely, before doubt could crawl back in. "We talk about you, you know. You're not some secret we erased. You're their auntie, Tay. Always have been."

Her lips trembled. "I don't know if I deserve that. After everything. After what I've become."

I took one of her cold hands in both of mine. "You deserve a family. You always did. Nothing you've done can change that."

For a long moment we let the silence surround us. The smell of pine and lilies comforting us both, the smell of our childhood, our home.

Then, heart hammering so hard I thought it might crack me open, I said the words I had only ever dreamt of saying since she left:

"Do you want to come for dinner? We're having a roast. The kids would love to meet their Auntie. They've been waiting a lifetime ... literally! Please, Tay. Come."

She pressed a hand to her mouth, shoulders trembling with quiet sobs.

"Ben ... I don't know. I'm only just starting to feel like I can forgive you. Coming here today ... it was a huge step for me."

"Please, Taylor," I urged, my voice raw and quivering.

"You'd really want me there?" she whispered, her voice cracking.

"I've wanted you there every single day since you left," I admitted, heat of tears stinging my cheeks.

Her eyes widened, tears spilling freely now. Her lips pulled into the smallest, trembling smile.

She met my gaze for a heartbeat. "Okay."

And in that fragile, impossible moment, it felt as if the gaping wound that I'd carried for years, was finally beginning to close. The old wounds from so many years ago were finally beginning to heal, and with them, hopefully my sister's resentment toward me.

Chapter 35

Danny

Saturday 2nd December 2022
Age 28
Emily's House, Portsmouth, UK

It was strange how quickly Em became part of my life. Back in September, if you'd told me that the woman I'd stumbled across in the Three-Legged Cat would be tugging at my sleeve in a frosty car park three months later, I would have laughed. Probably choked on my drink. I might have dismissed it as a nice idea that wasn't meant for me and my fate. And yet there she was, arguing with me about the 'proper' height of a Christmas tree. Em contested my every tree suggestion as if there were some official list of Christmas tree standards I'd somehow missed.

There we were, cheeks pink from the cold, breath puffing in little clouds into the December air, surrounded by rows of pines and firs.

She was adamant we needed one "as tall as us both put together." I, ever the practical realist (or buzzkill), kept pointing out the obvious: the ceiling height, the mess from the needles, the fact that our tiny car could barely fit a few shopping bags, let alone a twelve-foot pine.

"Sure," I said, "and while we're at it, why don't we hire a crane?"

Her eyes sparkled, clearly thinking I was joking. I wasn't. But she just laughed and tugged me toward the biggest tree in the lot. And I thought, with a sinking sense of doom and delight, that this was exactly how it would go: Em, chaos incarnated, dragging me into the ridiculous and somehow making it feel like Christmas magic.

"Where's your Christmas spirit, Scrooge?" she teased, holding the tree upright like a trophy, as if sheer enthusiasm could magically turn it into a living room-sized pine.

I couldn't help smiling. That same jolt I'd felt in the pub was still there - but softer now, stretched into something steadier. It wasn't just sparks anymore. It was warmth, a slow, quiet glow that made the mundane feel … well, less mundane.

She caught me staring, the way I always seemed to, and her grin softened into something gentler, suspiciously like she'd finally concluded that my gawk was somehow charming. "What?", she questioned.

"Nothing," I said, shaking my head, though my chest was full of everything. The dizzying, almost ridiculous relief of no longer questioning who I was. The comfort of her hand brushing mine as we both reached for the same branch. The simple miracle that somehow, our two messy, hectic stories had ended up on the same page.

And then, anarchy erupted. We were laughing, tears in our eyes, attempting to jam the tree into the car like a pair of drunken sumo wrestlers trying to squeeze into skinny jeans. The back seats were pushed down, the tree jutting between the front seats, its tip scrunching against the windscreen. Did it fit? Technically, yes. Legally? Probably not.

We clambered into the car, both beaming with ridiculous pride at our jamming skills. The sight of one another, framed by a wall of stubborn pine, set off another round of laughter so loud it almost scared the passing pedestrians.

On the drive home, Em launched into a spirited commentary on the upcoming school Nativity plays and the spectacular failures of the dress rehearsal. She dissected every wrong note, every misplaced angel, and the ongoing 'shepherd hook incident', as if the fate of the entire holiday depended on her next move.

As she spoke, my thoughts kept drifting to how absurdly lucky I was. For the first time in fifteen years, I'd actually felt Christmassy. Not just the kind of flickering, commercialised tinsel-fuelled Christmas that made you grit your teeth in December, but the warm, ridiculous joy that sneaks up on you when you're not looking. And in a sudden, almost terrifying moment of clarity, I realized: maybe it wasn't Santa's fairy dust at all. Maybe it was love. Or at least a dangerously close approximation, wrapped in pine needles and Em's relentless enthusiasm.

Upon finally wrestling the tree inside Em's house, it was immediately obvious... she had been right. Norman (yes, Em had named the tree Norman) looked like the unruly monarch of the living room, brushing against the ceiling, leaning dramatically to the left as if daring anyone to question his authority, and filling the house with a dizzying mix of pine and exhilaration.

"And in here is everything we need!" she enthused, presenting a pile of cardboard boxes marked 'Xmas Decorations' like she was a telesales presenter unveiling the latest must-have gadgets. I half expected her to give me a free set of fairy lights if I signed up for the "holiday joy subscription plan."

We started with the lights, carefully winding them around Norman's branches.

Then came the silver tinsel, thrown on with joyful abandon. Each piece was a different length, a different thickness, shimmering in its own way. Norman, it seemed, had impeccable taste for asymmetry.

Then, of course, came the baubles. A riot of colour and size, each one carrying its own secret backstory. Some were shiny, some matte, some questionably chipped. Each time one clinked against another, it sounded like tiny glass bells celebrating our complete lack of coordination.

No star was going on top (nor would fit), Norman didn't need one, he was the star! He himself commanded all the attention.

Leaning against me, Em whispered, "Best decision we've made yet."

"Yeah," I said, squinting at the lopsided spectacle, "it's a shame he's wonky though."

"I've got just the thing," she said, disappearing upstairs like a magician summoning her final trick.

Moments later, she returned with her Book of Fate. Nonchalantly, she jammed it under one of the legs of the tree stand. Norman immediately tilted, groaning ever so slightly in the way only a tree with personality can. The baubles clinked and chimed like a drunken windchime, an orchestra of pandemonium celebrating our victory.

"Perfect," I said, still marvelling. "But won't you need that?"

"Meh," she shrugged, leaning against the wall with the kind of serene confidence that made me question my own life choices. "Whatever it says, our story is all that matters now … and when I say 'our,' that includes Norman."

I nodded solemnly, because really, when it came down to it, Norman had earned his place in this relationship.

Chapter 36

Frederick

Thursday 16th April 2020
Age 62
Frederick's Home, Portsmouth, UK

I woke with a start at six. These days it was the restless dreams that woke me up, prowling at the back of my mind every morning. Not dreams of battles past (those I've long made peace with) but of an invisible enemy, one that crept through our streets and silenced so many. The virus. It had a way of making the future feel uncertain, even when our Fates told us the outcomes. It kept me to a soldier's timetable whether I wanted it or not.
My Fate reminded me:

"You will spend another day in lockdown, same as yesterday and the same as tomorrow. You will do your usual loop with Gunner. Tonight, you will join your neighbours in the usual 'Clap for Carers'. The evening will end in an announcement to extend this lockdown further."*

No surprises today then. Not even the addition of more weeks to this never-ending lockdown.

I flip the kettle on. Mug filled with strong tea, black as it came. Gunner's breakfast sorted before mine, he'd never forgive me otherwise. Spending these weeks indoors had taught me resourcefulness all over again. Supplies were harder to come by and the supermarkets run rationed provisions, in spirit as well as in law.

Online delivery slots were as rare as hens' teeth. I'd learned to make a decent baked sausage hash with whatever was left over. Not bad, considering the circumstances.

I was fortunate, in my 'young' age of sixty-two and with my health holding steady, that I hadn't been ordered to shield. No letter from the NHS telling me to remain inside at all costs.

That small blessing meant Gunner and I could take our daily allowance of exercise: one walk, no more, no less. Not far, never any further than a three-mile radius of home. No buses were running for leisure and therefore there was no chance of meeting Barbara down at the dog park. But at least we could put one boot in front of the other.

The streets were eerily quiet, like Sunday mornings dragged out into infinity. Rows of houses sat in silence, curtains twitching now and then. A neighbour would nod from across the way, but no one came close. That two-metre gap had become a wall between us. Strange times indeed.

The air was cool but carried the edge of Spring. There were blossoms bursting through regardless of the pandemic, oblivious to human troubles. I realised I'd not paid such attention to the nature outside my own garden in years. Perhaps it took a crisis to slow a man down enough to notice.

The birdsong seemed sharper, louder. With fewer cars on the roads, their calls carried clearer. Almost like Mother Earth was reclaiming the silence.

Gunner, of course, had no interest in blossoms or birds. His delight lived on every lamppost and tree stump, each one a message board waiting to be read.

Loyal as ever, Gunner's tail wagged with the certainty that nothing in his world had shifted. He had scents to discover and his own to leave behind.

Our loop took us an hour, half through the neighbourhood, half through the woods.

On the streets, I saw little glimpses of resilience. Children's rainbows painted on tree trunks, signs of encouragement hung in windows, chalk hopscotch puzzles scribbled across pavements. Some affirmations were updated every day. It brought a smile to my face. These simple marks were reminders that life, although interrupted, carried on.

Then to the woods, which was like entering a different world. Untrodden earth, sun shimmering through new leaves, a stillness broken only by Gunner's panting and the crunch of twigs. Out there, I could pretend for a while. Pretend that the daily death toll on the news wasn't climbing, that there weren't refrigerated lorries turned into makeshift morgues in the cities and that the clap on Thursday nights wasn't for people working themselves to exhaustion in hospitals I dared not visit. Out there, it was just me and the dog, soldier and comrade, walking familiar ground in unfamiliar times.

Returning home, I scrubbed my hands raw with soap. Funny, after years of training in decontamination drills and operational hygiene, it was still this tiny ritual that now stood between safety and sickness. I watched the water circle the drain, thinking of how easily things slipped away.

The day stretched ahead. In the Army there was always a plan, an order of march. Here, it was just me against the silence of time. I filled it how I could. The radio droned on in the background with BBC updates, though I had to switch off when the talk turned to "rising figures" and "ventilator shortages."

Too much of that and the walls seemed to close in.
Instead, I sharpened a pencil and picked up the daily crossword. It kept the mind ticking over.
By late morning I put myself through a few old routines, press-ups and sit-ups beside the sofa. Nothing spectacular, but enough to remind my body that it still had fight left in it.
Gunner sat watching with that tilted head of his, eyes full of questions, as if to say, "What's all this for, old man?" The truth was simple: it was to keep myself sharp, ready, in shape for what the next few years demanded of me.
Lunch was simple: tinned soup and toast. Supplies had to be rationed, not because the shops were empty, but because every trip out carried a risk. I never thought at my age I'd be calculating whether a walk to Tesco was worth gambling my lungs.
The afternoon blurred into reading and dozing. If there was any silver lining, it was that the books I'd been saving for some far-off rainy day, were finally coming off the shelves and into my hands.
I'd tried video calls once or twice, though they always felt strange, like talking to a photograph that answered back. Still, I rang David, just to hear that steady, familiar voice I'd always found comforting.
David reminded me not to overdo the walks, then launched into tales of the DIY projects keeping him busy and the improvements he'd made to his garden. I laughed at his easy humour and felt grateful, more than ever, to have a friend so uncomplicated and steady by my side.
Evening came on slowly. Gunner was restless, picking up on my own moods no doubt. I gave him a chew from the cupboard and settled for beans on toast myself. Not a banquet, but warm and filling.
At eight o'clock sharp, I stepped outside with the neighbours. Pots banged, hands clapped, whistles blew. 'Clap for Carers', week four, I think.

The sound carried down the street, a strange kind of unity. I stood there clapping too, though I'll admit, part of the whole thing felt hollow and purposeless.

It was good to honour them, the doctors, the nurses, all those frontline lads and lasses, but applause felt small compared to the fight they were in. Still, for a few minutes, it bound us together, strangers waving from driveways at a distance.

Back indoors, I pour a tot of rum. I sit with Gunner at my feet and turn the news on, keeping the volume low. More numbers, more warnings. They announce that the lockdown is to be extended another three weeks. Necessary, I know, but heavy all the same. Three weeks in Army terms is nothing. Three weeks in a silent house feels like forever.

I turn off my lights by ten. I lay in bed listening to the quiet city, stilled in a way I have never known. Gunner snores at the foot of the bed.

Another day ticked off. No parades, no medals. Just a man, his dog, and a world on pause.

Chapter 37

Emily

Saturday 11th December 2022
Age 27
Emily's House, Portsmouth, UK

I'd been practically buzzing all week. Danny and I had tickets for a light trail and I'd been counting down the days like a child. I'd bought them months ago (which was very organised of me), and even gotten two, just in case someone wanted to come along with me. If not, my mum would have been perfect company, always cheerful, always ready to sprinkle a bit of festive sparkle wherever she went. But Mum could step down for this one. I had Danny, and that was more than enough.

I woke early this morning, stretched, and, though night still clung to the sky, threw back the curtains. My breath caught.

The world outside had transformed overnight.

Nineteen centimetres of snow lay thick and soft, blanketing the rooftops and gardens like a fluffy white quilt. The hedges sagged under the weight of the fresh snow, and the branches of the old oak opposite my window glittered.

Frost clung to every window ledge, turning all the houses on my road into miniature ice-palaces.

The usual drab, grey Portsmouth morning had vanished; even the lampposts looked magical, halos of light caught in the snowfall. Footprints traced delicate patterns along the pavements, hinting at early risers braving the cold.

The rest of the world seemed hushed and still, the snow had muffled every sound and whispered a soft, frozen peace over everything.

Danny was supposed to come over for a late lunch before we headed to the light show. I'd been imagining it all week: the cosy warmth of my tiny kitchen, laughter spilling over mugs of hot chocolate, my gloved hand in hers as we stepped out in our woolen hats and scarfs.

But as I glanced at the car keys on the counter, a little knot of worry tightened in my stomach. I turned on the kitchen radio. The host's voice sliced through my apprehension with the news that made my heart sink: smaller roads in the area were mainly closed, larger ones littered with abandoned cars.

My shoulders slumped. I plodded over to Norman, the Christmas tree. His lights twinkled cheerfully, but even Norman seemed to hang his branches a little lower, as if he too, felt my disappointment.

I sat at my window, staring out at the snow, feeling an odd mix of awe and sadness. The world was beautiful, yes. But utterly inconvenient.

Then my watch pinged with an email. I caught the subject line before I'd even had chance to lift my finger: "Light show cancelled due to snow." Great. Just … great.

I sank back, a little gasp escaping me.

I called Danny immediately, my voice betraying me before I could even try to mask it. "Hey…" I started, trying to sound casual, but my throat tightened and I

had to swallow hard. "They … um … they've cancelled it. Because of the snow."

I could hear the sympathy in Danny's voice instantly. I tried to pull myself together, but the disappointment felt heavy, like a wet scarf wrapped tight, weighing heavily around my shoulders. I'd been dreaming about how perfect and romantic this would be. The glow of the fairy lights reflecting off her beautiful eyes, the cosy warmth of holding hands and laughing as we wandered from display to display. I'd imagined little moments of magic, the kind you only get in movies, and now all of it had vanished before we'd even left the house.

I laughed a little, trying to convince myself I was okay. "I guess Norman and I will just have to make new plans," I said on the phone, looking over at the flickering tree. "You'd think our tree could cheer me up, but even he's looking a little glum."

Danny chuckled softly, but I could tell she felt my disappointment too. And maybe, just maybe, that made the day a little less bleak, because at least someone understood exactly how utterly heart-breaking this felt.

"Hold tight, Em," Danny said, her voice bright even through the phone speaker. "I have a plan, and I think you'll like it just as much."

"What is it?" I asked, already imagining all sorts of possibilities.

"You'll see," she said, and hung up before we could even exchange goodbyes.

I stared at the blank screen, a little deflated but also curious. I decided to get dressed anyway, shaking off the dejection. Snow days had a way of turning all plans upside down, but I wasn't going to sulk all day.

I wandered around the house, considering my options. I could have baked: gingerbread, cinnamon buns, anything that made the kitchen smell like Christmas.

I could have curled up with a blanket, a mug of something warm, and one of the dozen books I'd been meaning to read since July.

I could have even tackled the pile of laundry I'd been avoiding for a week (but that one was less festive).

Instead, I found myself pacing, glancing out the window at the snow-heavy streets, and occasionally muttering to Norman. "Don't look at me like that. You're not helping either."

The hours drifted by. Danny still hadn't called back. Where was she? Stuck somewhere? I hoped not. I tried calling her a few times, but each attempt ended in the cruel little click of a failed connection.

By mid-afternoon, I started to feel like the snow had trapped the entire world and maybe me along with it. But then there was a knock at the door.

Danny appeared, cheeks flushed from the cold, dragging in two enormous boxes. "Fairy lights?" I asked, raising an eyebrow.

"You said you wanted a light show," she said with a mischievous smirk. "So I've brought you a light show!"

Before I could protest, she had the boxes open, wires and tiny bulbs spilling onto the living room floor.

The first challenge: untangling them. Strands twisted around each other with stubborn determination.

One strand refused to light up. We shook it, we twisted it, we swore at it (just a little). Finally, Danny gave it a heroic flick, and miraculously, it blinked to life.

We teetered on stools, draping lights across the mantelpiece and bookcases, trailing them down the stair banister, and looping them up through the curtains.

At one point, a rebellious string wound itself around my ankle, nearly sending me headfirst into the now emptying stack of boxes. Danny barely stifled a laugh as she lunged to steady me, and I shot her a mock glare that dissolved the instant our eyes met.

We unearthed bubble-wrapped bundles of 3D light figures of reindeer, snowmen, and other festive creatures clearly meant for outdoors - but they looked perfectly at home perched on the spare bed. On the wall above it, we hung a neon sign that blinked: "Dear Santa, I can explain..." Perfect.

Hours slipped by in a blur of wrapping, twisting, rewrapping, and occasional exclamations of, "Where is the end?!"

Each new strand added more sparkle, more disarray, and more laughter. Finally, when we stepped back to admire our handiwork, the house had been transformed.

Every room, every corner, shimmered and twinkled. Norman, our tree, looked more gloriously ridiculous than ever, now dazzling in neon blues, reds, and greens, a blinking testament to our makeshift, magical winter wonderland.

We flop onto the sofa; both our faces adorn victorious grins. "I think this might actually be better than any we could have got tickets for," I admit, there is a warmth beginning to spread through me which had nothing to do with the central heating.

Danny reaches over and takes my hand. "Told you I had a plan," she said.

And just then, I realise this was what I'd been missing all these years. Not a tidy (massive) tree, not the rules of symmetry, but the chaos of loving someone enough to fill the house with light, just because we could.

Chapter 38

Taylor

Monday 18th May 2020
Age 35
Ben's Family Home, The Flat Above the Florist, Alton,
UK

The program said I was ready, and for the first few weeks it felt true.

I stayed clean through Christmas, through New Year's, through all those early months. Ben was a lifeline, letting me crash on the sofa bed in the already cramped flat, always with a quiet smile that made me feel safe.

I even bought a notebook to start writing again, jotting down little hopes like a child with a fresh exercise book. Poetry, book ideas that had rattled around my brain for years, lists of places I'd like to visit one day.

Then March came. The news was all virus, lockdown and death counts popping up across every app. Supermarkets stripped bare. The world shrinking smaller by the day.

I hadn't comprehended how much I leaned on the routine. The meetings in the church basement, the soup kitchen for a hot meal and a chat, the rhythm of other people. One by one, it all shut down.

My phone buzzed with "we're moving online," but Zoom isn't the same as a room of faces who get it.

There were no quiet nods of recognition or hand on your shoulder when your voice cracks. Just a screenful of boxes, people's eyes darting to their own reflections, the silence always heavier once you click "leave meeting."

At first, I tried to keep the shape of my days. Tea in the morning while saying my daily affirmations softly to myself, letting the words sink in like a gentle reminder that I was still here, still capable of trying.

I made the bed properly, smoothing the covers like they had shown us in rehab, as if straightening the sheets could somehow straighten my own tangled thoughts.

I would use my 'once-a-day exercise allowance' to walk round the local lake, letting the cool air brush against my cheeks. The sky stretched wide above me, a quiet reminder that the world still existed outside of the flat's four walls, that there was still space for breathing, for hope. I watched ducks drift lazily across the water, felt the gravel crunch under my trainers, and for a few moments, it was enough.

I rang John from the rehab centre once or twice, his voice calm and familiar on the other end of the line, always reminding me not to be too hard on myself. I text the girls from the group, exchanging silly little updates. We laughed over our attempts at banana bread, joked about trying to follow Joe Wicks' ridiculous workout videos at home with the kids, and for a little while, the world didn't feel so small and empty.

But the walls here were thin. Above the florist you could hear everything - the ping of a new online order, the clatter of buckets as Rose cleaned up after the day's deliveries, the jingle of the bell above the door when Ben or Harry dashed out to deliver orders locally. Sometimes, I'd hear the faint strains of music from a neighbour, or the low hum of the fridge, and it was as

if the world existed right on top of me, pressing in from all sides.

Sometimes, when it was quiet enough, I heard my own thoughts too clearly, sharp and insistent, like they had been waiting years to reach me. Old regrets, little anxieties, deep routed cravings, sharp memories; they all circled in my mind. I clenched my fists, tried to push them away, whispered to myself that this, too, was part of recovery.

Still, I held on. I told myself this was just another kind of rehab, another test of patience. Every day I stayed clean was still a victory, wasn't it? Even if I didn't feel victorious. Even if the victory was small and almost invisible, I told myself it counted.

I wrote more in my notebook, filling pages with scraps of my life and pieces of my heart:

A poem about the empty shelves in the supermarket, and how strange it felt to see a world suddenly stripped down to its bare bones.

A memory of the first time I saw the sea after rehab. How infinite it had looked, the waves folding endlessly over themselves, and how small, but safe, I felt standing there.

A prayer for Mum and Dad, that they were somewhere watching over us all in this flat and keeping us safe.

Some nights, I wrote more private things too.

Notes to myself that I hoped no one else would ever see. Little confessions of loneliness, tiny sparks of hope I wanted to hold on to, even when the world felt frightening and closed in. Writing became a lifeline, each word a small tether to myself, a way of saying: I am still here. I am still trying.

By April, the cravings were undeniable, subtle at first, soft whispers in the quiet of the evening, little nudges that I could easily dismiss. But slowly, insidiously, they grew louder, until they became a roar I couldn't ignore.

I told myself I could ride it out; at thirty-five, I didn't have it in me to fall again. I had survived too much worked too hard. I had Ben and my notebook. I had those small, careful routines that had become my anchors.

Even though I was still sleeping on the sofa above the shop, wrapped in Ben's family 'bubble', the silence around me grew heavier.

Nights stretched endlessly, the darkness pressing closer, and I found myself listening too hard to the sound of my own breathing. Every creak in the floorboards, every drip from the sink, sounded like it might be a warning, or a secret code I was failing to read.

Old numbers still lived in the back of my mind. I swore I'd deleted them, wiped them from my phone, erased them from my memory - but apparently only the phone had obeyed. Faces, voices, familiar sensations of a world I thought I'd left behind, floated into my thoughts uninvited. I imagined the feeling, the hollow relief that always came with a hit, and I recoiled from it, both terrified and oddly drawn.

By early May, I rang the rehab reception directly. I knew I needed to go back.

The voice on the line was kind but flat: "We can't take anyone new right now. COVID restrictions. Try the phone helpline, love."

I hung up and stared at the wall for hours. How do you recover locked inside with nothing but your own head for company?

I walk the block, wear the mask, keep two metres from strangers - but inside, I'm right back where I started all those years ago: chasing, craving, bargaining with myself. I tell myself tomorrow I'll call someone else, try again. But tonight, it's just me, the ghosts of old habits, and a world outside that's too dangerous to step into, even for help.

Chapter 39

Danny

Saturday 24th December 2022
Age 29
Danny's Flat, Waterlooville, UK

Tomorrow Em and I are off to our respective parents' homes, otherwise known as the annual "pretend we're normal and not secretly terrified of small talk and weird, slightly soggy red cabbage side dishes" exercise.

Tonight, though, tonight is just for us. Christmas Eve, my tiny upstairs flat, and somehow, despite its usual bedlam, it's starting to feel like an actual festive sanctuary rather than a hoarder's halfway house.

Em is currently wrestling the pièce de résistance: the stockings.

Two perfect matching red stockings (ordered online at the start of December, arriving fashionably late yesterday) now hang above my fake fireplace like twin beacons of holiday ambition.

She's dressed in a Mrs. Claus outfit, cute rather than sexy, thank God, because if she'd tried sexy, I'd likely have melted into a puddle of embarrassment.

Or drool.

Or both.

She's laughing softly, brushing imaginary lint off the mantle like she's hosting the Queen.

"Maybe we could fit a third one on here someday," she says, pointing at the empty gap beside mine. Her eyes twinkling with mischief.

"Are we … getting a cat?" I ask, voice casual but hope clinging to every needy syllable.

She winks. "Maybe," she says. Dangerous. Vague. Perfect. I feel like I've just been handed a mystery wrapped in glitter.

I sip my hot chocolate, which I have enhanced with extra chocolate squares, because apparently self-indulgence (and high cholesterol) is mandatory on Christmas Eve. It's basically liquid therapy, and I'm prescribing it for every patient from now on.

Em is humming along to a Christmas playlist that is 90% cringe, 10% jazz covers of songs I vaguely recognize from long-forgotten adverts, and I can't decide if I should join in or quietly mourn my taste in music.

She jumped up to sit on the kitchen island opposite me, head falling forward and resting against my shoulder. I resist the urge to nudge her backwards in a 'you're ridiculously cute' way because honestly, I'm already dangerously close to spontaneous emotional outburst, a condition I like to call 'Christmas Eve with Em Syndrome'. I'm sorry to announce, its terminal.

I glanced at the bookcase behind her and my Book of Fate, wedged between the medical works (that remind me I'm a responsible adult) and the poetry and romance novels (courtesy of Em) that have somehow crept into my flat and now refuse to leave! The juxtaposition of my anatomy diagrams and treatment charts, against her dreamy writings, just feel right. Like my life is quietly telling me it's okay to be a bit of a jumble.

Outside, the street is quiet, apart from the occasional car gliding past. The fairy lights from the neighbouring flat spills in, painting the walls in strange, warm patterns that are either charming or an epilepsy sufferer's nightmare. I lean back, let my head fall onto Em's lap and allow the cosy commotion of stockings and chocolate-coated mugs settle around us. The flat smells faintly of cinnamon, pine, and whatever questionable candle we had picked-up last weekend from Home Bargains.

I catch myself wondering about my Fate and whether I should read it? If I should keep letting myself fall this deeply, or should I be sensible and guard my heart? I hadn't even thought to read it in a long time, so long it now felt like somewhat of a relic. Strange how some things just fade, and other things stick, stubbornly.

I think about how certain Em is about us, so certain that she'd stopped reading her Book of Fate altogether. Her words echo in my head, "Whatever it says, *our* story is all that matters now." The conviction in her voice had unsettled me, not because I doubted her, but because I envied her certainty. While she could close her Book without a second thought, I still felt the weight of mine pressing against the shelf, daring me to look.

I look up at Em and asked, half-curious, half-looking for trouble, "have you read your Fate since we met?"

Her head bows towards me, her face all soft and dramatic, and like she'd been rehearsing this moment for a Netflix special replied solemnly, "No! Because the moment we met, I knew you were the one I'd been looking for. *The Love of My Life*."

I snort so hard I nearly inhale a marshmallow. "Very smooth. Almost too smooth. Have you been practicing that line in the mirror?"

Em ignores my cynicism and continues with full Shakespearean flair. "For once, I don't feel like I need to keep replaying and rereading the day, hunting for details I might have missed. I just know. You're my everything!"

I sigh, partly because she'd managed to turn my scrappy little flat into a rom-com set, and partly because, against my better judgement, my heart had actually fallen harder than ever before. "You're ridiculous," I mutter.

"Plus," she adds quickly, completely ruining the tender moment, "I couldn't take my Fate out from under Norman. He quite likes being propped up on it."

I laugh loudly. "So let me get this straight. The only thing standing between you and destiny is... Norman the Christmas Tree?"

"Precisely." She gave me a very grave nod.

Before I could make another joke, her expression shifts, a flicker of suspicion narrows her eyes. She sat up straight. "Wait. Why? Have you read yours?"

I wave my hand dismissively, as though the very idea was beneath me. "No. I never paid attention to it anyway. For once I actually like the way my story is going."

Em squints her eyes further, clearly unconvinced. "You're sure? Not even a cheeky peek since we met?"

I grin, "Em, if I had read it, don't you think I'd be milking it for all it's worth? Quoting dramatic lines at you in bed? Saying things like, 'The book foretold this kiss, and lo, here it comes'?"

Her laugh was so sudden and loud it startles me. She shoves me lightly off her lap.

"Fine. I believe you. But if I catch you sneaking a peek, I'm confiscating it. Doctor or not, you're not above bedtime story supervision."

"Deal," I said, raising my mug in mock solidarity. "Besides, I don't need a book to tell me what's next. I've got you, Norman, and possibly a cat. That's enough fate for me."

Chapter 40

Ben

Friday 11th February 2022
Age 37
Green and Grow Florist, Alton, UK

The phone in the flat rang late in the afternoon. Quinn, who had been upstairs sketching designs for her "wanna-do" tattoo portfolio, answered it. I could hear her voice muffled through the ceiling, casual at first, then sharp with urgency.

A minute later she came flying down the stairs, heavy-footed, nearly tripping over herself as she burst through the door. Bell clanging, she thrust the home phone out in front of her.

"Dad - it's the doctor. The doctor's on the phone."

"Doctor who?" I quipped out of instinct, my mouth moving before my brain caught up.

Quinn didn't laugh. Her face was pale.

"Dr. Carter, or something. It's about Auntie Taylor."

The joke curdled in my throat. "Oh."

I took the receiver, my hand suddenly clammy.

"Hello, is this Benjamin Green?" It was a woman's voice, kind but measured and professional.

"Yes ... yes, it is," I stammered, forgetting for a second that it was, in fact, my name.

"My name is Dr Danny Carter. I'm calling about Taylor Green. Is she your sister?"

"Yes. Yes, she is. Is she alright? Where is she? I haven't heard from her since... God, Summer of 2020. Is she okay?"

"She's with me now, Mr. Green," the doctor said gently. "She's safe. We're working with her, supporting her in her recovery."

I shut my eyes. The relief punched me in the chest, tangled with dread.

"I knew," I whispered. "I knew she'd started using again."

"Mr. Green, part of recovery is about rebuilding a support system. It's taken a lot for Taylor to allow us to make this call, to let you in. You'll need to remain patient and sensitive."

"I tried to call her," I blurted. "Every day, at first. Then once a week. I know her voicemail by heart. I thought ..." My voice cracked. "I thought she was gone for good."

"I understand. She hasn't been ready until now. But she asked us to reach out."

A silence stretched. I could almost hear my sister's voice on the other end of the line, as if she were hovering in the room, listening, deciding whether I was worth the risk.

"What do I do?" I begged. "Tell me what I can do. I just - I want her safe. I want her home. I want her sober."

Dr. Carter outlined the steps: a new phone number for Taylor, ground rules for communication, a gentle encouragement to keep things light, supportive, not suffocating.

I scribbled it all down on the florist's notepad, pressing so hard the pen nearly tore the page.

When she finally hung up, I sat in the silence of the shop. Quinn hovered nearby, her big eyes wet, needing answers.

"Is Auntie Taylor okay?" she whispered.

"She's … she's trying to be," I said. My throat closed around the words.

Quinn sat down beside me, leaning her head on my shoulder. We stayed like that, staring at nothing, listening to the hum of the fridge through the ceiling.

And in my head, the questions wouldn't stop: Was it me? What did I do wrong this time?

Did I push her away by being too busy, too buried in online orders, trying to keep the shop afloat during lockdown? Was I not there enough? Did I let her fall?

The anger came next, at the virus that had made everything harder, at the fractured system that only caught people on the way down if they were lucky, and at myself for still not knowing how to save her.

But beneath the anger was something fiercer: resolve. Taylor was my sister. My stubborn, wild, beautiful little sister. And whatever it took - whatever patience, forgiveness, or strength - I would give it.

For the first time in years, I thought about my Book of Fate. Maybe I should open it, see where this chapter ends, find out whether she survives, whether she gets clean for good.

Or maybe it's not my Book I need to open. Maybe it's hers.

Chapter 41

Frederick

Saturday 3rd July 2020
Age 62
Frederick's Home, Portsmouth, UK

I woke early again, as always. Old habits. Six o'clock. First thing, kettle on, strong tea brewed, Gunner fed before me. He's a regimented bugger, never lets me forget it. His bowl must be filled before I so much as butter a slice of toast. That dog has more discipline than some of the men I served with.

The streets outside were quiet, still that odd silence we'd grown used to since lockdown began back in March. There is no hum of cars, not even kids kicking about on the pavement, just the postman rattling his trolley past, whistling behind his mask.

While eating my toast, I spotted a different van outside the adjoining house, number 56. A moving van, back doors yawning open, a woman alone, hauling out flat packed furniture and boxes.

I reached for my Book of Fate after breakfast. I can't say why, but I had a feeling today would matter. The page was clear enough:

"Emily Puddle will move in next-door, to number 56. Not today, but she will soon cross your path. She is central to your story, right to its end. Today you will keep company only with Gunner."

Strange words, but then Fate never wasted its ink.

I stepped to the window, tea in hand, to see this Emily Puddle a little clearer: a younger woman, late twenties perhaps, dark curly hair tied back in a bun, arms full of boxes she could barely balance.

On her own, by the looks of it. No man in sight.

Hard to believe she managed it all herself, but she did, trudging back and forth with a determination I recognised from somewhere.

She stacked open boxes of books against the front step, carefully checking each label before carrying them methodically inside.

At one point she looked over and caught me peering out the window. I gave a brief nod, nothing more. She returned it with a smile, quick, easy, unguarded.

I told myself not to linger, but the truth is I did.

Curiosity always did get the better of me. From my spot I noticed the way she worked. Not rushing, not flustered.

Yet there was also a chaos in her too, the good kind. It wasn't clumsy so much as spirited. A sort of charming disorder, as though her energy spilled out faster than her plans could keep up. Full of life, unafraid to make a mess of it, remembering to smile and carry on.

By midday, I put together my lunch. There no pubs open, no café fry-ups, not even a chippy unless you queued half an hour and stood on chalk-marked lines.

I'd got used to keeping it simple: soup from a tin, a couple of slices of bread and a banana for afterwards.

I sat in the back garden with my lunch, Gunner nosing about the borders, while the muffled thump of boxes and scrape of furniture drifted over the neighbouring hedge.

In the afternoon I caught glimpses of her again. She'd started on the garden already, lining up plants by the wall, tugging any overlording weeds out of the border. Delivery men dropped something off, large and flat-pack by the looks of it, and she directed them with a calm authority.

Even Gunner noticed her, head tilted, ears pricked up each time she walked near the hedge.

I didn't introduce myself today. It was too soon for that, and besides, rules were still rules. Two metres apart, wait until Fate said so. It was safer to observe, to let her settle. But I knew, deep down, that things were shifting. Quiet, predictable days, just me and the dog and the silence of lockdown, might be ending.

And if there's one thing the Army taught me, it's this: when Fate gives an order, you damn well pay attention.

Chapter 42

Emily

Saturday 31st December 2022
Age 27
Danny's Flat, Waterlooville, UK

The flat smelled of chicken tikka masala and onion bhajis. Danny had insisted it was a New Year's Eve tradition, "better than soggy supermarket party platters," she had said earlier, waving a ladle at me. A full-blown Indian-inspired feast to celebrate the end of the year.

The selfie we took at our 'light show' still sat proudly on her mantlepiece, in the frame I decorated for her as a Christmas gift. It makes me smile every time I see it, our cheeks pressed together, fairy lights glimmering around us, the kind of picture that looks like it belongs on someone else's Pinterest board, not my actual life.

Danny lounged across the sofa, her hair ruffled, cheeks warm and rosy with laughter, watching a TikTok where a duck waddled its way through a clumsy dance. Her laugh was loud and infectious, and the thought crossed my mind that I didn't ever not want this. Want her.

I had been rehearsing the words all evening. Lines had played and replayed in my head like a script I kept botching. But then, with my heart hammering, I took the plunge.

"Danny ..." I drew out her name, my voice soft and tentative.

She didn't even look up at first. "God, that's never a good sign. You say my name like that when you're about to confess to something. What did you do? Don't tell me you've killed off Norman!"

I laughed, half-nervous, half-relieved at her usual sarcasm. "No. Not yet."

She finally lifted her head, eyebrow cocked, smirk forming. "Alright Em, hit me with it."

I swallowed, painfully aware of every detail about her, her eyebrows slightly raised as she met my eye.

"Would you ..." I hesitated, then pushed the words out in a rush. "Would you move in with me?"

For a heartbeat there was silence. Then her grin spread, slow and dazzling. "Em ... are you serious?"

I nodded quickly, fumbling in my pocket until my fingers brushed the cool metal. I pulled out the little silver key, my hand shaking.

"Completely serious. I couldn't imagine my life without you. Your mess, your cynicism ... I want it all. Every day."

Her eyes softened, and she took my hand, curling her fingers tight around mine before I could lose my nerve. "You're ridiculous." She leaned forward until her forehead rested against mine. Her voice dropped to a whisper, playful but thick with emotion. "Of course I'll move in with you."

Relief flooded me, with a hot and overwhelming feeling. I pressed the key into her palm. She curled her fingers around it forming a fist, holding it tight like it was more than just a newly cut key.

As we sat together, I let all the feelings overwhelm and flood my brain. I could never wish for more than her.

The clock ticks closer to midnight. I pull her against me on the sofa, my chin rests on the top of her head.

Outside, distant fireworks crackle. On the TV, the countdown begins.

"Ten … nine … eight …"

Danny brushes her thumb across my cheek, trailing the line of my face. "Seven … six … five …"

Her gaze catches mine again, eyes sparkling. I kiss her softly, perfectly in time with the TV broadcast - "three … two … one …" - as London erupts in fireworks.

The world outside explodes in light and colour, but all I see, all I feel, is her.

"Happy New Year," she murmurs against my lips, her breath warm, her smile brushes against mine.

She holds the little key up between us, grinning. "So, this is it, huh? The grand merging of fates. Just promise me you won't hold an intervention every time you discover my socks stuffed in the sofa cushions."

I laugh, nudging her shoulder. "Absolutely no promises."

My eye drifts to her worn Book of Fate (currently forming a plinth for her slightly festive aloe vera.) "Think we should check if our future involves living in a sock graveyard?"

Danny presses her forehead against mine, her voice drops to a whisper. "If those pages ever dared to say otherwise, I'd tear them out."

She kisses me then, deep and certain, her hand still clutching the key.

In that moment, surrounded by fireworks and the hum of a brand-new year, I know this isn't just another chapter. This is where our story really begins.

Chapter 43

Taylor

Saturday 13th May 2023
Age 38
Lisa's Home, Southampton, UK

New streets. New walls. New faces I couldn't place. It felt as though the world had been wiped clean and painted over, a map with no compass, designed to keep me lost.

I left Ben's flat without a word to anyone. I couldn't stay, not with the shadows of everything I had ruined crowding the walls.

I already missed Harry, Quinn, and little Sky more than I could bear. But it was the ghost of the life I might've had that hurt the most.

My fate was written, and I had to accept that not every story ended in light and bliss. Some stories just curled in on themselves, dark and unfinished.

I drifted along the south coast, following dealers like breadcrumbs, hunting for the next hit. That was when I was introduced to Lisa. We met through a dealer, she was older than me but not by much - late forties, maybe.

Lisa offered me a roof when I had nowhere else to go. She wasn't gentle, but she was kind in her own way, although not in the soft way people think of kindness. She gave me warmth, a bed, a plate of food … and the drugs that kept me from falling apart completely.

I told myself it was survival. But survival had become slippery. The nights were spent sweating, shaking, chasing a high that slipped further away each time.

To repay her, I did what I had to. Petty thefts that left my chest heavy with shame: a stolen wallet, a shirt grabbed off a rack, trainers off a shelf, a watch that wasn't mine, food stuffed into my bag before the cameras could capture me.

The shame was there, always, but it felt muted - muffled beneath the relief of having a place to rest my head and a momentary silence from the gnawing through my bones.

Tonight, the city feels alive. Eurovision fever. The streets are draped in flags, people spill out of the pubs in sequins and glitter, voices raised together in songs from countries they'd never even visited. Cheers carry down every alley.

From Lisa's window I can see faces lit by the glow of phone screens and televisions. Everyone is celebrating, laughing and belonging.

And then there is me. Curled on the edge of a stranger's windowsill, my heart feels heavier than ever. The joy outside sounds like it comes from another planet, one I used to live on but can never return to.

I tell myself tomorrow I will stop. Tomorrow I will claw my way back. Tomorrow I might even call Ben. But tomorrow always hovers just far enough out of reach.

I scroll through my phone, staring at Ben's name, at the unanswered messages I can't bring myself to reply to.

Thu 12 Nov 2022

Thinking of you and them today, Tay. Where are you? Please just let me know you're safe. xx

21:33

Sun 1 Jan 2023

Happy New Year Tay! We are hoping we may hear from you this year … Quinn especially. She keeps asking about you. Lots of Love xx

00:27

Mon 13 Feb 2023

You don't have to do this alone. Please come back Taylor! xx

23:14

Or just reply! Anything …

23:37

Fri 28 April 2023

Hey, I was sorting out my wardrobe today. I've something of yours Taylor, please come home. xx

18:16

Today

Eurovision tonight Tay. Do you remember when we used to watch it with Mum and Dad? How he used to get so outraged by the scores? We will always be here for you xx

20:18

Each word cuts deeper than the last. I can't answer. Not yet. Maybe one day. Maybe not ever.

I feel older than thirty-eight, as if the years have been stolen out from under me. My body is tired, worn thin, but somehow, I keep moving.

One small step at a time, through shadows no one sees. Survival, yes. But survival with no end in sight, no book to tell me when this will all conclude.

Chapter 44

Frederick

Friday 12th February 2021
Age 62
Frederick's Home, Portsmouth, UK

The afternoon sky was pale and brittle, that peculiar February grey that made the world look fragile, almost half-formed.

I leaned against my gate, mug of tea warming my hands, watched the first stubborn shoots of Spring push through the soil. The bulbs I'd planted three years ago were growing strong, their green tips like small victories against the cold.

Over the spindly hedge, I could see Emily crouched by her little hand-dug pond, her fingers probing the murky water. I'd been hearing about the arrival of frogspawn for a week now, her excitement audible to everyone on the street.

"Morning, General," she said, glancing up and brushing a stray lock of hair from her face. Dark circles shadowed her eyes, the unmistakable mark of someone burning the candle at both ends.

"Morning, Miss," I said with a chuckle. "How's school going? Have you got another holiday soon, or they just fused it with the lockdowns?"

She laughed, a soft, tired laugh. "I'm exhausted. But yes, it's half-term … it's been a long slog."

I chuckled, shaking my head. "I can imagine. Classrooms… they're a different kind of battlefield from anything I ever faced. And trust me, I've seen a few proper ones."

She straightened, squinting at the pond. "You have no idea. And now, with the new COVID restrictions … it's like the rules change every day. Yesterday we were supposed to do one thing, today it's something else. Teaching Maths through a screen, juggling check-in calls with parents … it's a miracle anyone learns anything at all."

I nodded, letting my mind drift to my own days in uniform, where everything had been clear: orders, consequences, routines. There was a simplicity to it, a comfort in knowing exactly what was expected.

Civilian life had none of that.

"But at least things are starting to lift a little. There's light at the end of the tunnel, even if it's faint. A slow grind but people get used to it. Humans are stubborn in that way," I supposed.

Emily's gaze wandered toward the corner of my garden where Gunner was nosing through a patch of daffodil sprouts, his nose buried in the damp earth.

"Oh, he's lovely," she said fondly. "I'd love a dog someday… but my life right now … I don't think I could give one the time it deserves. Not until all this COVID is really over."

"Ah," I said, leaning a little further over, into a prominent gap in the hedge, smiling. Something in her words made me realise she hadn't read forward in her Book of Fate in the way I had. "Gunner's been my best mate through thick and thin. And he's still got a life ahead of him. Lots more gloomy mornings like this. One day… you'll have Gunner … a Gunner … a dog!"

My words stumbled out, awkward in their sincerity.

She laughed then, sounding lighter now, less weighed down. "Maybe one day. I'll get there."

We lingered a while, letting conversation drift between gardens, dogs, books, and the slow crawl of the world toward normality. There was a quiet comfort in it, a small island of calm shared across two gardens.

It took me some time to figure Emily out when she moved in next door, but I realised I couldn't have asked for a better neighbour.

My Fate had been right about this, as always, her company at the end of my story was not a footnote, but a lightening of the final chapters.

"I should get going inside, dinner is on," she said, offering me a tired but genuine smile. "Thanks for talking, Sir. It's … nice to have a neighbour who listens."

I tipped my mug toward her. "Anytime, Miss Emily. Anytime."

The garden settled back into its quiet rhythm. Gunner's soft sniffing, the faint scrape of soil under his paws, the distant hum of the city waking up for a Friday night.

Small moments, perhaps insignificant to anyone else, but sometimes they were enough. Enough to remind you that the world, heavy as it seemed, could still feel a little lighter. And sometimes, the quiet victories, daffodils breaking through frost, a friend's smile, a dog's wet nose, were all the medals you really need.

Chapter 45

Ben

Saturday 13th May 2023
Age 45
Ben's Family Home, The Flat Above the Florist, Alton, UK

Business had been better than I could have dreamt. The shop was thriving, orders tumbling in daily. Walk-ins, phone calls, and online sales piling up faster than we could process them. Rose's subscription idea, born in the grim days of COVID-19, had become the steady heartbeat of the place.

People liked the comfort of knowing that, once a month, a fresh bunch of blooms would arrive at their doorstep, tied with twine and scented with whatever the fields had to offer.

This month, wildflowers threaded the arrangements, but the true stars were the peonies - fat-headed, in shades of blush pink and rich burgundy, their petals curling open.

Tonight was family night.

Once upon a time, I had dreaded it, too much noise, too many squabbles. Now, because they happened so rarely, I found myself clinging to them, treasuring the pandemonium like it was gold dust. All the kids were here, crammed into the flat, their laughter ricocheting off the old walls. We were like cuckoos in a blue tit's nest, barely fitting, but somehow all the warmer for it.

It reminded me of my childhood, those Eurovision nights with Mum, Dad, and Taylor in this very room, though back then the sofa was scratchier, and the television a bulkier square with a picture that flickered if you breathed too close to it.

I remembered the uproar when televoting was introduced in the late nineties, Dad ranting that it wasn't fair, that countries were voting for neighbours, not the music.

Mum would just laugh, feet perched on the footstool, tapping out rhythms with her toes while marveling at the costumes "like aliens on roller skates," she'd say, or "someone let their curtains walk on stage."

This year felt different. Special. The UK were hosting Eurovision 2023 in Liverpool Arena, on behalf of Ukraine.

The stage design was something else. That sea of lights and screens, LED walls and a floor tiles, rotating panels, sweeping arcs that made every entry feel like stepping into a different world.

Yet I couldn't shake the sense that it would have meant so much more if the whole family were here. Tonight, the absence of Taylor pressed especially hard, I missed her with an ache I couldn't soften.

Taylor had been gone so long, lost in outreach services, hostels and months of silence. When I came across her Book back in April, I almost opened it, almost let myself search for the answers it held. Where she was now, where I might go to find her, to help her.

But I had sworn to Rose that I wouldn't read my own Book of Fate, and in that moment, I bound myself to the same promise for Taylor's. Her story wasn't mine to read.

When she left here I tried not to smother her with texts, though I wrote many, hovering over 'send' before deleting them.

Tonight, though, I sent one. Simple, a reminder of old times.

Delivered. As always. Unanswered.

Rose sat on the sofa with the kids piled against her. Sky's eyes wide as the glitter and sequins stormed across the screen, she didn't understand all the voting or history, but she was entranced by the dancers spinning beneath a rain of sparks.

Once the final song ended and points were tallied, we tucked the kids into bed. Rose disappeared for her bath, steam whispering under the door.

I stay on the sofa, TV dead, the room too quiet. Thoughts of Taylor fill the silence, sharp and insistent. My reoccurring nightmares had returned: her lying on cold concrete somewhere, lost in a city that didn't care. I realise that I cannot stay here any longer. I pull on my coat and step out into the night.

I walk further than I mean to, past streets I scarcely ever had reason to travel. My eyes scan benches, doorways, shadows under bus shelters. As though she might appear, curled small in the cold. As though the echo of Liverpool and the whole contest might reach her, wherever she was.

Of course, she isn't here. But I continue to search.

Chapter 46

Taylor

Sunday 12th November 2023
Age 39
Lisa's Home, Southampton, UK

The morning light shone in unapologetically through the ratty curtains. I woke with a phantom weight on my chest, not quite a pain, more like a memory that had edged itself into my bones overnight.

The date hit me the way a train hits a crossing: sudden and unstoppable. My parents' anniversary has always sat in the back of my head like a tune I can't forget; today it played loud.

Lisa was already up. I could hear the kettle rumbling through the thin wall and the clink of spoons against mugs. The radio muttering on about current affairs with a detached voice that made everything sound the same - wars, weather, politicians - all blurred into background noise.

When I dragged myself into the kitchen, Lisa was stood by the counter in her dressing gown with her hair pulled back. She glanced at me only briefly, as if she'd already read the shape of my morning before I had opened my mouth. Already knew what I was going to ask.

Even so, I had to ask.

I asked her for a bigger hit than I usually do. I needed more of it on a day like today.

The words came out cracked, too fast, slipping from me like something broken loose. They tasted of vinegar on my tongue, sour and corrosive, and the moment they were in the air I wanted to swallow them back down.

Lisa didn't blink.

Her face stayed still, unreadable, though her hand paused for the smallest second over the sugar jar. Then she carried on as if I hadn't asked for anything unusual at all, stirring her coffee with slow, unhurried turns, her eyes fixed on the spirals in the cup rather than on me.

The silence she gave me was heavier than any answer. She put the teaspoon down, wiped her hands on her dressing gown, and touched the side of my face in that way she does - not tender, not cruel, just decisive.

"Alright," she said. "I can sort that for you."

The assurance was a promise and a command. It was exactly the kind of comfort that costs you something.

Lisa leaned forward on the counter, eyes bright and hard as she laid out the bargain. "There's a new Mac in the tech refurbishment shop window," she said, casual and dangerous, as if naming it made it smaller. "You're the one who can do it, who can steal the laptop. You'll do it quick. I'll sort the extra you need in exchange." Her voice was steady.

My stomach folded. I felt the assignment land inside me like a stone. I didn't ask how to steal it, and I wasn't going to ask, because asking would make it real in a way I couldn't undo.

Instead, my head filled with a fog of shame and worry: the shame of being 'the one' who she thought would be able to steal it, the worry of what would happen if I didn't do it.

I pictured the refurbishment shop, a narrow, cluttered place where the air smelled faintly of dust and overheated plastic. The fluorescent lights overhead, casting every corner in an unkind light.

I avoided thinking of any further specifics because even thinking of techniques felt like a betrayal of whatever scrappy honesty I had left. Instead, I catalogued the risks: alarms, eyes, the hush that follows when something wrong is suddenly obvious. I imagined the staff watching me, not unkindly, but the kind of observations that weighed up every movement and every hesitation. My hands went cold at the thought of being seen, of the small but immediate panic that would follow.

Then the excuses my mind offers to soften the edges began to flood in, my need to feel anything but this ache.

The idea of feasibility became less about logistics and more about whether I had the nerve to do something I would spend the rest of my life apologising for.

Guilt came in waves and in small, sharp things.

"You don't have to do it," she said, though her voice was thinner than I wanted. She watched me with that patient, transactional calm, her eyes measuring how far I'll fall before I hit the ground.

I felt torn: the pull of needing to numb the day and the bitter certainty that saying yes would carve another line into whatever was left of me.

I pressed my palm flat to the notebook hidden in my pocket and tried to remember my parents, to find a small piece of me that still refused.

I pictured my Mum and Dad, their faces clear in my mind, warm and familiar even in their absence. Today, that absence felt almost obscene, like trying to celebrate a birthday in a dark room with no candles to light.

A hunger rose in me - not for food, but for something real, something I could hold onto: to be clean, to earn my own money, to pay rent, to do even the smallest thing that meant I was moving forward instead of just drifting in this fog of drugs and half-promises.

I wanted a life I could touch, a proof that I could still matter, that I could still belong somewhere. Instead, I was bargaining with myself in the dark, trading pieces of dignity for that short burst of relief.

I kept thinking of my Fate. I imagined holding the book in my hands again and flipping to a page that told me if this spiral had an end, if this desperate line of choices turned into something softer. Would it tell me I'd survive this? That I'd make a different choice today? Or would it read like a ledger, recording each small surrender like an account I couldn't settle?

It felt like my Book of Fate would've been a handrail I could clutch when the floor beneath me tilted, steady and real, and not having it left me teetering on the edge.

Lisa watched me while I considered her request. She angled her head as if measuring my thoughts. Lisa gives me what I need to get by, even when what she gives is the reason I must ask again. I love her in parts and I loathe her in others. Both feelings are honest and neither saves me.

I go back to my bed and sink onto it, letting the weight of it all press in. I pick up my battered notebook and write the date in the margin. I press so hard the nib cuts into the paper, leaving an indentation mark that feel almost like small, stubborn proof I exist today.

Writing still steadied me in a small way; words are a kind of tether. I try to be honest with myself about why I am considering stealing: not pride, not malice, but a raw need to feel present, to buy myself a minute that wasn't just waiting for the next crash. Even as I think about it, I know "need" and "want" are blurred by the same shaking hands.

The anniversary pressed at me like a question without punctuation: what are you willing to lose to feel something other than grief?

I fold the notebook closed. For a moment I allow myself a memory - my mother humming as she folds laundry while my father sits opposite her at the kitchen table gluing together a broken ornament - and I let the memory be both beautiful and painful without demanding it solve anything.

Then I breathe, counted to ten, and wait to see which side of me would speak louder.

Chapter 47

Frederick

Tuesday 21st February 2023
Age 65
Frederick's Home, Portsmouth, UK

The garden was a damp February mess. Mud clung to my boots, the grass a sludgy mess, and the rose bushes bare.
I had spent the morning clearing last year's dead growth, tossing it into the garden waste bin. Gunner patrolled beside me, tail wagging, occasionally nosing at the ground or barking at an overambitious pigeon.
I paused with my secateurs in hand, thinking about what I had re-read this morning in my Book of Fate. Today marked two years to the day until it happens. The shot. The end. My death.
So, it felt of great importance to reread the last chapters again today. The pages were curling with wear, yet the ink was still sharp under my eyes.

A grim little entry for today:

"You will spend the morning in your garden, where you will notice Danny Carter struggling with boxes next-door. For the first time you will converse. You will offer to help but find yourself laughing and gardening together instead. You will realize how both Danny and Emily are central to both your life and your death."

I'd long since stopped panicking over these things. Fate had a habit of showing you the finish line before you reached the first hurdle, and there wasn't much point fretting over what I couldn't change. Still, it left a sour taste, a reminder that time was moving, relentless as ever.

I turned my attention to the hedge, something instinctive in me scanning the perimeter. Emily's garden was quiet, no laughter or wobbly melodies being sung. But someone else was there, juggling boxes in a slightly frenzied way, clearly struggling along alone. I had had glimpses of her before.

A kind woman, always making Emily laugh, but I hadn't formally met her. I thought how this was obviously the long-awaited Danny Carter.

The Book of Fate had hinted she would play a part in my end, intertwined with Emily and, by extension, me. My army instincts pinged: protective. No harm would come to Emily under my watch, not if I could help it.

I cleared my throat, leaning over the boundary hedge. "Need a hand with those?"

Danny looked up, a box teetering in her hands. "Depends," she said with a grin. "Do you come with heavy-lifting insurance?"

I chuckled, "No. Just muscle memory and years of hard graft. Frederick, pleased to meet you."

"I'm Danny. And no worries, I can handle a box or three."

Not wanting the conversation to end so quickly, I fumbled for something to keep it going. My eyes cast downwards and landed on thin and scraggly hedge that I had been peering over. "Looks like our hedge could use a bit of attention," I said, nodding toward the spindly boundary between our gardens.

Just then, Gunner caught wind of the new intruder and erupted into barking.

"Gunner, quiet! Come here!" I snapped, summoning him to my side. He trotted over obediently, tail wagging, while Danny laughed a rich, easy laugh that somehow carried across both our gardens.

She crouched down, leaning through the gap and held out her hand. Gunner sniffed it cautiously and then gave a cautious lick.

"Hello, Gunner," she said, grinning. "Do you live here alone with this charming brute?"

"Mostly," I said answering for him. "He's in charge. I just follow orders."

Danny crouched down to scratch behind Gunner's ears, and he leaned into her hand, tail wagging ferociously. She straightened, smoothing her jeans, and tilted her head. "You know," she said, eyeing the unkempt shrubbery, "if you want, we could sort this hedge now before Em gets back in from school. Two sets of hands are usually better than one, right?"

I raised an eyebrow, sizing her up like I had a dozen times in the army before letting anyone anywhere near my perimeter.

As if to soften my scrutiny, she added, "I've got my own shears. Just don't blame me if the top ends up a little lively."

I shook my head. "Lively, huh?" I said, chuckling. "If it doesn't end up looking like a battalion formation ... well, don't say I didn't warn you about the consequences. Get the rest of your boxes in and I'll get the groundsheet."

Once her boxes were all inside, Danny came through my gate and into the garden. Crouching beside the hedge, we began planning the most tactical manoeuvre. She tapped a finger against her chin, pretending to study the terrain. "Soldiers and their hedges," she said with a mock-serious tut, grinning. "Even the bushes are afraid to misbehave."

She had a way of making even trimming a hedge feel like a proper mission - tumultuous, unpredictable, and entirely too enjoyable. I found myself sniggering, and for a moment, I forgot about the cold wind and the usual quiet of my garden on a Tuesday in February.

We worked side by side, passing shears back and forth and sharing stories. All the while, she made fun of my regimented pruning method.

Conversation flowed easily, full of the banter I had been missing, laughter, and little glimpses of honesty. By the time that the hedge looked respectable, I found myself thinking about Emily and Danny together. How intwined Emily already was in my story, how Danny also now belonged in my life, how their presence together added colour to my grey days. Danny had a spark, Emily had a warmth, and both were part of the same chapter that my Book of Fate had been hinting at for years. Protecting them felt natural, instinctive.

I could see now, more clearly than ever, that my life, regimented and sometimes solitary, had room for people like them.

People worth laughing with, worth looking out for. People who made the days count, even when there were only seven hundred and thirty-one of them left.

Chapter 48

Emily

Wednesday 18th October 2023
Age 28
St. Agnes' Primary School, Petersfield, UK

The children were losing their minds over Halloween. Strips of white tissue paper still clung to every surface like a ghostly Jackson Pollock installation from our paper-mâché session.
Slightly off curriculum? Probably.
Educational? Debatable.
But let's be honest: if "creative disarray" isn't in the curriculum somewhere, it should be.
Earlier one child declared his ghost was "a zombie unicorn that secretly works as a DJ," and somehow everyone nodded as if that was a natural career path for a ghoul. I'm pretty sure that counts as creative writing if nothing else, it's imaginative storytelling in its purest form.
The day flew by, mostly because the kids have finally figured out our new Year 3 routines, and partly because I may have accidentally ingested an entire thermos of coffee before lunch.
Honestly, these kids are wild little characters. There's Ishaan, who could either grow up to negotiate world peace or become a professional complainer, and Sienna, who narrates everything like David Attenborough documenting endangered insects.

And then there's Raymond, who spends every moment asking questions like, "but what if the zombie unicorn ghost gets stage fright mid disco?" - I don't know, Raymond, let's call it 'artistic tension'.

Three o'clock hit, and the classroom erupted into a chaos that looked like a bag of squirrels had been let loose. Book bags fly, coats go missing (the same glove vanishes every week), and I wave goodbye to them one by one.

Although this time I'm not saying, "see you in the morning," it is "see you later." Because tonight … tonight was the horror show disguised as professionalism: Parents' Evening.

Ah, Parents' Evening.

That special kind of punishment contracted into your salary, where the thirty minutes needed per parent gets crammed into ten-minute slots

You speed-run through the children's work while your mouth dries up, you laugh at jokes that aren't funny, and stand-up mid-sentence like some sort of awkward time-lord when the ten minutes are up. All this assuming parents are on time and your own nervous over-talking hasn't pushed the schedule into next week.

Meanwhile, Danny's at home, probably cooking something that could bring peace to war-torn countries: a cheese-laden, perfectly seasoned, spaghetti bolognese. Nights like this are one of the many reasons I love her. The thought of coming home to that after surviving a small army of parents makes the dry mouth, full bladder, and existential dread worth it.

Parents streamed in. Some brought their children along with them, the kids radiated self-pride at every tiny triumph scribbled across the pages of their workbooks.

Some parents clutched their Books of Fate, reading aloud ominous prophecies: "Your child will become a doctor." "Your child will still be living with you at 42 due to a tragic lack of ambition and drive." It was all terrifyingly specific and self-fulfilling.

Other parents came alone, which was slightly less chaotic, but far more awkward when you are mid-praise for a paper-mâché creation of a ghost zombie unicorn DJ hybrid and the child isn't there to smile and confirm that backstory.

Of course, some parents brought gifts. Chocolate (critical fuel for surviving the seven o'clock slot), flowers, or occasionally, a single lost sock retrieved from the bottom of a book bag ... a heroic act.

Mr. and Mrs. Green come through last, nervous looks on their faces, Sky holds up a slightly scruffy but heartfelt bouquet that she'd made herself. Handmade gifts always trump the classic Tesco's '#1 Teacher' mugs, which feel more like passive-aggressive bribes. Sky had written a little note in her careful cursive on the tag, thanking me for "making skool fun," and I smile so hard I almost forget that the overlording clock is ticking.

I watch this little family bounce off each other, pride practically glowing from them when they look at Sky's work and I have a moment of envy, or maybe hope.

One day, I think, I'd like to be on the other side of the table. Listening to another teacher describe my own tiny human, made with Danny, narrating the universe in their own style and sharing their latest spooky creations.

I think about sneaking a peek at my Fate when I get home. Maybe I can check if it has a tiny human or two in there, already causing trouble. But then I remind myself of what Danny always says when the Books are brought into conversation: half the fun is not knowing.

After all, life is way more entertaining when the pages are blank, the stories are unpredictable, and the zombie unicorn DJ ghost hasn't attacked the teacher yet.

Chapter 49

Ben

Wednesday 18th October 2023
Age 45
St. Agnes' Primary School, Petersfield, UK

Rose came back from the school run with Sky, the bell above the florist door chiming as they walked in. The shop always feels brighter when Sky arrives, her voice tumbling ahead of her like petals scattered on a path. On the way home she had asked Rose if she could make a bouquet for her teacher. She'd noticed the sunflower earrings Miss Puddle often wore and decided the flowers had to be all yellow.

Normally I'd tuck in other shades - splashes of purple, flashes of red - because yellow alone can look gaudy, but today I stepped back and let Sky take the lead. She wandered between the sizeable buckets. Her tiny hands reached up, her head tilted this way and that. She lingered over the chrysanthemums, counting softly under her breath, deciding whether two or three gave the balance she wanted. Watching her, so thoughtful and deliberate, I could see her mother in her more than ever. She had Rose's precision, that quiet florist's instinct for when enough was enough.

It felt different, noticing her in this way now the older two had gone.

Harry was off chasing history in Oxford, and Quinn beginning her first year as an art student in Edinburgh. Both out there blooming on their own stems, away from our vase. I'm so proud of them it almost aches. But the flat feels empty without their colour, and Sky feels it too - especially Quinn's absence. She used to trail after her sister, and now Rose and I must find ways to keep her rooted and occupied.

So today, the answer was flowers. Once she'd gathered all she could carry, I bound the stems with twine, smoothing them as I would for any customer. Rose gave her a pen and tag, and Sky climbed onto the counter stool. Bent over the card, tongue poking out in concentration, she scrawled her message in her best joined up handwriting. I tied it on with ribbon, curling the ends until they bounced like tendrils.

Tonight was parents' evening. We'd been through dozens before, but this one had a different weight. Sky's start to the year had been unsettled. Miss Puddle had spoken to us at the gate about her calling out, getting distracted, even sneaking off to play in the toilets. Our little wildflower, always cheeky but never unkind, was suddenly struggling to stay within the rows. We'd spoken at home about respect, even enlisted Quinn to give her some sister-to-sister advice over the phone.

Rose believed much of it was down to transition, Year 3 is more rigid than Year 2, with a sudden absence of the play opportunities in which Sky thrived. This alongside the shock of Quinn leaving home was sure to cause disruption.

Still, we braced ourselves for what we might hear.

Driving up, the crescent moon hung above St. Agnes'. We had walked through these doors countless times over the last eighteen years, but at night the place always looks strange, the familiar play equipment seen in moonlight rather than sun.

Stepping into Sky's classroom, I was struck by how stark the Year 3 felt compared to those of earlier years. The cheerful rug was gone, replaced by islands of bigger desks; the walls, once alive with children's drawings, now displayed word charts and grammar rules. A gravestone-shaped poster announced, "Said is Dead," its surface crowded with synonyms. Even the reading corner had matured, chapter books arranged neatly by genre where once dog-eared picture books had been piled high. The room still held warmth, but it struck me how quickly our youngest was being asked to grow tall.

Sky, clutching her bouquet, walked shyly to Miss Puddle. Her voice trembled as she explained why she'd chosen yellow, and Miss Puddle's reply was equally unsteady as she knelt to thank her. Watching the two of them exchange that gift, I knew we'd done the right thing. Sometimes a bunch of flowers says what a parent cannot.

We sit together and began to speak about Sky.

Miss Puddle pulls out a 'Now and Next' board that she had been using this week and assures that it is already helping Sky stay on track. The relief I feel between Rose and I is tremendous.

Then she asks if we want to see Sky's work. We leaf through her Maths book, then her English. Her teacher begins to read aloud a story Sky had written about a scarecrow in a pumpkin patch. The sentences are simple, but they flow with a natural rhythm.

Rose's eyes shimmer, and I feel the same. No matter how many times you've sat in these meetings, hearing your child's words on the page never loses its sting of pride.

Sky's storytelling startles me, so fresh, so alive. A seed of something neither Rose nor I had ever planted. And then, unbidden, my thoughts turn to Taylor. My sister had always loved writing, spinning tales and stories. Sky's story carries echoes of hers, and for a moment it winds me. I force myself back to the present.

At St. Agnes' no one expects parents to peek into their Book of Fate, to see what is to become of their children. That choice comes at eighteen when they receive their own books. Tonight, I am grateful for that. Sitting with Rose and Sky, the scarecrow story between us, I don't want to know what flower she might become.

It was enough to see her beginning to blossom, roots deepening, petals just starting to show.

And as I look at her, my youngest and last child, our last flower still in the vase with us, I feel the familiar swell of pride, fragile and fierce, and as golden as the chrysanthemums now brightening her teacher's desk.

Chapter 50

Danny

Saturday 11th November 2023
Age 30
Emily and Danny's Home, Portsmouth, UK

There was a sharp ring from the doorbell late morning. Em was curled up on the sofa, a blanket over her legs, completely absorbed in a romance novel, in the kind of page-turning focus that made the rest of the world disappear. She didn't even look up. Clearly, the fate of the world could wait.

I went to the door and there stood Frederick, ramrod straight as always, Gunner sitting neatly at his heel as though he'd been born trained. Frederick doesn't arrive anywhere; he reports for duty (clipboard optional, but somehow expected).

"Hey General, you alright?" I asked, stepping aside.

"Yes. May I come in?" he replied, clipped and calm, like asking permission was a formality.

He marched in, Gunner padding silently behind him. Em looked up then, finally, and broke into a grin. She adores that dog and insists it's mainly because he's better behaved than the kids she teaches.

Putting the book aside, Em went to put the kettle on. She always remembers the details, two sugars for me, none for Frederick. He takes his tea as if it were punishment, no milk, no sugar, just boiling water and the tea bag.

Frederick sat down carefully, back straight and hands folded, Gunner parked loyally by his boots.

Once the tea was distributed, Frederick began to explain the reason for his visit. His voice was low and deliberate when he began. He informed us that he had read his Book of Fate and therefore he knew what he had to do. "Operation Interflex", he said. A UK-led training programme for Ukrainian soldiers. He would be putting his years of Army knowledge, his endless drills and his discipline to use once again. He'd been waiting for this, he admitted. Counting down the years until he could redon a uniform.

The pride was there in his eyes, a light I hadn't seen in a while. He obviously missed it. Missed the structure and the purpose.

"And Gunner?" I asked, glancing down at the dog, who had not so much as twitched since arriving.

Frederick nodded firmly. "That's why I'm here. I know where I am going, and I know Gunner will not be with me. You two will look after him until I am back."

He said it not as a request but as an assignment. A handover of duty. Congratulations: you've just been drafted to Operation Paw Patrol!

I looked over at Em. She was already smirking. "Not the third we expected," she remarked to me. "But a solid compromise."

I laughed, but there was truth in it. A long-term partner, a house, and now a dog. It all felt like pieces slotting into place. Like being ... well, a grown-up. Yuck. We hadn't read our Books of Fate like Frederick had, and consequently had not prepared for Gunner.

Yet, today proved that life was better with surprises. Frederick promised Gunner's bed, food, and toys would be brought over soon. "The whole kit", as he put it, and "the Army never travels light".

After we finished our tea, I offered, "Would you like me to tend to your garden, Fred? I know it's winter, but I can keep on top of the weeds for you. Maybe even give the hedge another little trim!"

"Only if you have time," he replied, voice softer now. Then, with that old soldier's precision, "I can leave you with a key anyway. In case you need something for Gunner down the line."

Em, of course, couldn't resist. "Oh, don't worry, General, I'll make sure Danny doesn't let the brambles take over."

Frederick smiled, a quick flicker across his face like sunlight on steel. His own way of showing thanks.

When he finally stood to leave, Gunner looked up at him, ears pricked, waiting for the command. Instead, Frederick gave him one long pat on the head and said simply, "Stay." And Gunner did. Sat there like he knew his orders had changed.

And just like that, our household had grown by four legs and a tail.

Once Frederick had left, the place felt weirdly quiet.

Em sat back down with her romance novel, pretending to be casual, but every two minutes darting her eyes to Gunner, who was walking around the room like a sergeant surveying his new barracks.

I decided to establish dominance, which involved me saying "sit" in what I thought was a commanding Frederick-like voice. Gunner blinked once at me and then looked away.

Em clapped her hands. "Sit!" she chimed. He sat immediately.

"Excellent," I muttered. "He's not my dog. He's yours."

"That's fine," she said sweetly. "You can just be the one collecting his samples from the garden."

I gave Gunner my best stern look. "Hope you're ready for NHS-level care, mate. No private healthcare here." Later, when I went upstairs to dig out blankets for a makeshift bed (for Gunner not me). I spotted our Books of Fate. Our dusty relics sitting untouched on the bottom shelf of the bedroom bookcase, gathering more lint than wisdom. I wondered if under today's date 'Dog Mum' was scribbled somewhere in the margins.

When I came back down, Em was on the rug, scratching behind Gunner's ears, laughing as he tried to roll onto her lap like a thirty-kilo toddler. Lucky dog. "Not the baby I'd dreamt of," she said again, as she looks up at me with that grin that makes me forget my own name. "But at least there will be less interrupted nights."

I raise an eyebrow. "Give it a week. You'll be up at three in the morning, in a dressing gown and soggy slippers, whilst supervising the Great Lawn Sniffing Operation. You know from Fred, Gunner's very particular about where he leaves his business!" I jest.

"Somehow you've forgotten who's going to be dealing with the deposits," she smirks. "I'm just the fun mum, remember?"

She laughs and I lob a cushion at her. Gunner snatches it mid-air and presents it to her like some loyal knight. Traitor.

So yes, today we became dog foster parents. Frederick didn't just leave us a pet; he drafted us into a new unit. And while I will continue to moan about it for appearances' sake, I admit – underneath it all, I'm excited.

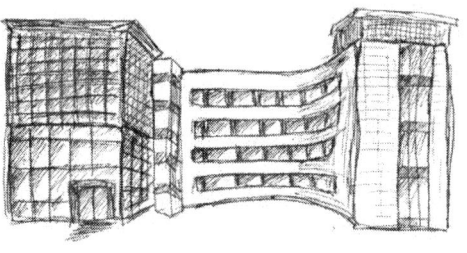

Chapter 51

Taylor

Saturday 17th February 2024
Age 39
Queen Alexandra Hospital, Cosham, UK

I woke to the sharp, antiseptic smell of the ward and the soft, rhythmic beeping of the monitor beside my bed. My head throbbed and my stomach churned. A hot flush of embarrassment ran through me.

How had I gotten back to this point?

I wanted to hide under the blanket and pretend I wasn't here, but the IV in my arm tethered me to reality, and the nurses' careful eyes reminded me I wasn't alone.

The nurse, Emmanuel, approached clipboard in hand, with a calm, friendly smile that felt completely non-judgmental.

"Morning, Miss Green. How are we feeling today?" he asked. I mumbled something about being better, trying not to look at him directly, trying to disappear into the bed.

Emmanuel didn't push. He checked my pulse, blood pressure and temperature, asking in quiet, patient tones if I'd slept, if the lights were bothering me and more generally what I liked to do when I wasn't in here.

"Your observations are stable," he said after a moment. "We'll keep monitoring you. You did the right thing coming in." His words were kind, but I still felt the shame of the overdose curling around me.

Breakfast arrived, tea, cold toast and some squared melon pieces. I nibbled on the toast quietly, conscious of the other patients around me. In the bed opposite, a woman scrolled through her phone, glancing up from time to time. From behind the curtain next to me, someone hummed softly to themselves, I assumed as they ate.

A different nurse came over to check I was eating, her ID badge partly hidden behind a set of pens clipped to her pocket, and gave me a small, encouraging nod. She noticed my notebook on the bedside table. "Is that yours?" she asked, tilting her head. My cheeks warmed immediately.

"Yeah ... I write kids stories sometimes, poetry ... or just thoughts" I admitted quietly. She smiled, gentle and encouraging. "Would you like to share some of your stories? Not right now if you don't want to, but I'd love to hear them. I love reading to my kids every night."

I hesitated, fingers curling around the worn cover. "I ... I have a few," I said meekly. "Not finished though."

"That doesn't matter," she said. "I'd love to hear them."

I flicked through the pages and read one aloud, the shortest story. My voice trembled at first, but gradually steadied as I went on.

The story followed tiny mice, scuttling through a tangled forest in search of the perfect winter home. I had forgotten how much I loved helping them solve their little challenges, finding clever ways through the twists and shadows of the trees. With each sentence, a quiet joy stirred in me, the simple triumphs of the mice reminding me why these stories had once meant so much.

She listened, asked questions, suggested ideas I hadn't thought of, and I scribbled notes. Speaking aloud felt like a gentle lifting of a weight I hadn't realized I'd been carrying.

Later, Dr. Hurd arrived. He asked about my mental health, medication, and support network. I answered honestly. He said what happened wasn't failure, it was needing help, and now I had it.

I tried to believe him, though the shame still lingered stubbornly.

The day passed in a strange, comforting rhythm. Emmanuel came by repeatedly, checking my vitals, offering snacks, and asking considerate questions.

Another patient arrived in the bed to my left, a young girl with dark circles under her eyes. She whispered a quiet hello, waiting nervously for the next poke or prod. I offered a small, tentative welcome, and after a long pause, she spoke.

She'd broken up with her boyfriend and, for a fleeting moment, thought she'd go out like Juliet, only to realise he was not her Romeo. I felt a strange ache of recognition, thinking about how everyone here carried their own private storms. Some of them might seem small from the outside, but to the person living them, they were the size of the world.

Our conversation was cut short when a social worker appeared, and the curtains around the girl's bed were pulled closed.

I focused on my notebook, scribbling down story ideas that had been stirred by the nurse's earlier questions. When she came by again, she listening as I read a few aloud. She laughed softly at the silly ones, asked about my characters' motivations, and told me I had real talent. I felt a spark of pride, fragile but alive.

Meals passed quietly. I ate slowly, more out of routine than hunger, noticing the small rhythms of the ward, the low hum of heaters, footsteps in the corridor and whispers between patients.

There was something both unfamiliar and reassuring about the ward. I found myself appreciating the little gestures of care: Emmanuel straightening the folds of my blanket, the mental health liaison team stopping by to show me a grounding technique, the social worker's quiet, measured words to the girl beside me.

When my medication came, the nurse explained each pill, each dose. I swallowed them, listening carefully, feeling a little more secure knowing I was being watched, supported and guided.

I heard my phone buzz on the side table, and for a moment I hesitated, my hand hovering over it. When I finally looked at it, the screen lit up with a message. It was from Lisa. My chest tightened a little. I tapped it open and read her words, careful not to let anyone see me flinch.

Today

> Taylor, you've had plenty of time. The debt isn't going away, and neither am I. Pay up before things get messy. I will find you.
> This is your last chance.
>
> 18:10

I pressed the phone to my lap and closed my eyes, trying to steady my breathing. The ward was quiet, just soft footsteps in the corridor and the low hum of machines, but Lisa's words felt louder than anything around me. I kept telling myself I was safe here, that the nurses would check on me, that I couldn't be reached easily. But the knot in my chest refused to loosen, twisting tighter with every second.

I picked up my notebook, thinking maybe writing could quieten my mind.

My hands shook as I scribbled: "I am safe. I am in the hospital. I am still me." The words felt hollow, like a fragile shield against a storm I couldn't stop.

My stomach churned, and I forced myself to take slow breaths, listening to the distant beeping of the monitor beside my bed.

Emmanuel comes in to check my vitals, and I try to smile, to act normal.

"Feeling okay?" he asks, concern in his eyes.

I nod, swallowing hard, hiding the panic I can't shake. He lingers for a moment, then leaves, and I return to my notebook, writing furiously, trying to make sense of the fear.

I can't let it get inside me. I can't. I must stay here. I must stay alive.

Even as I write, the phone sits beside me, silent now, but I know it will buzz again.

My hands hover over it, tempted to delete the message, to block Lisa, but I can't. I feel trapped, caught between the security of the hospital walls and the reach of a threat that seems to follow me everywhere.

I flip back to the story I'm writing about the mouse, tracing the new details I've scribbled in the margins. Even here, even now, there's more to me than this fear. There are people who see that I'm more than the hopeless, talentless junkie I've been led to believe I am.

I write one last line before letting my eyes close:

I am still here. I am still me. I can still dream.

Chapter 52

Frederick

Saturday 25th May 2024
Age 66
Frederick's Home, Portsmouth, UK

I had finally returned home after my time in East Anglia, training young men under 'Operation Interflex'. It had been demanding and exhausting, yet incredibly satisfying work.

Watching raw recruits transform into disciplined soldiers capable of defending their country filled me with pride.

My body and mind bore the marks of years in the Army, and six months of pushing these lads had reminded me that my age was not just a number. I was tired.

Not broken, but definitely tired.

It was time to hand over responsibility to someone younger and fitter. That was the reality.

I unlocked and opened my front door.

And halted immediately.

The living room had been transformed. A 'Welcome Home' banner hung across the wall. Balloons bobbed in clusters. A platter of sandwiches, cakes, and assorted finger foods occupied the dining table like a small tactical operation.

Emily and Danny sat there beaming. Gunner, my dog, was practically vibrating with excitement at Emily's heels.

I felt something I hadn't felt in years, the faint warmth of family.

"General!" Emily jumped up, practically glowing. "Welcome home! We've been counting the days!"

Gunner ran over and was instantly back at my side, my faithful companion.

"Permission to report, Commander Frederick? You've been gone too long," commanded Danny.

I chuckled, sitting down while shaking my head. "You two … I don't even know. This, all of this, it's … unexpected. This and looking after Gunner, I just … how can I thank you?"

"You don't have to," Emily said softly. "We just wanted you back."

Danny grinned. "Mainly to stop Gunner from writing his own letters to you because he missed you. We can't have him getting any ideas about personal correspondence."

Gunner barked brashly, as if to confirm the suggestion. After letting the moment sink in, Danny gestured toward the back door. "Come on! Let me show you the operation you didn't know you'd been redeployed to."

I followed her, and with theatrical flair, she opened the back door.

The garden was something I couldn't have imagined in my wildest dreams. Every detail spoke of time, care, and deliberate thought.

Bluebells and forget-me-nots carpeted one edge of the garden. Tall, proud foxgloves lined the back fence, standing at attention like soldiers in formation, their speckled throats catching the sunlight. Punctuating the lawn were scarlet poppies glowing against the green, while the peonies swelled with buds ready to burst. Honeysuckle crept up the gate, buds perfuming the air, mingling with the warmth of the May sunshine.

Lining the patio there were sweet peas in pots, reaching eagerly for the light, their vivid blossoms bright and cheerful, tiny flags of welcome.

And there, in the far corner, a small wild pond had been constructed from a half-barrel, carefully lined and filled with water. Water lilies floated lazily on the surface, while iris shoots pushed up with sharp precision, already reflecting the sun in their glossy green leaves. The water ripped gently with disruptions caused by a tadpole or an adventurous insect.

Bees hummed lazily among the flowers; birds flitted between branches calling to each other with brisk cheerful trills.

Danny grinned. "We can move the pond if you don't like it General, but there are still a few tadpoles in there, courtesy of Em going a bit overboard with frog spawn."

I took a slow breath. "It's perfect. I ... I don't know how to express it. I'm overwhelmed."

Emily took my hand, her eyes as warm as her touch. "You don't have to. We just wanted you home, Fred."

Danny leaned in conspiratorially. "Also, be warned. Gunner's now your subordinate, and he takes his new nighttime cuddle duties very seriously."

Gunner grumbled and then padded back over to me. I scratched behind his ears and chuckled softly. "You've missed me too, haven't you, boy?"

"Yes, sir," Danny said mock-saluting. "All jokes aside, General, we'll really miss having him with us at night, he's such a wonderful hot water bottle."

I laughed, shaking my head, but inside I thought, "You'll have him back soon. Forever, I hope."

Gunner whined softly, torn between excitement at seeing me and loyalty to Emily and Danny. I crouched down. "You'll have them back soon," I reassured him. "But I intend to savor my last tour of duty with you first."

After Emily and Danny leave, I sink into the sofa, surveying the decorations, the food, the garden visible through the door.

My Book of Fate never prepared me for this. Years of knowing my life in meticulous detail didn't predict the simple joy of walking into a home full of friends, love, and unexpected kindness.

Even after decades of service, after following orders and missions with precision, life still finds ways to surprise me. And as much as I try to maintain discipline and order, I feel gratitude, happiness, and dare I say it, a sense of belonging. A feeling of being part of a real family.

Chapter 53

Emily

Friday 8th December 2023
Age 28
Emily and Danny's Home, Portsmouth, UK

We dragged the Christmas decoration box out tonight, me handling it like a holy ritual, Danny acting like she'd been handed a detention slip.

The box was so battered it could have passed as a reject from the junk modelling pile. Inside: fairy lights were tangled with strands of silver tinsel, and a jumble of old baubles in every shade of the rainbow.

In honour of our new traditions, we draped the fairy lights around the house. It didn't glow with the blinding brilliance of our previous 'light show', but it carried the same cheerful, creative chaos.

"Do you think we should try and tidy them up a bit?" I asked, tilting my head at a particularly droopy section.

"Christmas isn't tidy, Em. We've been through this already! When have we ever been tidy?"

I laughed, nodding in both agreement and surrender.

This year, of course, we had fostered a new tree: Firnando. Shorter than Norman had been (rest in peace), but twice as wide. "Chonky but proud," Danny declared. I had to admit, Firnando was glorious in his own bulbous way.

We decorated together, Danny carefully stuffing bald patches with tinsel, while I gave orders about bauble spacing. "That one's too close to the gold" I pointed. "Symmetry kills Christmas spirit," she muttered, dangling a bauble in exactly the wrong place just to wind me up.

As I hung our stockings, I froze.

Two of them, mine and Danny's, side by side. And the glaring gap where a third one could be. Here we go again!

I couldn't help but think of kids, of how badly I wanted one. Of how long the pathway of IVF would be.

Danny must've caught the look on my face because she nudged me with a grin. "We could still get a kitten in time for Christmas. Put a fish-shaped stocking up for it. We could call it Blizzard?!"

I laughed. "You do know a cat isn't just for Christmas, right?"

But then Danny's face softened, and she leaned back against the sofa, suddenly serious. "Maybe it's time we actually plan this properly, Em."

So, we did.

Cross-legged on the floor, mulled wine in hand, fairy lights flickering around us, Firnando standing guard. We finally talked properly about IVF.

The NHS rules made me want to scream.

It was a total postcode lottery. Some areas still funded a round or two for same-sex couples, but here in Portsmouth it wasn't covered, and I was already twenty-eight. And that was before even thinking about the BMI restrictions. I'd have to shed a third of my body weight just to get through the door.

By the time it would take me to lose that weight safely, I'd probably be thirty-five, the cut-off age in most places. Then we might not qualify at all.

Private IVF was the reality staring us in the face.

And oh, the costs. It would cost at least £8,000 for a single cycle, with medication, blood tests adding another £2,000 on top. The London Sperm Bank were offering first time discounts on 'vials' but they still totaled £1,500.

At best, we'd be looking at £15,000 after all the hidden costs. And that's per round.

Most people needed more than one go.

Danny in her not very helpfully Doctor-mode pointed out that at least there was a 30% chance it would work. Urgh.

It felt impossible.

Danny tried to keep it light. "So, we remortgage the house, sell my kidney, and maybe flog Firnando on Facebook Marketplace. Easy."

I lightly smacked her arm. "Have some dignity, Firnando is part of this family too, thank you."

But then she said something that floored me. "What if I sell the flat? It's sitting there empty. Just my Pokémon cards and some old photo albums gathering dust. I don't need it. Fifteen extra minutes on top of my commute isn't the end of the world, Em. We're not getting any younger."

I wanted to protest, but her hand found mine. "It's not about the flat. It's about us. About having a chance."

So, we did the stupid thing; Googled it all properly. The full process.

It started with hormone injections to make my ovaries go into overdrive, producing not just one egg but loads. Daily jabs for around two weeks, bloating, mood swings. Then the egg collection itself. Romantic, right?

I watch TikTok videos of women sobbing over pregnancy tests, cycle after cycle, their bank accounts draining as quickly as their hope. But there are also stories of miracle babies, of it working on the first try, of it being worth every injection, every penny, every ache.

By the time I put my phone down, I know two things: IVF is terrifying.

I want it anyway.

I climb into bed. Danny stirs and mumbles, "Before you ask, were not naming our kid Firnando."

"Fine," I whisper. "But the middle name Blizzard stays."

And under the glow of the fairy lights, still twinkling faintly in the hall, I lie awake - half scared, half hopeful.

Chapter 54

Ben

Tuesday 12th November 2024
Age 46
Ben's Family Home, The Flat Above the Florist, Alton,
UK

It was the anniversary of my parents' death.
Every year it felt heavier, like the day itself had weight I couldn't shake off. Rose was downstairs, running the shop. I could hear her laughter drifting up through the ceiling, mixed with the sound of the bell above the door jingling in rhythm with customers' movements. I had come upstairs under the guise of needing paracetamol for my ever-persistent headache.
I sat on the side of the bed, staring at the door of my wardrobe. My eyes traced the wood grains as though the lines themselves would tell me something I couldn't find in words.
The wardrobe doors trembled with my unspoken desire to open them and reach for my Book of Fate. I knew exactly where it was: wedged at the back, pressed between Rose's and Taylor's Books. It felt almost alive, daring me to take it, to read it.
I didn't want to break my promise to Rose, but just one glimpse couldn't hurt, could it?

I already knew she was my one and only love. We'd had our three children, and we were both too old for more. What secrets could this book possibly hold that I didn't already know?

I opened my book.

And then I couldn't stop.

I reread my life from my eighteenth birthday. The excitement, the anticipation, the triviality, and beauty of those days. How Rose had called the landline and I had picked out my Nirvana t-shirt to wear to the cinema (I still owned that t-shirt). At that moment, I had no inkling it would be the last birthday I would ever spend with my parents.

I sped through the entries of 1996: romantic dates, considerations of my future, the cloning of Dolly the sheep, the official divorce of Charles and Diana. Rose and I had sung Wannabe lying on wet grass, staring at the stars, our laughter echoing into the night.

And then I saw it.

12th November 1996

I knew what was coming before I even read the words.

"You will stand at the side of the road, frozen. Blue lights flashing all around you. The red Ford Escort mangled, unrecognisable. A paramedic will place firm hands on your shoulders, turning you away. But it is too late. You have already seen them."

My Mum and Dad. Both gone, gone forever. They had headed out to get *me* a nineteenth birthday present. The blue Renault Clio I had been obsessing over from the local garage.

They had only just left, telling me to look after Taylor while they popped out to pay the rest of the bill and drive it home.

I have never forgiven myself for what had happened. How could I? I had wanted my own car so badly, even though I already had access to theirs whenever I needed it.

It was selfish, and the guilt had burrowed into me, deep and unrelenting. I knew I had to protect Taylor, but she, too, blamed me.

I read on, reliving the trauma of the aftermath, each stage of grief I had endured so far.

I skimmed over the turn of the millennium, the quiet panic of Y2K that, thankfully, had never come to pass. I lingered on the early years of running the florist with Rose, barely adults ourselves, stumbling through invoices and deliveries, learning the hard way what it meant to keep a business, and life, afloat. I felt the ache of Taylor leaving for the first time, that hollow emptiness when she went missing.

And then I cried again at the births of Harry, Quinn, and Sky - their tiny bodies, the softness of their cries, the overwhelming rush of love that had never left me, that had only grown heavier with each passing year.

I stumbled over the Brexit vote, the political chaos, the divisions it caused in families, friendships and businesses. I spluttered through details of COVID, the fear, the uncertainty, the endless newsfeeds and the isolation. How it would have been so much easier if we'd had time to prepare for it.

Through the years, I saw my own small victories and failures, the mundane and the monumental, all chronicled in painstaking detail. Every heartache, every moment of joy, every trivial quarrel and every miracle small enough to go unnoticed by the world was recorded here.

I read past where Taylor left us again, waking to find her gone, and the weight of it spreading slowly through the entire family.

Every entry, no matter how distant in time, drew me back to her. Each time Taylor was mentioned, I read with bated breath. I wanted to know where I would see her next, when she would be ready to forgive me, and if I could understand what I needed to protect her from.

I close my eyes and draw in a slow breath. The book rests open in my lap, heavy with the pull of the past and the weight of the future, of everything that had been and the fragile truth of what was still to come.

My gaze drifts to her book, sitting untouched across the room. I remember when the brown padded envelope had arrived on 20th June 2002, at the florist's door. I had kept it safe for all these years, meaning to give it to Taylor if she ever asked.

But she never had. Like us, I assumed, she had no desire to know how our Fates were to unfold.

Yet I have the answers right here, the knowledge of where she is, what she's doing, the silent trajectory of her life. And still, the lack of conversation between us stretches on, endless and unbroken. I wonder, fleetingly and with a jolt of panic, if she's even alive. Her book is thick, its spine heavy with untouched secrets. There's so much in there but I can't bring myself to cross that line.

So, I decide I'll continue to read my own book only to the point where Taylor is mentioned next. Just enough to know when and where I'll see her. This time, I'll be ready. This time, I'll do it right.

Chapter 55

Danny

Friday 9th August 2024
Age 30
On the Fjord, Olden, Norway

I had taken two whole weeks off work - two glorious weeks - something I hadn't had since I started med school, which felt like a lifetime ago. But in the spirit of ticking off our DINK (Duel Income, No Kids) bucket list, we'd planned a proper break.

The flat had sold, subject to contract, and we were just waiting for the final completion date to receive the money. We would get more than enough for three rounds of IVF, and I felt ridiculously proud. Especially since Em was about to put her body through something no 'mum-to-be' self-help book, no matter how thoroughly read, could ever truly prepare her for.

We'd decided on the Norwegian fjords. Not a hot holiday, not a crowded resort. Just a rented van, winding roads, mountains, and scenery so perfect it made my phone camera feel inadequate. Our base was Olden, a tiny village squashed between towering peaks and glacial rivers. Em's eyes sparkled as she took it all in.

"I can't believe we're actually here," she said, staring at the crystal-blue water. "It's … like a postcard."

"Exactly," I said, grinning. "Except, unlike the postcards we've seen, I can't see any trolls. They're probably lurking just under the water, waiting to pop up and demand we perform some sort of Viking initiation ceremony."

We'd booked a kayaking trip that morning. I had seen people paddling across the fjord near Olden, looking impossibly serene, and I begged Em to let us go - even though she knows my idea of serenity usually ends with bruised shins or me panicking about balance. She gave in.

The guide handed us dry suits. Which turned into a comedy show. Em's face scrunched as she wrestled her head through the neck hole.

"You know," I said, trying not to laugh, "I think you just relived childbirth. That's basically labour 2.0."

"Shut up," she growled, tugging the suit. "This is entirely different! Although just as traumatic for everyone involved!"

Once suited, we shuffled toward the kayaks, looking less like adventurers and more like budget astronauts. I could see the doubt in her eyes, and admittedly, I felt it too, but the moment we pushed off, something clicked. We found our rhythm, paddling together like we'd done it a hundred times before.

The fjord stretched endlessly. Steep cliffs, waterfalls, peaks dusted with snow. The water was so still, I felt like a walking metaphor, floating in a mirror, pretending to be competent.

"This... this is perfect," Em murmured from behind me in the kayak. "I could stay here forever."

"Yeah... except for the frostbite," I teased. "And your complete inability to survive without one of your three meals a day."

I felt her glare bore into the back of my head.

"I skipped lunch the other day!" she shot back triumphantly.

"Wow," I said, grinning. "Living life on the edge, huh?"

Our Norwegian guide paddled alongside while we tried to maintain dignity. "This fjord," he said, voice booming, English perfect, "was carved during the last Ice Age, roughly ten thousand years ago. The glaciers were massive, moving slowly but powerfully. They shaped these mountains."

The guide leaned closer, lowering his voice. "Beneath the water, orcas sometimes pass through here. They dive hundreds of metres down. They come to these fjords when they're injured or pregnant, it's a haven for them."

Emily gasped. "Pregnant orcas, under us? Right now?" I raised my eyebrows. "Yep. You're essentially kayaking over killer whales. No pressure."

"I knew signing up for this would be dangerous," she said, gripping the paddle like it was a lifeline. "And not in the fun way. In the 'I might actually get eaten by an orca' way."

We paddled on in silence for a while, letting the quiet wash over us. Occasionally I pointed out a waterfall or a tiny red house clinging to the cliffside. The fjord felt endless, yet intimate, like it had been waiting for us.

"I can't stop looking at it," Em whispered. "It's like the world paused just for us."

"Exactly," I said. "Just us two, for now"

Later, as we return to shore, Em flops dramatically. "I'm officially a kayak expert now. I survived the orcas, the dry suit and your terrible jokes."

"You're officially amazing," I say, pulling her close and kissing her. We laugh, help each other out of the suits, and I feel a deep, quiet contentment. Soon, once the flat is finished, we'll start our baby journey. But for now, we have this: two weeks of just us, the mountains, the fjords, and laughter that makes the bite of the cold feel like nothing.

And I know this perfect, ridiculous, breathtaking adventure will carry us through whatever fate comes next.

Chapter 56

Frederick

Friday 13th September 2024
Age 66
Frederick's Home, Portsmouth, UK

Friday 13th, unlucky for some, I suppose, but I never bought into all that codswallop.

I sat in the chair by the window, Gunner at my feet, watching the drizzle blur the edges of the houses across the street.

I kept my Book of Fate open in front of me, its spine worn from years of handling and travelling around with me. I re-read the last few chapters of my life. The words felt heavier today than usual. In five months, it would all be over. That part of my Fate was as clear as the regimented lines of a parade ground.

'You will hear the crack of the bullet first, and then the impact - strange, dull, like pressure bursting inside your chest. Warmth will begin to pour down your back, and your breathing will become wet and shallow. You will close your eyes and then feel a warm hand holding yours. They will try to stop the bleeding. You will die at 14:31. Age 67."

I wondered, as I always did, if it could be changed. Could there be a mistake?

Could Fate have misprinted something, or maybe a page stuck in the wrong place?

The thought made my stomach twist. Fear. I hadn't felt much of it in decades - not during COVID, not during field exercises, not even during deployments. But now, staring at the inevitability of my own end, fear settled like fog across the moorlands of my mind.

And yet, in the fog there was also clarity. Every step had built me up to be ready for this moment. Ready to face it with precision, dignity, and a soldier's acceptance.

I thought about Barbara. I often thought about her. Sometimes I thought of her in the mornings, sometimes in the quiet of the park. I wondered if, in another life, we might have seen more of each other, if we might have been more than friends. Perhaps in some other fate we were walking Ernie and Gunner together every Thursday, laughing at their little leaps and antics, swapping stories as the autumn wind tugged at our coats.

I wondered if Ernie was still running across Braemar Dog Park, if the grass still bent under his tiny, determined legs. I made a mental note to myself: in the next few months, before it was too late, I would go down to Braemar and maybe see her again.

We still had time.

Just a little.

Enough to share stories, perhaps even a quiet afternoon together, with both dogs chasing a ball in the drizzle.

I looked down at the Book again.

Today's date.

"Today you will begin your preparations for the end. You will write your will. You will plan to leave Gunner in the care of Miss Emily Puddle and Dr Danny Carter. You will split the rest of your assets between Amnesty International UK and the future children of Miss Emily Puddle and Dr Danny Carter. 20:80 ratio. You will walk Gunner through the drizzle and have fish and chips for dinner."

I exhaled, letting the words settle. It was precise, measured. Black and white. The kind of instructions I could understand and follow without hesitation. I liked that. The clarity reminded me of military orders - concise, unambiguous, leaving no room for doubt.

I opened my laptop and logged onto the online will-writing service.

My fingers moved automatically, trained over a lifetime to follow procedures, to tick boxes and fill in forms, to make the correct calls even under pressure. The process was simpler than I'd feared. Each question had an answer, each instruction laid out clearly. 'Beneficiary', 'executor', 'distribution of assets'. I filled them in carefully, methodically.

Gunner nudged my knee, bringing me back to the present. I scratched behind his ears, and he leaned into my hand, unaware that his world would soon change. He didn't know he'd soon belong to Emily and Danny, but I took comfort in knowing he would be well cared for. I knew they would let him sleep on the bed with them, as he could only do on special occasions at mine.

Completing the will felt strange. Oddly final. And yet, also oddly freeing. There was a strange relief in having every decision laid out for me, in seeing my Fate spelled out with the precision of a drill sergeant. I was not guessing. I was not worrying. I was following orders - my own, written by the universe itself.

I closed the laptop and looked at Gunner, then at the drizzle outside. I pulled on my coat, clipped on his lead, and stepped into the misty afternoon. The smell of wet grass and autumn leaves filled my lungs, and I felt a quiet strength settle over me.

Each step through the forest was deliberate. I walked as a man who knew the final mission, who knew the schedule, and yet who chose to savour the small, fleeting victories - the way Gunner's ears flapped in the wind, the way the drizzle caught on the branches above.

We stop at the fish-and-chip shop I always go to, the one with the paper cones and vinegar-stained tables. I order as the Book instructs, not because I'm hungry, but because it's part of the blueprint. I sit, Gunner at my feet, and eat slowly. Even as the wind rattles the windows, I feel oddly at peace. The world is uncertain, yes, but my part in it is clear.

Later, back at home, I make a note to go down to Braemar Dog Park - to see Barbara again, just once more, as Fate allows. And in the meantime, I live with the discipline and order that have carried me through decades. Each day dignified. Each task completed. Each memory cherished.

I've worked my whole life to be ready for this, and now I am. My hands shake slightly as I turn the pages of the Book again, but I tell myself I'm ready. I'll face the months ahead like any mission: with courage, precision, and quiet acceptance.

And in the back of my mind, beneath the discipline, there's hope, hope that even in the shadow of what's written, there can still be small joys.

Even with an ending foretold, there can still be laughter, walks, stories, and the comfort of my warm, wet-nosed companion by my side.

Chapter 57

Danny

Thursday 20th February 2025
Age 31
GP Surgery, Gosport, UK

There was nothing quite like a Thursday in February at a GP surgery. Bleak, wet, grey outside - fluorescent strip lights inside. Honestly, I thought the lighting was a form of low-grade torture, slowly leeching the life out of both patient and doctor until everyone resembled a sad mushroom.

Thursdays are my full-day clinics, which meant I was chained to the consulting room from eight a.m. until who knew when, a parade of coughs, sore knees, suspicious rashes, and people demanding antibiotics (just in case).

Old Mrs. McGuigan still insisted on seeing "her Dr. Danny" even when other GPs were available. She said I listened, which I knew was code for: I let her list every ailment she'd ever had since 1937 without sighing audibly.

I was halfway through explaining about viral upper respiratory tract infections when my phone buzzed.

An email notification popped up.

Normally, I would ignore it, at least until I'd finished explaining to the patient in front of me that antibiotics did not cure colds, or heartbreak, or Brexit. But something made me flick my eyes to the screen.

It was from the solicitors.

"Completion confirmed. The funds will be transferred by the end of the day. The property keys will be released by the estate agents."

Just like that. A black-and-white set of sentences on a tiny glowing screen. But what it meant, what it really meant, hit me so hard I nearly prescribed amoxicillin to a perfectly healthy (for her age) eighty-seven-year-old lady.

My flat. Gone. Sold. Done.

The money, real, tangible money, was finally coming our way. Which meant that Em and I could officially start our IVF journey.

I just stared at it for a second, while the poor patient coughed awkwardly, waiting for me to continue. All I could think was: Oh my God. This is happening. We're actually doing this. We're, dare I say it, going to be parents.

It felt surreal, like someone had pressed play on a film I'd been waiting to watch for years.

I had told myself over and over that selling the flat was just paperwork, just numbers, just bricks and mortar. But suddenly it wasn't. Suddenly it was the thing that unlocked everything else.

How did it feel? Equal parts relief, excitement, and sheer, unfiltered terror. Relief because the flat had just become a burden. Honestly, the damp patch in the bathroom had become so established it was probably on the electoral roll. Excitement because Em and I had been dreaming about this, planning and waiting for the right time. And terror because I was about to become responsible for a tiny human life. I could barely keep a succulent alive, let alone a child.

My immediate instinct was to text Em. Something quick, something witty: *It's done! Baby time!*

But then I stopped myself.

No.

This deserved more than a text squeezed between my patients. I wanted to see her face, to hug her properly, to celebrate.

Maybe with a Chinese takeaway. Yes. Crispy duck pancakes and prawn crackers (the true cuisine of romance).

I must have been grinning like an idiot because the patient in front of me looked genuinely confused.

"Doctor?" she asked, uncertainly.

"Yes, sorry," I said, snapping back. "Definitely not antibiotics. Try paracetamol, fluids and Netflix."

The rest of the morning passed in a blur. Kids with earaches, teenagers needing sick notes for exams, middle-aged men convinced that AI-ing their symptoms was equivalent to a medical degree. One chap actually brought in a printout of ChatGPT and asked me to 'confirm' that he didn't have lupus. I resisted the urge to tell him that if he brought in one more printout, I'd diagnose him with being a pain in my backside.

But underneath it all, through every consultation, every prescription, every polite-but-sarcastic explanation, my brain kept circling back to that email. To the fact that the money was moving. To the fact that this door was finally opening.

It was funny, really. For months, I had moaned about solicitors, estate agents, mortgage companies - every single step a headache. And now, with one simple email, it was all worth it.

The waiting, the chasing, the endless 'just one more form to sign'. Because now Em and I could take a step forward in our story.

IVF wasn't just this abstract, theoretical 'one day' plan anymore. It was right there. Tangible. Bookable. Injectable.

Injectable. Fun!

By lunchtime, I was still buzzing. I spilled soup down my white shirt (standard) and forgot to put the lid back on my coffee (again, standard). One of the nurses asked why I was walking around like I'd won the lottery, and I nearly blurted it out.

But no.

Em first.

Always Em first.

So I finished my afternoon clinic, jotted down a few final notes that future-me would not understand ("Pt v tired. Suspect toddler or existential dread") and packed up. As I shoved papers into my bag and fished out my car keys from under a pile of post-it notes.

The email popped back into my head again.

My flat was gone.

My money was coming.

My baby - our baby - was suddenly possible.

I drove home with a stupid grin plastered across my face, already rehearsing how to tell her. I picture her eyes lighting up, the way she'll hug me, how we'll order far too much food and toast the future with cans of Pepsi Max.

It's happening. We are doing this.

Messy desk, messy hair, messy life - but now, the future looks beautifully, perfectly clear.

Chapter 58

Taylor

Friday 13th September 2024
Age 40
Victoria Park, Portsmouth, UK

Friday 13th, unlucky for some, I suppose that includes me.

I had been out of the hospital for four months, but the smell of antiseptic was still strong in my memory.

They told me I was lucky to be alive.

Lucky, they said, like it was some small gift to be kept in a drawer. I had folded that sentence up and tried to tuck it somewhere safe, but it kept unfolding itself at night.

I had spent the last two months hiding in every shadow I could find, every dark corner I could wedge myself into. Daylight felt too exposing; I moved through it like someone avoiding the beam of a lighthouse.

I kept to side streets, to cafes with booths hidden in corners. People were following me wherever I went - I knew it, because I saw them in the corners of mirrors and reflected in windows, I felt their presence like a chill at the back of my neck.

It was the echo of their steps, matching mine as I walked, that made my stomach go hard.

I slept with one eye open, propped on my elbow.

They were coming after me because of the money I owed.

They wanted the money, they wanted to scare me into paying, they wanted to make an example of me.

The thing was, there was only so much I could get hold of. My needs themselves were barely met.

I stole food, hopped on trains that didn't check tickets, and slept wherever was dry. The maths in my head was constant and cruel – food, drugs, the blistering pressure of that owed number - it never added up.

I lied to myself some nights, told myself that I could earn it all back. I circled round to old connections like a scavenger, offering scraps of myself for quick cash.

I did what I could: small jobs, phone calls to people I had burned, apologetic texts, promises that tasted like rust. But those promises were like paper boats in a storm. Money came in dribbles and went out on everything else. There was never enough to fill that black hole.

Paranoia had become the furniture of my life. I described it to myself like a guest who had overstayed their welcome: intrusive, persistent, familiar.

My eyes catalogued exits, windows, strangers carrying bags that looked too full. I watched faces for the twitch that matched the way my hands shook.

When a car slowed at the junction ahead, my heart hit my ribs and I felt the urge to run.

Someone was following me yesterday. I had seen them slip behind me on the high street, matching my pace with a careful rhythm. I ducked into a charity shop and watched through a rack of coats as they drifted past the window. Their face was half-hidden under a hood.

I wanted to call the police.

I wanted to tell someone.

I did neither.

Sometimes I thought it might be Ben. My brother, who had always watched over my life in some way or another. The thought of Ben following me made my body ache in a different way. If it was him, then it was personal in a way that cut deeper. Family made everything mean more.

I had imagined him standing on the pavement, eyes hollow, a hard tenderness on his face.

I wanted to run to him and tell him I was sorry for leaving and that I would do whatever it took to get clean again.

I wanted to slam the door in his face and never let him in.

I wanted both at once.

It felt like time to go back to Lisa.

I had resisted the thought for weeks, made reasons for not knocking on her door, concocted excuses as to my lack of reply to her many messages.

Going back to Lisa felt like stepping into a house that remembered me, even the parts I had tried to leave in the gutter. I knew she would not pretend everything was fine. She would look me in the eye and tell me the truth I didn't want to hear, that debts were not just numbers.

Maybe she would help me make a plan. Or, help me carry out a plan she had already made.

I had been proud once, proud in the way people are when they insist they can handle things alone. Pride had been expensive. It had cost me friendships, jobs, the slow unspooling of a life that used to have small but consistent joys.

Now pride felt like a luxury I could not afford. Going to Lisa meant admitting I could not manage on my own. It meant handing over some part of myself that I had refused to give up. But when the night closed in and the footsteps outside seemed to come closer, the thought of those small admissions felt like oxygen.

266

The truth was messy and simple: I did not know who was following me for sure. I did not know how I would clear the debt. I did not know if I would be brave enough to knock on Lisa's door and say, "I'm back. I need help."

What I did know was that hiding in the shadows had worn me down until the edges of me were soft. The overdose had been a cliff I had fallen off, but I crawled back to shore, and since then I had been afraid of even dipping my toes into the sea.

I make a list in my notebook: call Lisa, look up the clinic contact, count the money in my bag, throw away the promises I can't keep.

Maybe tomorrow I'll do one of those things.

Maybe tomorrow Ben will come and find me.

Maybe tomorrow I won't wake feeling like someone's watching my every move.

Tonight, I try to sleep against this huge tree.

But mostly, tonight, I try to keep breathing - because breathing is simple, and it's proof that I'm still here.

Chapter 59

Ben

Friday 21st February 2025
Age 47
Portsmouth Harbour Train Station, Portsmouth, UK

Today was the day.

I carried a bunch of irises and pink roses in my hands. An odd combination, perhaps, but one I knew Taylor would recognise instantly. In my coat pocket I had stuffed her Book of Fate, it felt like time to return it to her and give her the chance to perhaps see where her story was going.

I had read mine, up to the entry leading me here, and I knew exactly where I needed to go to find her. The pages had laid it all out for me: the place, the time, even the weather.

"It will be a cold, dry day. You'll take the 13:30 train to Portsmouth and head to the bank. There, you'll catch a brief glimpse of Taylor - she won't linger. The sight of what she's become will leave you disheartened, yet your loyalty to her will endure."

I knew the clock I had to beat; the exact moment Fate demanded we cross paths again. For once, I wasn't going in blind. For once, I was prepared.

I had been rehearsing my words for days now, running them through my head in the quiet moments, editing them silently while brushing my teeth, or standing by the shop window watching Rose open-up for the day. My speech had become a rhythm, a mantra: the words I would give her to draw her back home, to remind her that no matter how far she had fallen, she wasn't lost to me. Whatever she has become, however disheartened I was, she is still my little sister.

I pictured her listening, the way her eyes might dart away when guilt grew too heavy, the way she might fold her arms and try to look defiant even when her heart was breaking. I knew she wouldn't make it easy. Taylor never had. But I was ready to tell her that whatever debt she carried, whatever chains she had wrapped herself in, we could face it together.

I didn't care if it meant driving her to every rehab in the country, sitting through every NA meeting ever hosted, holding her hand through every withdrawal and every relapse. If fate had written this into our story, then it was my duty to make sure the ending was not despair but survival.

I get off the train, tuck the flowers tighter under my arm, steady my breath, feel Taylor's book in my pocket, and step out into the big city of Portsmouth.

I head into town, Fate already written, but this time, I have the courage to meet it head-on.

Chapter 60

Frederick

Friday 21st February 2025
Age 67
The Hard Interchange, Portsmouth, UK

Today was the day.
This was what I'd been training for my whole life - drills, early mornings, hard choices - and the odd comforts that followed them.
I had one mission left.
It isn't loud or dramatic; there are no bugles, no parades. It is quiet and precise, the kind of assignment that suits a man who spent decades following orders and giving them.
I checked the list again this morning: will signed, beneficiaries named, Gunner's future arranged, letters left for those I love, small instructions for Emily and Danny about the house. I even polished my boots out of habit, more ritual than necessity, because rituals steady me.
All my loose ends are tied.
The paperwork is done, the calls have been made, and the things that mattered most have been said - clumsily, imperfectly, but honestly.
I feel the old readiness settle into my bones, the same calm that comes before a march.
I am ready to meet my fate - not because I'm unafraid, but because I have prepared.

I walk this last stretch with the same discipline and dignity I have tried to live by: steady steps, clear orders, and the peace of a job well done.

Chapter 61

Emily

Friday 21st February 2025
Age 29
The Bank, Portsmouth, UK

Today was the day.

The one I'd been dreaming of, scribbling hearts around in my head like a teenager with a crush.

Danny and I stood in the bank, next in line, clutching paperwork but daydreaming about babies.

Our babies.

I couldn't stop picturing it. Next Christmas with a tiny stocking hanging beside ours, a lopsided Halloween pumpkin carved with 'Baby's First Haunting'. Easter eggs hidden so badly even a toddler could find them. The thought made me grin so wide the man at the desk probably thought I was plotting a bank heist.

Danny squeezed my hand and it hit me again how far we'd come. Things had been so much lighter since I'd stopped clutching my Book of Fate like it was some strict lesson plan. I'd finally accepted I didn't need to know every answer.

"Do you think they'll have your nose or mine?" Danny whispered jokingly.

"Mine," I shot back immediately. "Otherwise, they'll never fit standard sunglasses."

She rolled her eyes, but she was smiling, the kind of smile that made my chest ache in the best way.

We were nervous, of course. IVF wasn't exactly an easy ride. It was needles, hormones, appointments, and more waiting than a GP surgery on a Monday morning. But standing here with her, I can't help but feel giddy. Because for the first time, it's not just a dream scribbled with doodles, it's real.

And whatever happens, I know we'll laugh through it, cry through it, and come out stronger. Together.

I have no idea what to expect, but my heart aches with the hope that soon I'll be expecting.

Chapter 62

Taylor

Friday 21st February 2025
Age 40
The Bank, Portsmouth, UK

Today was the day.
My heart was hammering so hard it felt like it might burst through my chest as the car jerked to a stop.
The dashboard clock glared at me: 14:29. Too late to back out.
I jumped out with two others. A man and a woman I didn't know but who clearly knew Lisa.
Their faces were hard, unreadable.
My body was shaking, but I shoved the fear down. There was no room for hesitation.
We had five minutes to pull this off. Five minutes to do something that would either work or ruin everything.
The air was cold and damp, smelling faintly of exhaust and wet tarmac. As my boots hit the pavement, I could hear the thump of my own heartbeat, loud enough to drown out the rest of the city.
We burst through the bank's doors, the bell ringing like it was announcing the end of the world.
And then I saw him.
Ben.
My stomach lurched.

What was he doing here? He wasn't meant to be here. Not today, not anywhere near this. He looked straight at me, and I saw recognition flash in his eyes.

There was no time for hesitation. I yanked the mask over my head, the one I'd been handed, fumbling as I pulled it down over my face.

The plan was simple.

Go straight to the bank clerk behind the desk.

The man I'd entered with would do the talking.

Hands up. No one gets hurt.

We take the money.

And we leave.

Five minutes.

Easy.

But nothing ever goes as planned.

Once inside, everything changed. The bank wasn't just walls and counters and numbers. It was people. Real people. Their eyes were wide with fear, their hands raised in instinctive surrender. My mind froze for a split second, and that split second was enough to make the plan start to unravel.

A woman with short hair moved in front of another lady, her hands trembling as she pleaded, "Please just put the gun down." Her voice cracked, and for a moment it stopped me cold.

I raised the gun, shaking, thinking I could still push through, thinking I could still make it happen, but then I saw her properly.

Recognition hit me like a punch to the stomach. I froze. The gun wavered in my hands. She wasn't just anyone. I'd seen her before. That face. Those kind eyes. I could never forget her.

It was Dr. Carter.

The world tilted. The plan that had felt so clean and mechanical before now seemed impossible, a nightmare constructed of flesh, blood, and addiction. Her eyes met mine and the kindness left, replaced by fear.

I couldn't move. My finger pressed against the trigger, but my body refused to obey.

I wanted to drop the gun. I wanted to run. I wanted to dissolve into the shadows and disappear forever.

The man I'd come in with was shouting, his voice jagged, cutting through the charged air, and the woman at the desk was trembling so violently I thought she might collapse. All I could hear in my head was a single, horrifying thought: I can't.

But my hands betrayed me.

The gun wouldn't lower.

My fingers clench around it, cold and rigid.

Chapter 63

Frederick

Friday 21st February 2025
Age 67
The Bank, Portsmouth, UK

Today was the day.
I couldn't be late. Not for this one. 14:30 on the dot.
I saw the bank ahead.
Routine, precise, everything in place.
A man with flowers lingered in the doorway. I elbowed past him without a second thought.
"Move!" I shouted.
The moment was sudden and violent.
I lunged, tackling the person pointing the gun at Danny and Emily. In the struggle, the weapon became trapped between our bodies.
I heard the crack first, sharp and alien, and then the impact - dull, strange, like pressure exploding inside my chest.
Warmth poured down my back. My breathing became wet, shallow, and ragged.
I close my eyes and feel Emily's hand warm and steady in mine.
Danny is shouting something, frantic, precise. I can hear her trying to stop the bleeding.
I think of Gunner, I know he will be safe, cared for and loved.

Mission complete.
My story over.
Soldier down.

Lizzie Rose

Chapter 64

Taylor

Friday 21st February 2025
Age 40
The Bank, Portsmouth, UK

Today was the day I killed a man.
Was that... my gun?
My hands shook violently as the thought hit me.
What had I done?
My mind raced faster than my heartbeat. It was an accident, just an accident, but the word felt hollow, useless, swallowed by the chaos around me.
I glanced frantically around.
The two I'd come in with were already moving, sprinting toward the door, their footsteps pounding like warning drums.
I had to go. I had to run.
Blood roared in my ears, my pulse hammered in my temples, and every instinct screamed at me to disappear before it was too late.
As I run toward the door, I catch his eye. Ben.
My stomach twists.
He isn't meant to be in this part of my story.
Not today, not here.
The look on his face is shock, disappointment - something I can't read fast enough before I force myself past him. My legs carry me faster than my mind can comprehend - desperate, terrified, alive.

Chapter 65

Ben

Friday 21st February 2025
Age 47
The Bank, Portsmouth, UK

Today was the day I saw my sister kill a man.
I couldn't move.
My body had betrayed me, locked in frozen, helpless shock. Around me, the chaos unfolded like a nightmare I couldn't wake from. My Book had said I would be disheartened but nothing could have prepared me for this.
Sky's teacher was on her knees, hands trembling as she cradled the old man's lifeless body, murmuring words I couldn't hear but felt in every shiver that ran through me.
Nearby, another woman pounded desperately on his chest, her face twisted in terror, as if sheer force could somehow bring him back.
The screech of sirens pierced the air. Police stormed in, barking orders I barely registered. "Stay where you are! Don't move!"
I stood frozen as the bank transformed into a crime scene, sirens wailing and flashing lights painting everything in harsh red and blue.

They led me to the police car. The flowers in my hand drooped, petals already wilting as if mourning alongside me.

A sharp voice cut through the noise. "You saw the shooter, yes?"

I swallowed, my throat tight, words catching in my chest. "Yes ..."

"Can you give us a description?" they pressed.

I shook my head. Taylor's book was heavy in my pocket, but the weight of my loyalty was heavier still.

"No ... I'm sorry ... they were wearing a mask."

The words land like stones, heavy and suffocating, and the world around me crumbles.

Today was the day I saw my sister kill a man.

Chapter 66

Danny

Friday 21st February 2025
Age 31
The Bank, Portsmouth, UK

"Time of death, 14:31. Frederick James Garrison is deceased," I managed.